◇—◇ PRAIS|

THE PERFECT PLACE TO DIE

★ "Fans of true-crime murder mysteries
won't want to miss this one."
—*BOOKLIST*, STARRED REVIEW

"[This] novel will appeal to readers excited about an account of
gruesome historical events steered by an intrepid young woman."
—*KIRKUS REVIEWS*

"[An] entertaining thriller… Moore deftly captures
the bustle of 1890s Chicago, as well as the near-
claustrophobic feel of *The Castle*."
—*PUBLISHERS WEEKLY*

"True-crime buffs will appreciate the passages at the
beginning of each chapter, which are excerpts from
serial killer H. H. Holmes's published confession."
—*SCHOOL LIBRARY JOURNAL*

ALSO BY BRYCE MOORE

Perfect Place to Die

Don't Go to Sleep

A FAMILY OF KILLERS

BRYCE MOORE

sourcebooks
fire

Published by Sourcebooks Fire, an imprint of Sourcebooks
P.O. Box 4410, Naperville, Illinois 60567-4410
(630) 961-3900
sourcebooks.com

Cataloging-in-Publication Data is on file with the Library of Congress.

Printed and bound in the United States of America.
VP 10 9 8 7 6 5 4 3 2 1

For Michaela, at last

CHAPTER ONE

*"The manner of murdering was the same in every instance.
The victim seemed first to have been struck upon the head
with a hammer, and then to have had his throat cut."*

—The New York Herald
(New York, New York), April 10, 1874

———

F ATHER SHUT THE DOOR AND sat down on my bed. "Warren,
we have to talk."

If you had a knife, you could stab him in the eye.

"What about?" I asked, hoping my tone stayed level. The Voice
inside my head didn't come all the time, but when it did, it was all I
could do not to get up right then and check to make sure no knives
were near. My room didn't have much in the way of furniture: a bed,
a dresser, and a table for my washbasin. One of mother's needle-
works of a sunset hung on the wall.

"Your mother's worried, and I can't say she's wrong this time.
About you. We—" He shook his head and clenched and unclenched

his fist. "Something ain't right with you, and we want to know what it is."

"I'm fine," I said, but my mind was focused on the different places a knife might be hiding in my room. I wouldn't have brought it in, but someone else might have, and what if it were there this instant, and I were to get hold of it? What would stop me from following through on that thought? The picture was so vivid in my mind. Father. The knife.

I got off the bed, unable to stop myself. Just a quick glance through my dresser, though then I had to move my other trousers aside to make sure a knife wasn't hidden there. Nothing under my shirts either.

"You ain't fine," Father said. "You ain't been fine since we come back from California. At first we figured it was just a phase—just another way Warren was being Warren, separating your food, fixing the way the furniture sat in a room—but this…this *whatever it is* you're doing now is far from fine."

There was no way I'd be able to check the whole room properly. Not with Father right there staring at me, asking me questions. So I fell back on my second option: folding my arms tight against my body and keeping them there. I couldn't hurt anyone if I didn't move my arms. It wouldn't matter if a knife was there or not.

Assuming the temptation didn't overwhelm me.

Father stood and strode over to face me, placing a hand on my shoulder. "Stop. I'm trying to talk to you about the very thing you're doing, while you're doing it, and you're telling me nothing's wrong?"

If only he knew getting closer to me only made the Voice whisper more suggestions into my ear. I hugged myself more tightly, imagining I could squeeze the evil out of me, even if I knew I couldn't.

"You need to tell me," Father said. "I promised your mother I wasn't leaving this room until it was out and settled. No more excuses. No more fancy words to talk around it. What ain't you telling us?"

It's not that I hadn't considered telling him before. I dreamed about it at night sometimes, and the expression of horror that crept over his face each time I admitted what I'd been thinking about was something I never wanted to see in real life. So what could I tell him that would be enough to make him leave me alone?

Nothing would satisfy him but the truth, and the truth was the one thing I wasn't going to give him.

So, instead, I stood there with my arms around me and my eyes squeezed tight, trying not to think of the many ways I might kill my father.

Twist his neck just so.

Wrap the curtain sash around his throat.

Get the rifle and—

On and on and on.

He had to give up eventually.

Except the time kept passing. Outside my room came the sound of Mother downstairs baking bread and yelling at Adelia to churn the butter. Father still stood there, his arms on my shoulders, his gaze intent.

"Is it something I done?" he asked.

I couldn't just leave a question like that hanging in the air. "No," I said. "It isn't—you haven't—you're one of the best things in my life. If anything, you're the one making me less—" I cut off. That had been too close.

"I ain't leaving," he said.

A pit of dread settled into my stomach. Perhaps he was serious after all, and if that was true, then it meant the time had finally come, no matter how much I'd tried to push it off. I'd have to come clean. Have to admit to him just what an awful person I was turning into.

And once he knew? Father was the one I'd always been able to go to with my problems. He'd talked me through the pain of losing Ferris, our dog. Taught me how to ride a horse. Showed me everything he knew about tracking and life in the wilderness. The moment he found out, all of that would be gone. No one could love a *thing* like me.

I tightened my jaw. I wouldn't do it. Right now, my family just thought I was strange, and that was something I'd made peace with years ago.

Mother had moved on to stew, from the smell of it. I tried to think about other things. Our house wasn't large—just two floors with four rooms on each floor—but it was so much nicer than anything we'd lived in before. Made from real lumber instead of logs, with an actual floor. Back in California, Wyatt, Adelia, and I had slept in an open loft tucked into the rafters, with Father and Mother down below.

Life was supposed to be better. And it would have been, if I hadn't been broken.

Father hadn't moved.

Maybe I deserved it. It would be safer for my family to know. Better for them, even if it was worse for me. Was keeping the truth from them the first step toward me finally giving in to the Voice?

After an entire hour, my shoulders slumped. My arms were aching from having been tense for so long. Father would find out eventually. Better to get it over with now.

He sensed the change in me, and he led me over to my bed, where he sat next to me. "What. Is. Wrong?"

The words got stuck in my mouth, too timid to come out, but Father sat there patiently waiting.

At last they came, slowly, but once I began, it became easier. "Before we left California, I—there was this boy who confronted me while I was out target shooting with my Remington. I...you know how you used to take me target shooting, back before everything happened?"

"You could hit anything you looked at."

Not quite anything, but close enough. From the time I'd been old enough to walk, I'd been attracted to guns. Father had me go out hunting with him not too many years after that, and right away he'd seen something different in me. "It's like he was born to do it," he'd tell everyone who came by. "The Bullock blood, showing itself again." I thought I'd explode, I was so proud. It had become a part of who I was—a way I might measure up to everything my older brothers had already done.

I continued, unable to look Father in the eye. "On the way back from California…I know the boy didn't mean anything by it. He was about my age, but he said some things about me that I didn't take to. Before I knew it, my revolver was in my hand, and I had it leveled at his chest. I didn't even think. It just happened, and I was *so close* to pulling the trigger. I wanted him dead so bad, I ended up throwing the gun down and riding off."

"That's what happened back then with that Palmer boy?" Father asked. "You said you weren't well, and Wyatt come back with your gun, but he only said you'd left in a hurry."

I nodded. "I'd never known I had a temper like that, but I swore to myself I'd never let that part of me out again. Except it felt like something I couldn't shove back inside. I kept having these…thoughts. Vivid images that came out of nowhere. I could be plowing the field or cleaning up from supper, and suddenly one of them would appear. All of them violent. Evil. And they kept getting worse."

His forehead furrowed in confusion. "Evil?"

"Just now, when you walked into the room, I thought about stabbing you through the eye. Yesterday, it was kicking Adelia down the stairs. Horrible things."

His hands stiffened, and his face froze, as if he was worried about giving something away. It was the exact expression I'd been dreading. "But you don't do any of those things...right?"

"Of course not!" I said. "But only because I worked out a way to keep everyone safe. At first, I just said to myself I'd never pick up a gun again, but the images got bloodier and more detailed. Eventually I decided that whenever I entered a room, I'd check it for weapons. Anything I might use to hurt someone. If I can't be sure I've checked the whole room, I hug myself tightly. I can't do anything if I can't use my arms, after all."

"Warren, you ain't making sense. Of all my children, you was always the cautious one. You cared more for keeping your room spotless than you did for getting in a fight. You spend half your time buried in a book."

I'd pictured him being horrified. I hadn't thought he might not believe me at all. Somehow, that was even worse. "People change," I said. "You know how Virgil was when he came home from the war."

"People change when they see the sort of things you see on a battlefield. But this? It's hogwash. You're worrying about nothing and getting yourself worked up when you should be off avoiding chores."

He had to understand. "What am I supposed to do when I'm using the plow and I suddenly get the urge to run someone over with it? To see what it would be like to hit a body at full speed? Or if I'm working with a pickax and want to bury it in someone's head? I'm not making these things up. I really get those thoughts. I wish I didn't, and I've tried so many things to be rid of them, but I can't."

A shadow of unease crossed behind his eyes. "There's a difference between having a thought and acting on it," he said. "If I was responsible for every little idea that came to me over even the course of a week, I'd be behind bars. It don't matter. You don't do anything about these thoughts. End of story."

I dropped my eyes to the floor, studying the wood grains of the pumpkin pine boards. "They're getting worse."

"What do you mean, 'worse'?"

"More frequent. More specific. Bloodier. It's not as if every murderer started out that way. You told me that yourself. They grow into it. So what if that's what I'm growing into now?"

"You know better than this. I been justice of the peace for more than a third of your life. You been with us on the wagon train to California and back again. You think you're like that beast who attacked his bunkmate in the middle of the night with an axe? He was drunk half the time and never had a good thing to say to no one. Maybe all these thoughts you're having are a sign I've been too easy on you. Anyone with the time to think such things needs more work around the farm."

"But I—"

He forced a smile and then threw his arm around me in a half hug. "No. You need to let this drop, Warren. It ain't healthy. Maybe you're doubting who you are, but can you at least believe me when I say you're wrong? If you'd only stop worrying about this so much, I'm sure it would just go away."

I was glad I didn't have to make eye contact with him. "You think?"

"I know," he said. "You're a Bullock. That means you're not afraid of violence if there's no other choice, but you also ain't gonna go out and turn into a murderer. Justice is in your blood. So stop all this searching rooms for weapons or hugging yourself or anything else. Try it for a month. I'll keep an eye on you and stop you from doing anything wicked. Trust me, okay?"

"Okay," I said, trying my best to force some optimism into my voice.

"Good." He stood and walked to the door, then paused and turned to look at me one more time. "I love you, Warren. We'll get through this together."

The door closed behind him.

I wanted to throw up. A fierce pain had developed behind my right eye. Had his speech had been too fast? Was he too quick to break eye contact with me? Father might have seen more than his share of violence over the years, and he might be trying his best to hide it, but that didn't mean he wasn't unsettled by what I'd just told him.

Worst of all, after he tried his best to support me like that, how could I keep searching rooms right in front of him and not seem ungrateful? I'd give anything if I really were the sort of person the Bullocks could be proud of. It was fine for Father to assume I'd never do anything wrong, but I couldn't have the luxury of that conviction. Not if I didn't want to actually hurt anyone.

I'd have to just get better at hiding what I was doing.

What else were you supposed to do, when you knew you were a monster and no one wanted to believe you?

CHAPTER TWO

"The scene Thursday was too horrible to give a faint description of. Seven bodies in various stages of decomposition were lying on the ground by the side of their open gates, their skulls broken in and their throats cut from ear to ear."

—The Daily Memphis Avalanche
(Tennessee), May 14, 1873

———

TRYING TO HIDE MY HABIT was torture. I'd walk into a new room, and my heart would start pounding in my ears. It felt like someone was pulling down on my insides, and I had to take deep breaths to even have a hope of staying calm.

However, as long as no one was in the room, no one could know if I'd checked for weapons or not. I started being first for everything. First downstairs in the morning. First to supper. First to the fields. I couldn't do as thorough of a search as I wanted, but I could do enough to let me breathe. Father took it as a sign of how successful our talk had been. "I'm proud of you, Warren. See how easy things got once you put your mind to it?"

He didn't hear me sobbing into my pillow at night, terrified of what might happen the next day.

The worst thing about it was how much I hated myself for everything. No one else had to deal with anything like this. I was seventeen, and I couldn't even control myself not to cry? It was shameful. Up until my talk with Father, I'd been grateful my family had been so accepting of me and that I'd never had to admit what sort of person I truly was.

I didn't have that luxury anymore.

A month after Father had banned me from checking rooms, he rushed into the parlor at 9:04, just before I was going to bed.

"Quick," Father said. "Come with me."

I glanced from my book—Thoreau's *Walden*—to check the clock, wondering if perhaps I'd gotten the time wrong. What could be so important at nine? "Something in the house, or—"

"Get your hat," he said. "It'll be a ride."

I placed my marker in the book and laid it down just so on the side table before getting up to follow Father out the door. It wasn't that I *had* to read from 8:30 until 9:15 each evening; it was just my routine. Normally Father understood and let me keep my schedule. So I reminded myself this must be something important, though that didn't make me fidget any less with my hat as I went out to the barn. Things just felt wrong when they got out of order.

The temperature had dropped since I'd come in from plowing. My shirt was still slightly damp from sweat, and I'd grabbed a coat when I went for my hat. Father hadn't bothered with a lantern. The full moon cast a silver glow over the fields; it was bright enough to read by, if you had to.

Father grumbled about how long it had taken me, then kicked his horse into a gallop. I clicked at Surrey to follow, still wondering what we were doing. All the animals had been in the barn when I'd gotten Surrey, and we weren't heading toward town. Had one of the neighbors had an accident?

I would have just asked, but when he was like this, asking him would only get me silence. When a Bullock was on a task, everything else disappeared. Father's horse quickly outdistanced mine. It was an animal bought for speed. Surrey was more of a horse of all trades, and he'd been plowing for most of the day. I felt bad making him do this so soon after we'd finished, but I bit my tongue.

After a mile, Father took out a torch and struck a match to light it. In the guttering firelight, he veered off the road and into the fields, heading for the North Fork Spring. Did it have something to do with the river then?

You could drown someone in the river. It wouldn't take more than a minute. Wide eyes. Thrashing limbs.

I dug my thumbnail into my finger, pressing hard so I could focus on the pain instead of the Voice. *Stay focused, Warren.*

A group of mounted men waited in the middle of the field, not a light to be seen among them. A pit opened in my stomach, making me forget all traces of my reading schedule and my comfortable spot by the fire.

"Put out that light, Bullock," one of them said as we approached. The moon was bright, but everyone's hat blocked the light from their faces, casting each of them in shadow. "You want him to see us comin'?"

"I want you to go home and leave this to me," Father said, his voice clear and confident.

Another one spoke up. "You ain't justice of the peace no more, or did you forget you lost the vote?"

There'd been accusations of vote tampering, but the results had stood. "A vigilance committee is the last thing we need. Warren and I can go over there and take him into custody, same as I've done a hundred times before."

I tried to search the faces of the other men with us, looking for anything that might let me know who they were. If I could just *talk* to some of them, maybe I could stop this from becoming what Father feared. He'd taken me to my first hanging when I was seven. A man found guilty of robbery and murder. Bullocks needed to know all parts of the law. The hangman misjudged the weight when he measured, so when the man fell through the trap door and the rope went taut, his head was pulled clean off his body.

My opinion of hangings hadn't improved from there, even if the scene still replayed in my mind, ten years later. The Voice loved a good hanging.

Each man was a stranger in the night. I might have been searching their faces, but they were all focused on one thing. One man.

Someone rode up to Father and stopped a foot away. Even there, the angle of his hat made him hard to recognize, though I thought it might have been Mr. Cogburn. "You gonna shoot us?" he asked.

Father's pause felt like an eternity. Then his shoulders sank an inch. "No."

"Then steer clear and mind your boy." He leaned forward and grabbed the torch from Father's hand, then dismounted and stomped it out on the ground.

The group peeled off in two as half the men circled to cut off any chance of his escape.

There had to be something I could do. For a moment, I pictured myself standing up and calling for reason, but Father would have already tried, and if he had failed…

Why had he brought me? I couldn't be involved with this. It might be exactly what the Voice needed to complete my transformation into a monster. But I couldn't just ride off without trying to stop this.

Get the rope. Tie the noose. Slip it over his head and see the fear in his eyes. Watch him kick as he—

We were twenty yards away when the condemned man heard us coming, waking from his sleep and yelling in surprise. He hadn't had a campfire, and the next few seconds were a jumble of fighting shadows. A gun fired twice. Someone hollered.

"Got you!"

As quickly as the action had started, it was over. Someone struck a match, and torches blazed to life, casting a ruddy glow over the area. The man had his arms tied behind his back, blood streaming from a blow to his left temple. His head lolled forward, unconscious.

The other men whooped, riding their horses back and forth, staring up at the trees.

"Here's one!" someone shouted. "Grab a rope!"

"We can't do this," I blurted, my nerves causing my voice to tremble. If I didn't do something to show the Voice I was resisting, there was no knowing what would happen. The crowd went silent all at once, almost as if a lightning bolt had clapped down next to me. Twenty pairs of eyes turned to me, and I backed Surrey up a few steps in surprise. The pit inside me only gaped wider. All those people. Staring at me. I cleared my throat. "I don't know what he did, but we should bring him to—"

Someone grasped me by the arm.

"It's too late for that," Father muttered, then raised his voice. "Well, come on. You were the ones so antsy to do this. Sooner this is done, sooner I can sleep."

He grabbed my reins when I tried to ride off, jerking Surrey's head around to face the tree. I couldn't raise my eyes to watch, though my mind was only too happy to fill in the details. I'd pictured hanging someone countless times the past few years.

I might not have wanted to watch, but I couldn't plug my ears. Couldn't stop from hearing the rope as the noose was tied, the way it swished through the air as it looped over a branch. The way the mob cheered all at once and the stranger woke up. He screamed like a panther, inhuman and piercing. He couldn't find any words.

And then he didn't say anything at all.

The crowd quieted, and you could hear every grunt as the man struggled for breath. Every creak of the limb as his legs kicked to find purchase that wasn't there. The sounds stopped.

A moment or an hour later, the men were talking again, though I couldn't understand a word they were saying. I sat on Surrey, staring at the way the torchlight cast shadows on the blades of grass. I hadn't been part of this, had I? It didn't count, did it?

The Voice only laughed.

Father released my reins. He jerked his head for me to follow. Instead, I rode off in the opposite direction, trying to get away from what I'd just experienced.

I didn't ride far. I wasn't familiar with the area, and I didn't want to risk Surrey's footing in the dark. So I went down by the river and watched the silvery reflection of the moon on the water. Tried to block out the memory of those sounds and the sight of the man hanging from the tree, his head slumped forward, his feet dangling.

My entire body felt numb. Like I was detached from myself somehow. I bit my tongue until it almost bled.

That hadn't been right. It might have been normal, but just because something was normal didn't make it good. It was almost worse to know I'd have to see those men around town. Buying tools at the general store. Laughing together as they gathered in the square. I hadn't focused on the faces, but they still came back to me, lit by the torches. Daniel Cogburn was the barber. Alan Ladd worked a farm just a few miles down from ours. They had wives. Children.

And not a single one of them would feel bad about what they'd done?

I wasn't sure how long I stared at the North Fork Spring, but at some point, I got back on Surrey and rode home.

"We should have stopped it," I told my father as soon as I stepped into the kitchen. The fire in the stove was long dead, and the room was already chilly. A candle on the table provided the only light.

He glanced up at me as he poured another drink, then snorted in dismissal. "You might as well try stopping the Mississippi. The man stole ten horses and shot at the Ladds as he rode off, and this ain't Philadelphia."

Shove his face into the embers. The hiss of the fire on his skin. The smell of burning flesh.

My eyes flicked around the room, and it was all I could do to keep from hugging myself, but I had to see this through. "What if we'd—"

"You heard them. I'm not the justice anymore. I don't have any right to interfere."

"Should that matter to a Bullock? Did anyone see the man actually commit a crime?"

Father's head jerked to the side as if I'd slapped him. "Ladd found him with horses from three different farms. It ain't like he borrowed them. If we'd brought him in, he'd have been found guilty soon enough and faced the same fate."

I kept my eyes on the table, wishing I'd been more assertive, but I was already treading far too close to anger for my comfort. "Why even bring me then? Why did I need to see that? Are you trying to make things worse?"

Father kicked back the whiskey in a quick swallow, then poured again, not responding. Outside, the spring peepers and the crickets seemed louder than ever. Far too tranquil.

"Listen to me," I said.

He sighed. "Warren, what happened out there was going to happen with or without us. I don't like that they did it, but it's them that did it, not us. Why did I bring you? You were the one going on about being some kind of monster. Live as long as I have, and you see there's a monster inside every person you pass. The trick is not listening to it, and you don't need all these extra rules to keep that from happening."

"It isn't—"

"I saw your face out there tonight. You weren't enjoying what they did to that man, but there were some people—people you think are good—who were. You ain't no different than anyone else. You're better, actually."

"Why didn't they listen to you then? Why couldn't everyone just—"

"Even if I'd been justice of the peace still, stopping that would have meant I'd need to draw iron on some of my neighbors." Father stood and stomped over to stand between me and the table, stopping just short of pushing against me with his chest. All I could see now was his half-unbuttoned shirt. The smell of whiskey washed over me as he spoke. Tonight had taken more of a toll on him than I'd thought. He always got meaner when he drank. "If you want to stop something violent, you need to be ready to get violent yourself."

Get a rope and hang him. See what he thinks about it then.

I turned away from him. My book still sat on the table by the fire. I should have been in bed over an hour ago. "They would have listened to you, before."

He stared at me, silent, and in that moment, I saw Father in a new light. In my eyes, he'd always been this unstoppable force of nature. You might as well try to stare down a tornado as get in his way. But for a moment, I saw him as just another man. Full of hopes and doubts just like anyone else. It made me want to take the words back that hung between us, but he spoke first.

"Maybe yes and maybe no. And maybe I'd have tried to stop

them if some random horse thief was worth the effort. But he wasn't, and I didn't, and I'll sleep just fine tonight knowing he's dead." He wove his way out of the room, and I didn't know what to say to stop him.

CHAPTER THREE

"For several months different persons have been disappearing very mysteriously on the route between Independence and Osage Mission. Nearly a dozen people had suddenly dropped out of sight in this way, and the matter was exciting a great deal of talk throughout southeast Kansas."

—Chicago Daily Tribune
(Chicago, Illinois), May 13, 1873

———

G EORGE AND HIS BABY HAVE gone missing," Father said at the kitchen table.

"Missing how?" Mother asked as she handed the bowl of peas to Adelia.

"He was supposed to be here a week ago, on his way back to Iowa."

"Maybe he was delayed." Mother's tone still said she was only half listening.

Arsenic is tasteless. They'd be dead in hours, writhing on the floor, vomiting blood. And no one would—

I bit down on my tongue, hard. The pain made the Voice quiet.

Father stared at the far wall, chewing slowly as he mulled something over. In the background, the clock ticked its way toward six. "It don't set right with me," he said at last. "I'm gonna have to go see what's held him up."

That caught Mother's attention. "It's almost May! You can't just leave the farm in the middle—"

"Newton's planning on stopping here on his way north to meet back up with his family anyways. He don't have a farm he's tending to at the moment. He can keep an eye on things for the week it'll take me to go see what the trouble is."

"George isn't even family," Mother said, setting her cup down more forcefully than she ought. The Voice was thrilled by the tension in the air.

"His father saved my life. I promised him I'd look out for his son, and a Bullock always—"

"Keeps his promises," Mother finished. Adelia had mouthed the words along with her.

Father glanced between the two of them. "It's about time Warren stepped up some, anyway."

My eyebrows shot up. "Me? I—"

"You're seventeen," Father said. "Old enough you could be well on your way to your own farm now. I haven't brought up the issue, on account of…you being my youngest son. But it's high time I stopped treating you like a child."

Mother and Adelia looked at me, and we all knew what Father had started to say. Father had seven living children. Newton came from his first wife, and James, Virgil, Wyatt, Morgan, Addie, and I all came from Mother. Addie was the youngest at twelve, but she missed out on most of the Bullock expectations, with her being a girl and all. But try always being compared to people who were grown men the day I was born.

And being different, to boot.

I'd never been close with my brothers, though I wished it were otherwise, and it wasn't from a lack of affection on their part. But I'd never be able to measure up to them, and I always felt the difference when they were around, no matter what they tried to tell me.

"Still," Mother continued after another long pause, "surely it wouldn't hurt to wait one more week. He's coming from *Kansas*, after all. Heaven knows what sort of—"

"Sooner started, sooner finished. The man has a baby daughter not even eighteen months old, and he just lost his wife and son. I'd say he's already had more than his fair share of sorrow, and I'm the one who convinced him to move east to be with family. He might be laid up sick in Osage Mission, or maybe he had some sort of accident. Either way, I owe it to his father to find out. I'll be back in less than ten days. You'll see."

When Father made his mind up, there was no going back. Newton arrived the next day, and Father was gone the day after.

My oldest brother was thirty-five and easily irritated. Father said he hadn't always been like that, but when he came back from serving in the army during the Slaveholders' Rebellion, he'd changed. It's not that he was mean or spiteful, but he had expectations about what needed to be done, and he made sure you met them. Mother said some of it was because of the injuries he'd suffered during the war.

"Everything's harder when you're in pain all the time," she explained to me. "He puts up a good front, but even working around the farm is much harder for him."

Whatever the reason, it didn't change the fact he also thought the best way to get me to "grow up" was through hard work. If you listened to him, Father had been far too easy on me.

At least the Voice wasn't as loud when I could barely keep my eyes open from exhaustion.

A week passed, and there was no sign of Father. His ten-day promise came and went, and still no word. Mother's face took on more worry lines every morning, and Newton had to make arrangements for his family in his absence. Life around the farm grew quieter, as everyone couldn't keep from checking the horizon for a rider. Some passed by, but none of them was Father.

On the first of the month, I rode to the general store to pick up a few groceries for Mother. It was a short trip, and I enjoyed having time in the sun, even if it meant I'd have to be around strangers for a half hour or so. Most people in Lamar knew about me, but strangers still tended to get too close or want to shake my hand. I'd had plenty of practice slipping in and out of rooms as unnoticed as possible.

Handling a store full of knives, rope, poison, and axes was a different story, but it was one I'd had to learn to deal with years ago. It was a balance between trying to spend as little time in there as I could and taking enough time to avoid forgetting something and having to make a second trip. I forced myself to carry something the entire time or to keep my hands in my pockets where they wouldn't be tempted to do anything wicked, and even then I usually ended up sweating and breathing heavily within a minute or two of walking in the store.

It was no wonder most people gave me a wide berth.

The grocer, Mr. Crowe, saw me come in, but he was deep in conversation with a short man with a strong chin, broad hat, and patched clothing. The store wasn't that big, so his voice carried easily across the room. Despite that, I tried to keep my head down and ignore it. In and out. If I was quick enough, the stranger might still be talking while I was paying. Talking to the grocer meant not talking to me.

A single axe blow to the head would kill him in an instant.

No. In and out. Focus.

Except somehow in the middle of all that turmoil, one of his words caught my ear. "Murder" will do that.

"Two boys," the man was saying. "Couldn't a been more than twelve years old, findin' a body like that? I thought we'd put all that behind us with the war."

"And it was just floatin' in the water?" Mr. Crowe asked. I risked a glance at him. His face was twisted in disgust.

"Rottin' to boot. Me? I'd'a left it there. Dealin' with bodies is up to the law, but I s'pose a twelve-year-old wouldn't know no better. Nosy, them. And they got more than a noseful, from what I heard. Turned the body over to see its skull all stove in and its throat cut in a second smile, ear to ear. Head barely wanted to stay on the body."

My feet had planted themselves to the floor. My stomach roiled, but I knew I had to hear what the stranger had to say.

Mrs. Cutchins sniffed loudly, standing by the canned goods. When neither man looked over at her, she turned and left the store.

The man continued. "When they brought word to town, it didn't take a committee to see the connection. From what I hear, forty or fifty people have just vanished over the last year. Only a few of 'em was ever seen again, and them that were showed up in the same condition. Throat slashed, head stove in. Not that they've found most of 'em."

Mr. Crowe grunted. "It's Kansas. What else would you expect?"

The man nodded, jabbing his finger at the grocer a few times for emphasis. "Exactly right. You put that many new people all together in one place, you might as well stuff ten cats in a bag and hope they'll all get along. Sure, the law's looked some, but that close to Indian Territory? They got outlaw conclaves there to rival a small town in size. Full of men who'd slit your throat for a smile. Women too."

Forty or fifty people missing? Thoughts of Father pushed aside my hesitance around strangers and my terror of losing myself in violence. "Where w-was this?" I asked.

Mr. Crowe raised his eyebrows, but the stranger didn't know anything about me to notice. "Down about Independence way. Kansas, not Missouri, that is. Along the road from Osage Mission."

That was the same area Father had gone looking for George. "And n-no one knows who's been doing it?"

"No one knows, and no one cares neither. All too busy lookin' out for their own to care about their neighbor."

I shoved some money at Mr. Crowe, not bothering to count it, and practically ran out the door. Outside, I took deep breaths, staring at the ground and hoping no one was noticing me. Once I had myself under control, I hurried home to tell Mother and Newton.

"Father knows how to take care of himself," my oldest brother said. "I'd like to see the outlaws foolish enough to try to get the drop on a Bullock."

He had a point, but I also didn't miss the way Mother's eyes flicked to the distance and how worry lines began to appear on her face. Those lines only deepened when more travelers came through, bringing with them even more gossip about missing people.

With Kansas being so close to Indian Territory, you had more than your fair share of people with a less-than-passing relationship with the law. Cross the border, and you were outside the realm of anyone's jurisdiction. There were entire outlaw colonies in the area between Texas and Kansas, they said. Even the name of some of it—No Man's Land—was enough to make you wonder what exactly went on there.

So it wasn't that out of the ordinary to have people disappear from time to time. Ever since Lincoln passed the Homestead Act in 1862, almost anyone willing to come to Kansas and work the land for five years, growing crops and putting up shelter, got to keep 160 acres of it for free. Soldiers who'd served in the army longer than two years could get the land after a single year. With that many strangers coming to one place—with so many different backgrounds and opinions—it would be almost impossible to keep track of everyone. They kept settling the edges of civilization, after all.

The Voice, of course, found all this tremendously fascinating, whispering to me all sorts of situations that might have happened first to George and then to Father. Corpses with slit throats and shattered skulls danced in my dreams, no matter how many times I reminded myself how capable Father was.

As I went about my chores on the farm, I found myself looking at the horizon more often than usual, to the point that Newton had to chide me for shirking work. The pit in my stomach only grew.

At night in my room, I lay there, thinking through different scenarios. Perhaps Father had gone looking for George and come across the trail of these larger disappearances. It would be like him to want to follow that thread and see if he couldn't solve it, especially having lost the election for justice of the peace. Being a lawman was the same thing as being a Bullock, to him, and this would be a way for him to get that part of himself back.

Except he also wouldn't leave the farm—and Mother—for this long without at least sending word. Could his message have been waylaid? It wouldn't be surprising. Only, Father would have known it was possible for a single letter to go astray. He would have sent more than one and kept us in the loop.

My mind tangled itself up in knots as the Voice whispered all the grim fates he might have suffered, and I tried to convince myself everything was fine. As each day passed, that became harder to do, until I thought I might burst out screaming in frustration. What if Father was somewhere alone, in need of help? He'd be off to save one of us in an instant.

Who could save him? Newton was crippled and couldn't ride for long times at a stretch. Virgil and James were back east, the last we'd heard, and Morgan and Wyatt were somewhere near Omaha. We couldn't afford to take the time to send them word and have them come.

I found maps of Kansas and Indian Territory, staring at unfamiliar town names. Osage Mission. Cherryvale. Coffeyville. There was a lot of ground to cover. If Father had spent more time getting familiar with where he was going, would he have been home sooner? And what about anyone who went after him?

Father needed help now, and I could only see one way forward.

"I need to go to Kansas," I said at the kitchen table. It had been twenty days: ten more than Father had said.

The entire room fell silent, as if someone had thrown a blanket over everyone. In the background, the clock in the parlor was as loud as hammers.

A series of emotions flashed across Newton's face: annoyance, confusion, and—most disappointing—doubt. "Pass the potatoes, Ma." He dragged his stare off me and turned to Mother. She sat with her hands clasped in front of her, picking and twisting her napkin as if it had some answers hidden inside it.

When Newton repeated himself, she looked up, blinked, and handed him the potatoes.

"Aren't you going to say any more than that?" I asked, my stomach twisting. It was one thing to tell myself I wasn't up to the task, but to have Newton dismiss it so casually was far worse.

Adelia kicked me under the table, but I ignored her.

"What do you expect me to say?" Newton asked. "We all know why you're fixing to go to Kansas, and I can't say I blame you. But if there were ever anyone less equipped to go find Father, it's my youngest brother who can't even enter a room without getting the fidgets and can't look a man in the eye when he has to talk to him."

Newton sliced up his potato, his blade cutting through the skin every bit as quickly as those words had struck my core.

That knife is sharp enough to—

I shook my head clear. Forcing my family not to use knives at the table had never worked, but if it belonged to them, it didn't belong to me, and that made any potential weapon somewhat more acceptable.

"There's no one else who *will* go," I said.

Newton ate his potato in silence, then took a drink of whiskey. "Much as I hate to say it, that ain't the numbest thing you ever come up with."

"No," Mother blurted. "He can't—"

Newton held up his hand. True, he was from Father's first marriage, but Mother had raised him since he was two. That didn't mean he had much patience even with her when he wanted his way.

"Warren's a bright enough boy," he said, "but we all know he's not up to running this farm on his own. If my hip worked the way it ought, I'd be on the road myself by now, but I got Jennie and little Wyatt to look out for. Whatever Father went and got himself in the middle of, it's gobbling up people left and right. If Warren were up to the job, he'd be the right Bullock to do it."

Newton stared at me and forked a piece of potato into his mouth, his full beard moving as he chewed. "Thing is," he continued, "I got my doubts about that."

I pressed my lips together, trying to keep my voice steady. If I spoke rashly, I'd only give him more reason to say I was unfit. "I can do this. I'm ready." It was a line I'd practiced multiple times in my bedroom.

Mother threw the napkin down and exclaimed, "You're going to abandon us, just like your brothers!"

My jaw dropped. "I'm not abandoning anyone. I'm seventeen. Surrey can handle the trip with no troubles, and I could be there and back in two weeks. I sat down last night and calculated it all out. It shouldn't be that hard to dig around and find out what's been going on, and if I need help, I—I'll find it."

Newton placed his fork down and stared at me. "Why you figure it won't be hard? You saying you'll have an easier time of this than Pa?"

I felt the blood run to my face, but I forced myself to return the stare. "I'm saying I won't do what Father set out to do. I'm good at paying attention to details. I think things through, but I know I'm not like the rest of you. I wouldn't send me after an outlaw either. But I won't need to do that. As soon as I find the trail, I'll turn it over to someone who can do something about it."

"You can't go," Newton said.

"What?" I asked.

He picked up his knife and fork and began moving the steak and potatoes around on his plate again. "You heard me. You can't go."

"Why not?"

"I'll give you five reasons: you ain't me, you ain't James, you ain't Virgil, you ain't Wyatt, and you ain't Morgan."

"Just because I'm not as experienced as—"

"Not as experienced? That's like saying a foal ain't as experienced as a workhorse. The rest of us are all men, tested and true. Me, James, and Virgil are war veterans. Wyatt's already been a constable, even if he and Morgan are both too busy whoring around to care about anything else at the moment. What have you done? You won't even sleep in the same room as the rifle Pa gave you six years ago, let alone pick it up, and you get upset if your peas touch your meatloaf."

I managed to avoid staring down at my plate, where my food was neatly and precisely laid out. Instead, I slapped my hand down on the table, trying to get through to him. "I can do this." The Voice sent a thrill down my spine. This was skirting too close to violence. I had to stay calm.

"Having a tantrum ain't gonna help your case," Newton said. "This is the real world. It don't run according to a schedule. If you were talking about going to find a homestead of your own, I'd be all for it. But people are disappearing, and they ain't disappearing without someone being behind it. Someone with practice. If Father wasn't even up to it? If you go out there and start poking your nose around, what's to say you ain't gonna get disappeared yourself?"

"I'll be careful," I said. "You know how much attention I pay to detail. No one else out in Kansas is going to be doing that."

Newton leaned back from the table and folded his arms. "Fair enough. I wouldn't argue that any day of the week. You get your rifle. Meet me outside. If you can hit a bottle at twenty-five yards, I won't stand in your way."

It felt as if he'd punched me in the gut. I was supposed to not just hold a gun but *fire it*? "I—I d-don't—what—"

"No brother of mine is going to Kansas if he can't defend himself. People there ain't just gonna nod and go away if you ask them nicely. So prove to me you can do this one thing, and I'll help you pack your bags tonight."

Mother and Adelia both stared at me with twin expressions of surprise and worry. No doubt they'd assumed Newton would never stand for this. Then again, they also had to know just how hard it would be for me to do it. Years ago, sure. But now? I stood from the table and headed upstairs, my knees struggling to hold my body up. I'd given the Remington away, but Father had given me the Winchester five years ago, buying one for himself and one for me at the same time. It was before I'd realized just how dangerous I might become, but I couldn't come up with a good enough reason to get rid of it as well.

Three years ago, I'd moved it out of my room and into the hall closet. When Father had stumbled upon it there, propped up in the back behind the coats, he'd been so hurt, he couldn't talk to me for a week.

I rooted around in the closet and shoved the coats aside to stare at the rifle. It wasn't loaded, of course. I don't think I could have slept if I'd known a loaded rifle was just fifteen feet away from me, even if there were two doors between me and it. A box of bullets was shoved into the back of the top drawer of my dresser.

What use would it be for me to go on a search for someone as evil as I was if I lost all control before I even found them?

It holds fourteen bullets. You could kill your entire family in less than a minute.

The image was so clear: Newton, Mother, and Adelia slumped on the floor, lying in three spreading pools of blood. I rushed to my chamber pot and threw up my supper.

No. I couldn't do it. I'd leave in the middle of the night, perhaps. Without Newton's permission, and then—

And then I'd be in exactly the sort of danger Newton was insisting I recognize. I might not go looking for a confrontation, but that didn't mean a confrontation wouldn't come looking for me. Trying to face down someone as evil as I was? Someone who didn't even bother resisting the thoughts that came into their head? They'd kill me without blinking if I didn't have a way to protect myself.

If I wanted to do this, I needed to at least make people believe I was someone to be careful around. Having the rifle in a saddle scabbard might be enough to ward people away. I didn't even have to have it loaded.

Except I was never going to shoot a bottle with an empty rifle.

I set the chamber pot down and teetered to my dresser. My hand shook as I opened the bottom drawer and took out the box of bullets, staring at the small metal rounds. I grabbed a handful and did my best not to think about what I was doing, striding to the closet and grabbing the gun in one quick motion.

It was cool to the touch but not dusty. Father had taken care of it when I wouldn't, reassuring me it would be ready for me once I was back to myself. A Bullock needed a rifle.

I loaded the rounds, sliding each one into the chamber in succession. The rifle took care of the rest. My hands shook enough that I dropped several cartridges, but I got through the task eventually.

As I did, I scrambled to come up with a rule I could follow that would keep me in check. Better yet, a few rules. For one thing, I wouldn't point the gun at another person. Ever. And if I only fired it when someone else told me to, then there was no way I'd end up losing control.

It didn't make sense, but it was enough of a plan to let me go back downstairs.

When I went outside, the wind had picked up. The sun still had a few hours to go before it set, and Newton already had a green bottle set up on one of the fence posts. He was standing a ways off from it. Was that really twenty-five yards? It looked more like fifty. I'd been a natural back when I'd practiced shooting, but would that still be the case?

I stepped over to Newton. "It doesn't matter if I can hit that or not," I said. "It doesn't change the fact that I need to—"

"All your smarts ain't gonna do much if someone's really set on causing harm. Not unless you plan on boring them to death."

My face warmed, and I swallowed. Why couldn't it have been anyone but Newton here now? He'd always been the one to show the most disappointment in me. "But they—"

"Less talking. More shooting. Or slink back inside and don't bring this up again."

I studied my brother for a moment. He was twice my age. A fourth sergeant in the war. He'd put on weight the last few years, but every inch of him was still as intimidating as ever.

"Maybe you could come with me?" I said, feeling like a fool for the way my voice pitched up at the end of the sentence, making it sound almost as if I were begging. Mother and Adelia stood on the front porch about fifteen yards away from us, watching this all unfold.

Newton scowled for a moment. Then his face softened and somehow became even more lined. "I'd help you if I could, Warren. Heaven knows I want to. Father out there alone? It makes my skin crawl, but you get to be my age and you realize you can't always do the obvious thing. Everything has to be weighed, and me leaving my family and Ma could be the death of all of them. Sending me off to go poking around would be almost as bad an idea as sending you."

"But not quite as bad?"

He gave me a half smile. "Shoot, if you can. I hear you used to be pretty decent."

I'd already picked up the gun. I might have had thoughts of shooting my family, but I had yet to follow through on any of them, even if my palms were sweating with the stress of it all. *No pointing at people. Rules will keep you safe.*

With that thought planted firmly in my mind, I stepped forward, putting my brother well out of any danger. I let out a deep breath, squared my shoulders, and brought the rifle to my shoulder. Father had always talked about point shooting, getting so good with the gun that you aimed the same as you did when you pointed at something with your finger. He could have hit that bottle without thinking twice. It used to be easy for me too.

Just point and pull the trigger. Don't think about the wind or the elevation. Don't think about what the bullet could do to a person. Don't think about how you're not sure which you want more: to hit the bottle or to miss it. Don't think at all. Just do it. The more I thought about it, the more I'd confuse myself, the same as I always did.

I pulled the trigger, then cursed myself for having forgotten to cock the thing in the first place. Newton chuckled, and something inside me snapped in anger. I cocked the rifle, straightened my back, and fired.

The bottle exploded in a flurry of broken glass. For a moment, I couldn't believe I'd done it. The Voice cackled in glee, but I tried to ignore it. I looked back at Newton and hoped I sounded confident. "That answer your worries?"

He stood there for what felt like a full minute, his eyes flicking from me to the gun and over to where the bottle had been. "What were you planning to do if I said no?" he asked me at last.

I chewed the inside of my lip. "Ride off anyway. Father's in trouble, and I can't sit by."

He grunted, then jerked his head toward the barn. "Best get you packed up then, hadn't we?"

CHAPTER FOUR

"Benjamin M. Brown, of Cedar Vale, Howard county, Kansas. His head was mashed in and his throat cut from ear to ear! With the exception of a red and white handkerchief around his neck, he was entirely naked."

—The Emporia News

(Emporia, Kansas), May 23, 1873

I LEFT THE NEXT MORNING JUST after it grew light. My saddlebags were packed with enough food to last me a week, and Newton had added enough money to my savings to cover expenses for at least four times that. This shouldn't be a long trip, however. Riding by myself, I should be able to cover more than thirty miles a day, no matter what Newton said. My brother had tried to convince me to take his horse instead of Surrey. It would make the journey faster than Surrey could manage, but I wanted a mount I could rely on, and Surrey had always been the most dependable horse I'd laid eyes on.

"Don't go doing anything foolish," Newton told me right before I set out. "You stay on Pa's trail, but if it goes much farther into Kansas, you come get help. Maybe I can rope Wyatt into coming back, or Virgil."

"I can take care of myself."

"Not in some places, you can't," Newton said, his voice serious as a drought. "You stay away from western Kansas, and don't you even set foot in Indian Territory, no matter what."

"I saw plenty of the Utes and Cheyenne on the trail to and from California," I said. "They never gave us trouble. Are the others really that bad?"

"The tribes? No, they're peaceful enough for the most part. More interested in trading than killing. But I'm talking about the outlaws. The law don't head past that border, and there's plenty that know it. They'd kill a man for nothing more than his horse. You steer clear."

I agreed, mainly to get him to let me go. This should be straightforward enough. If I stuck to the well-traveled paths, I'd make Osage Mission by tomorrow night, as long as everything went according to plan.

And if you planned well enough, it usually would. I'd made a packing list, sketched out a rough itinerary, listed places I'd need to check, and inspected all my gear to make sure it was ready for a journey. My saddle, bags, clothes, food, map, pot, matches, flint (if the matches failed), rope, compass—everything was in order. Surrey was well rested and dependable, and he was freshly shod.

I hadn't accounted for the rain, however: a steady drizzle that started an hour after I'd set out and lasted the entire day, casting everything in a sort of half fog that made me feel like I was riding through a dream.

Surrey's hoof falls were muffled on the packed dirt, a constant beat that helped remind me I was making progress. The air was damp against my skin, but my oiled duster made a valiant attempt to keep the rain off my top half. My bottom half, on the other hand, was soaked through after an hour, the fabric cold and uncomfortable.

Even then, I felt lighter than I had in weeks. I was *doing* something, and it made me think anything was possible. I'd find Father, and we'd come back to smiles all around. For the first time in years, people would be proud of me. Plus, now that I was on my own, without anyone around I had to worry about injuring, it felt like I'd set down a weight I hadn't realized I'd been carrying.

He's dead. Murdered with the rest of them. Moldering in the ground as he—

No. For today, I could be positive.

I'd start at Osage Mission. It was where George Longcor had been headed, and it was where he hadn't shown up. Father would have gone there first. I'd ask at each place I came to until I found the spot where people stopped having seen Father or George. Likely George, since he would have been more noticeable, with his baby. That would pinpoint where they'd gone missing, and perhaps I'd hear some of the specifics of the other disappearances as well.

Kansas couldn't be as dangerous as it used to be. Yes, it had been one of the hotbeds of the fight between the North and South before the war, but the Slaveholders' Rebellion had ended seven years ago now.

As I rode through the fields, nodding to the occasional farmer or housewife I passed, the disappearances made less and less sense. Everyone'd had their fill of violence and more for four long years. Even the Osage had left peacefully, more or less. They'd sold the land to the U.S. government for ten million dollars, and it'd been a priest at Osage Mission who'd helped them avoid getting taken advantage of, from what I'd read. They'd gone on to buy land in Indian Territory.

No one should have been in any danger, as long as they stuck to the roads.

Camping that night was more complicated than I'd expected. I'd lived on the trail for weeks at a time, but we'd always had a wagon with us, and Father and my older brothers there to tell me what to do. At my age, I should have been better at taking care of all the chores that needed doing: rubbing Surrey down, lighting the fire, cooking supper, and settling in for the night. Taking care of my horse was easy enough, but I couldn't find dry wood that would take a match, so my supper was nothing more than hard tack and jerky, and I discovered I hadn't quite packed my bags tightly enough either. Rain had seeped its way inside my packs and gotten my heavy tarp soaked.

It was a wet, cold end to a wet, cold day, and in the morning, my skin felt puckered and sticky. My clothes were stiff, and my boots were almost too tight to put on.

The trip could only get better from here.

And indeed, the sun came out, and I began to regain my spirits as the miles went past. Surrey didn't go quite as fast as I'd thought he'd be able to, but I didn't want to push him. There were plenty of miles in front of me.

I'd looked at Osage Mission on a map, so I knew where to go but little else, picturing a small building off in the middle of nowhere, complete with men in black robes and a few nuns. I came upon the place when the sun was an hour from setting. I'd stopped squelching with every step Surrey took, but sores were forming on the inside of my thighs, and I still felt like a waterlogged dog.

The first thing I spotted was the mission itself: a cluster of ten buildings spread out across the plains. Most of them were still rough-hewn logs, but it had a stone church and a stone building that might have been a school or a dormitory. The ring of a smithy came from one of the far buildings toward the center, and the scent of baking bread wafted from another. Several boys scurried with their heads down, their eyes on the ground as they rushed between buildings under the watch of priests in black robes. To my right, nuns were doing the same thing over a group of girls.

But beyond the mission there was more. Much more. An entire town had grown up nearby, no doubt attracted by the traffic that came as so many settlers funneled into the area, each anxious to get their own 160 acres to claim. Back home in Lamar, the town was sixteen years old, and that had given it time to settle down some. Here it was all so new, the paint still looked wet. I could hear the bustle of excitement soon after I passed the mission complex.

Once I hit Main Street, the sheer variety of businesses was more than a little overwhelming. Two different attorneys, a hardware store, a harness shop, two shoemakers, two wagon makers, two lumber dealers, a butcher, a tailor, a druggist, a bank, four blacksmiths, a dentist, two furniture stores, three groceries, a painter, a doctor, a post office, a newspaper, a mason, a livery, two restaurants, two saloons, a gunsmith, a foundry, a photographer, and an auctioneer. It was twice as big as Lamar!

The streets were wide, the buildings mostly timber framed with flat roofs and an occasional balcony. It was less than sixty miles from my home, but there was no doubting I'd traveled to the frontier. The place was swarming with people: hurrying on errands, strolling with sweethearts, yelling, drinking, laughing— one man fast asleep on a front porch. Most of the men were armed, and half of them seemed eager to use their guns as soon as possible. I clenched and unclenched my fist, trying to ignore the churning in my stomach until, at last, it became too much. I tucked Surrey and myself into an alley off the main thoroughfare, where it was at least a little quieter.

I had a complicated relationship even with the people I knew well. Strangers were usually tolerable in small numbers. I couldn't tell where I stood with them. They'd give me odd looks for even small things like arranging the glasses on a table in a symmetrical pattern. How could you know what a stranger was thinking or what they might do?

Confrontations were the worst. They might berate me for looking at them wrong or saying something they didn't like, but how was I supposed to know what was fine and what wasn't? And when they snapped, I always worried I'd lash out at last. I had a callus on the inside of my right cheek from biting there each time. If I focused on the pain instead of responding, I was able to keep myself well away from anything that might make me want to give in to the Voice.

But this? That sea of faces in front of me felt like I was looking at an enemy host gathered to face me. How would I have a chance of getting through them all? Particularly because peppered through the crowd were all manner of revolvers, knives, whips, and clubs.

You could grab a revolver when someone passes by you. In seconds, you could fire all six shots into the crowd. You already have a rifle with you. It's only a matter of time until you use it.

I forced my mind back into focus. Father needed me. This was a problem just like any other. *Focus on the problem and not the fear. Break the problem down into a series of steps, and then work my way down the list.* The first step: find a place to sleep tonight.

A hotel sat opposite the alley I had picked. Taking a breath,

I walked Surrey across the street and hitched him out front, then went in to get a room. Whatever I was going to do, I'd need to be at least somewhat rested to start in earnest.

The accommodations were spare: a bed and a nightstand, with a dresser so rickety that I worried it might fall over if I tried to store anything in it. At least the barn for Surrey seemed well stocked and clean. My first order of business was looking for weapons, of course. My fingers were already itching to get to work while the innkeeper was still showing me the bed and pointing the way to the facilities. The moment the door was closed, I took the sheets off the bed, lifted the mattress, and checked each drawer. That still didn't feel right, so I removed each drawer from the dresser and ran my hands around the inside and outside of each one, confirming nothing was hiding itself from a visual inspection.

After I'd done that three times, I was finally able to convince myself the room was safe and that I wouldn't have to worry about being tempted while I stayed there. If yesterday I'd been relieved to be alone, today brought everything back with a rush. It was as if my journey had made the urge to keep others safe from me that much keener.

I'd delayed long enough. It was time to go back into the streets. I stopped in front of my door, my hand on the knob.

Why were my insides bubbling up like I was facing down some monsters from Greek mythology?

This was it. Father was missing, and I needed to do whatever it took to find him and bring him home safely. If I let myself consider any other possibilities of his fate, I'd be no use to anyone. I'd turn the knob, walk downstairs, and head into the town, asking people if they'd heard anything about George Longcor or Father.

What was the worst they could say to me? They might ask why I was nosing around, or they could laugh at me. Did that really matter? And why should my nerves override my concern for Father?

Forcing the worry deeper down, I opened the door and headed out.

For the first while, I just walked through the town, looking at the faces of the people and the signs of the stores. Should I approach a woman or a man? Someone old, or someone young? Would it be better to do it outside, or would they be more likely to answer if I were inside? A saloon, or a store? Several times I thought about how poorly prepared for this I was. Wyatt wouldn't have had these troubles. Any of my brothers should be doing this instead of me.

At last I sat on a bench outside a barber's, taking deep breaths and trying to calm myself. My palms were sweaty, my mouth dry. The last time I'd been this upset had been when I'd broken the axle on our wagon, riding it over too rough of a terrain. Mother had made me wait outside until Father was in from the fields, and I'd been convinced he'd kill me as soon as he found out.

Before I'd left yesterday, a part of me had felt like a mix between Mark Twain off to see the west in *Roughing It* and Auguste Dupin in "The Murders in the Rue Morgue." This was my big chance. My opportunity to prove to myself that perhaps there was hope for me after all.

Instead, I was behaving more like the white rabbit in *Alice's Adventures in Wonderland*, scurrying around, nervously accomplishing nothing. I had to be more than this.

Squaring my shoulders and biting down on the callus inside my cheek, I stood and headed into the first building I came across.

Of course it was a saloon.

The place was everything I'd imagined from stories. A long bar filled with men huddled against it, drinking or chatting with one another as the bartender scrambled between them, his face covered in sweat, his apron askew. Four different poker games were going on at the same time.

A few women circulated, smiling at the men and trailing their hands across shoulders. In the corner, a man was playing "Camptown Races" on an out-of-tune piano. Several men were leaning next to it, singing along.

If I'd thought the street was overwhelming, that was just because I hadn't seen so many people crammed indoors before. Before today, I'd never considered myself to be much of a rube. I'd lived in several states. I'd been to California and back. My family had been involved in local politics. But I'd always had the freedom to go where I wanted and do what I wanted. It just so happened that what I wanted never included "stay inside with too many people."

And why would it? People smelled, and they gave me odd looks and made me feel like I shouldn't exist. Worst of all, they made the Voice get louder. If I thought of hurting or killing people I loved, was it any wonder I thought even more about violence when I was around people I didn't care about?

You could punch that man in the throat.

This place would go up in flames with the right match in the right place.

The same weapons that had been in the street were here, only closer together and easier for me to reach. Instead of listening to the thoughts that streamed through my head as I stood at the entrance, I focused on the disorder instead. The messy state of the bar. The way the tables weren't lined up in a pattern. The puddle of spit around the spittoon.

If I was thinking of cleaning, I wasn't thinking of hurting.

A man shoved past me, cursing as he entered the saloon. I realized I was standing in the door like a sack of potatoes, and I moved to the side to gather my thoughts once more.

It wasn't enough for me to just enter the saloon. I had to talk to people. I considered joining one of the poker games for a few seconds before I tossed the idea. I'd have better luck just handing money out to anyone who wanted to talk to me, and it would be a miracle if I could ask a question at all, let alone try to play a game with strangers. The thought of touching those cards—that so many others had touched before me—decided me more than anything.

And didn't all poker games end in shoot-outs?

Instead, I walked up to the bar, hoping I didn't look as pale as I felt. *Just ask about George or Father, and then leave if no one knows anything.* Simple.

The bartender came over and cocked an eyebrow, wiping his hands on a towel as he waited for me to speak. I started to lean on the bar itself, then looked at it again and changed my mind. Better to stand.

I cleared my throat. "Yes—I was wondering if, well, I'm here to ask about, or at least look into—have you heard anything—"

His brow furrowed and he practically shouted, "You'll have to speak up. I don't hear too good on a quiet day. What are you drinking?"

My eyes flicked from him to the card games to the piano player to the women. A few of them glanced up and stared at me. They were going to ask what I thought I was doing. They could see the evil in my eyes, and they'd all stand up and—

I turned around and left the saloon, hating myself with every step, but just unable to do the thing I knew needed doing.

For my second attempt, I tried a general store. It would be easier to do this someplace quieter and at least generally familiar, and I didn't give myself time to get worked up about things for another. I just went straight to the first person I saw and said, "I'm looking for anyone who knows anything about George Longcor."

And that really was an improvement. But the person looked me up and down, shook his head, and walked on, leaving me staring at his back.

The next man I tried was old, bent with age, and extremely hard of hearing. I ended up shouting my questions multiple times, making even more of a scene, and he waved me away in irritation when he still couldn't understand what I was going on about.

Things did get easier. I got used to the odd looks, and after one old woman kept me talking for fifteen minutes about the bunions on her left foot, I became better at getting right to my questions. My heart still pounded in my ears some of the time, but I managed to barrel forward.

Unfortunately, none of that barreling produced any results. No one remembered seeing Father, but people had heard of George Longcor and the disappearances—I could see the recognition in some of their faces when I asked the question—but no one wanted to say anything about them. It was as if they worried passing on information to a stranger might end up hurting them later. I grew increasingly frustrated and hungry as the evening ran into night.

In the end, I went back to my hotel, collapsing into the cleanest chair I could find in the common room as I tried to catch my wits.

I'd bought a few hard rolls from a baker before he'd closed up shop, and I ate them now. They'd grown stale since they'd been made this morning, and their crusts bit into my gums. A fitting ending to the sort of day I'd had.

After a while, my attention turned to the other people in the room with me.

There were a couple of men speaking at a table, their voices low and intense. Interrupting them might not be welcome. Another pair—husband and wife?—were arguing about…luggage? It was hard to tell, though their faces were both flushed, and the wife kept wagging her finger in her husband's face. Again: not someone I wanted to approach. However, in the far corner, a mother sat cradling her child as she read a book.

Books and I got along just fine.

Did I have one more try in me today?

I walked over to stand in front of her. She was short, with blond hair neatly tucked under a bonnet and a plain green dress that came to her wrists and the floor. She had a strong jawline, and she muttered to herself under her breath as she read. "What book?" I asked, hoping my voice sounded bright and friendly, and not forced, the way it seemed to my ears.

She glanced up at me, then back to the book. "*A Tale of Two Cities.*"

"That's one of my favorites! Have you finished it already?"

That earned me more than just a glance. Her face brightened, and she said, "It's my third time."

From there, the two of us were off and running. I sat down next to her, and we talked for at least a half hour about different authors and works. George MacDonald. Lewis Carroll. Jules Verne. She'd actually been able to read the new translation of his *Twenty Thousand Leagues under the Sea*, and I was more than a little jealous.

"What brings you to Osage Mission?" she asked at last.

My insides froze up, and all at once, I worried that as soon as I told her my purpose, this whole conversation would disappear in a puff of smoke. I forced the words out anyway. "I'm trying to find out what happened to my father. He came here looking for George Longcor."

"That poor man who disappeared with his baby?"

And just that easily, I had the first real conversation about my quest. The woman—Mrs. Stewart—turned out not to know much more than I already did, but that wasn't the key part of that inter-action. I realized through it that just going up and asking strangers questions about a sensitive topic wasn't likely to get me anything more than suspicious stares. It should have gone without saying, and I was embarrassed that it took me as long as it did to figure that out, but from then on, my search would be much smoother.

That night as I lay in bed, staring at the ceiling and waiting for sleep to come, I realized something else: there had been a stretch of time today—an hour or two—when I was so focused on all my other worries that the Voice hadn't been as loud. I'd been thinking so much about talking to strangers and making a good impression and trying to figure out what to do next, the thoughts of killing and maiming people had been drowned out.

It sounded like a simple thing. Like something anyone else wouldn't have even thought worth mentioning. For me, however, it left me almost glowing inside. It was the first time in at least two years that I thought I might actually be able to redeem myself.

I woke in the morning and proceeded to go on a number of make-believe errands. Buying a loaf of bread from the baker. Getting my hair cut by the barber. And at each place and in between, I would strike up a conversation about anything. Asking someone for a recommendation for the best bakery or where I might put in for a job. Was I a perfect conversationalist? Definitely not, but I muddled my way through.

The Voice didn't disappear the same way it had yesterday, but perhaps that was because I was thinking about it now. Still, the more I focused on what I needed to get done, the less sway the Voice had over me. Was it my fear of talking to strangers? My senses being overwhelmed by everything else around me? I couldn't be sure, but I wasn't complaining.

Strangers were much more willing to offer advice than they were to talk about dangerous subjects, and once we'd talked for a while, I would mention that I'd just come to town the day before, which inevitably led to them asking why I'd come.

In that manner, I discovered a few key points.

First, almost everyone was convinced George was dead, which made it much harder to keep my fears for Father in check. I reminded myself of how he never backed down from any challenge and always came out on top. George might have been a lost cause, but Father was too much for anyone to overcome.

More important to my search, I learned that all the disappearances had happened in the same stretch of country.

Between Osage Mission and Independence, Kansas, ran a single thoroughfare called the Osage Trail. It wasn't much compared to the larger roads, but it was the main route people traveled from here to Independence and on to Indian Territory. Many people had disappeared besides George, though nothing seemed to connect them other than the location.

Ben Brown from Cedarville had come to Osage Mission to try and get a loan. He vanished on his way home, with some people claiming he had over two thousand dollars with him. He had a wife and two children, now left without a father or their savings.

Then there was William McCrotty, an Irishman from Illinois who'd been on the road with so little money, he had to ask for help to pay for supper. And John Phipps, a boy whose body was found partially eaten by wildlife. He'd had three hundred dollars with him when he'd left town, but it had been gone when his body was discovered.

Henry McKenzie was a war hero, liked by many. He was a skilled fighter, but it hadn't been enough to keep him from falling victim to the same person or people.

They were all men of various ages. Some had money, some didn't. Some could fight, some couldn't. Some were well-liked, some weren't. Many of them had stopped in Ladore, a place most said was nothing but a magnet for horse thieves and villains. In 1870, a group of men had gotten drunk and beat and robbed a hotel owner before assaulting the two young girls who worked as housekeepers at the hotel.

The men got in a drunken rage after that, killing one of their own and then splitting up, taking one of the girls hostage. A vigilance committee was formed, and five of the men had been caught and hanged from a tree, with the sixth being thrown in jail.

I knew all too well what that scene would have looked like.

There were any number of more outlandish rumors flying around, from the entire thing being caused by John Wilkes Booth to some sort of mysterious society that wrote to one another in code. One man went on for fifteen minutes about pieces of paper that had been found in the area with long strings of numbers on them. "My nephew saw them with his own eyes," he said. "And he doesn't have enough sense between his ears to make something like that up. Papers with numbers, they were. One after the other with no space between them. Mark my words. The whole thing's being caused by the Illuminati."

I thanked him for his time and moved on to the next person.

The most popular theory I heard was that a gang of outlaws was stationed near Ladore, lying in wait and identifying potential targets to rob. The ones who didn't have any money might have come across the gang's hiding spot.

After two days in Osage Mission, I felt more confident and able to tackle this search. Perhaps I wasn't a full Bullock, but maybe I had just enough of that blood in me to be able to at least succeed at this.

I'd ride off to Ladore and poke around town before proceeding on toward Independence. I'd make sure to only travel during the day. It was around forty miles, so I'd have to stop some place for the night, and sleeping outside in such a dangerous area seemed like a bad idea. As long as I found a spot at a roadside inn—with plenty of witnesses—I should be safe.

By then, I'd even developed a better cover story. Asking about Father hadn't gotten me nearly as many responses. A man with a baby stood out more in people's minds than a single man asking after that man with a baby, and George Longcor's plight was on many lips. When I told people I was one of his friends, trying to track him and the baby down, people were much more open to helping. Strangers searching after strangers were suspicious. Strangers searching after lost friends made people want to lend a hand.

If things went well, I might know who was at the root of this in a few days.

CHAPTER FIVE

"He never reached that home. Suspicions were aroused that
he had been foully dealt with, and every recess on the route
to Independence was searched by his many acquaintances."
—Frank Leslie's Illustrated Newspaper,
June 7, 1873

———————

T HE NEXT DAY DIDN'T QUITE go as planned. I headed out
according to schedule, passing up the breakfast at the hotel
in favor of a few fresh rolls from the bakery. They were much better
when they hadn't sat out all day.

I'd pictured the prairie as nothing but flat. A sea of waving
grasses and gusting winds and nothing else. While it might have
been plenty flat, it had more trees than I'd expected. Or at least, the
southeast corner of Kansas did. Which made sense. It wasn't as if
nature would care I'd passed from Missouri into Kansas. It would
take some time for the prairie to fully take hold.

It also had creeks both large and small to ford, even on a fairly straight path as the Osage Trail. The place seemed flat from a distance, but that was just because the grasses did such a good job hiding the dips and gullies.

It was a far cry from Lamar. Homes were spread out from one another, so at each place, you'd be lucky to see more than three other rooftops in the distance. Each homesteader got their own 160-acre parcel of land, after all, so that didn't lend itself to much in the way of towns.

As I rode, I forced myself to go up to each house I passed, worried I might miss a crucial clue that would help lead me to Father. People seemed more open than in the city, even if the answers were still the same. They hadn't seen George and had nothing to offer.

Halfway to Galesburg, I stopped by another homestead that seemed like a twin to at least four others I'd already visited. Neat rows of corn and soybeans in the field, a humble but well-cared-for cabin, and a man working out in the barn, fixing one of the harnesses.

You could twist the harness around his neck and pull, the leather squeezing the air from—

"Hello," I said, the words following a well-worn path by now. "My name's Warren Bullock. Sorry to bother you. I've been looking for a friend who's gone missing. George Longcor? He would have—"

"Another one, huh?" the man said.

I was so stunned by a different response that I didn't know what to say. "Another one what?" I asked at last.

"Friend of George's. Just like that other fella, a week or two ago."

I was off Surrey and standing in front of the farmer faster than I'd have thought possible. "There was a man looking for George? You met him?" My voice sounded desperate, but I didn't care.

The farmer, bald, with a few streaks of white in his beard, frowned at me. "You feeling all right?"

"He was maybe sixty, with a white beard and an expensive horse?"

"Yes, that's the man. He rode in and asked about that George, same as you. I told him what I'll tell you. Haven't seen him, but you can water your horse here before you head on."

"When was this exactly?"

He wiped his face with a red handkerchief and stared up at the rafters of the barn. "Exactly? Well, it was the day after I'd gone into Galesburg for supplies. That's always on a Wednesday, and this is… He came by ten days ago. But that's all I can say for sure. He was only here a few minutes."

I could have done cartwheels, I was so happy. "Thank you," I said. "Thank you!"

"Don't know what for. Is your friend George in trouble?"

I wasn't sure what I said in response or even how much longer I was there. All I knew was for the first time, I'd picked up the trail of my father. Ten days! He must have taken longer in Osage Mission than I had, likely because he had more of an idea what a search really entailed. But none of that mattered now. If I rode quickly, perhaps I could make up even more time.

Ladore was a cluster of white buildings along a main street, smaller than Osage Mission by far, though it had a railroad station and some of the commerce that came with it. Having heard so many bad stories about the place, I was nervous once again, despite my recent success. I plowed through the fear, to no avail. No one had seen George, though several people got protective as soon as I brought him up.

"We're not all bloodthirsty villains," a man next to the general store yelled at me. "We don't kill babies!"

You could ram your fingers into his eyes, ripping them out as they—

I bit down on my tongue as I tried to drown out the thoughts. After how smoothly things had gone yesterday, I'd stopped worrying so much about getting yelled at, but he'd lost his temper as soon as I'd said the name "Longcor." I stared at him for a few beats, frozen in shock, then turned and hurried away. While I might have gotten more used to dealing with strangers, I was still nowhere near ready to have an argument with one.

So I wasn't sorry to leave the town behind me and continue onward. But if Ladore really was the place where everyone was disappearing, then it stood to reason that once I was on its other side, I'd have more luck finding someone who'd actually seen the man and his baby.

I stopped at more farms now, so many that my questions began to feel like a routine. "Excuse me, sir. My name is Warren Bullock, and I'm looking for a friend of mine who disappeared a few weeks ago. You might have heard of him. George Longcor? He was traveling with a baby, so I think he'd be easy to remember. Maybe he stopped here for supplies or directions?"

Some people let me get through the whole speech. Others cut me off anywhere from "excuse me" to in between. But no one showed any sign of having actually seen the man. One or two said, "Another one, huh?" when I asked, which lifted my hopes again, though they refused to elaborate.

Zigzagging across the trail like that took more time than going straight, especially when I had to factor in time to find someone to talk to at each farm. The sun was already falling low in the sky, and I still hadn't had anything close to a clue since the morning. That one shining spot of success seemed much dimmer now. What was happening to Father? Could he have been taken captive somewhere? Was he close to death? If my incompetence led to his...

I stopped that thought in its tracks. There was nothing to do but keep going.

Ahead of me, a small homestead poked up over the horizon, just off the Osage Trail. Like many of the places I'd passed since coming to Kansas, it was almost the bare minimum of homes. A single log cabin around fifteen feet by twenty-five, with a raised front stoop and a crude window on either side of the front door. The glass glinted in the evening sun. To the right was a makeshift barn or stable, along with some animal pens and a water trough. The only unique aspect of the place was a small orchard that had been planted behind the house. The trees were so young, they were still little more than upright posts, but perhaps ten or fifteen years from now, they might have a chance of bringing in a regular crop.

It was the orchard that settled my nerves more than anything. Someone willing to plant something like that meant to stay in a single place for a while. There was commitment in those trees.

I could relate to stability.

As I drew closer, more details of the farm began to emerge. The cabin was made of rough-hewn logs still so full of splinters, you'd want to avoid leaning against it or resting your hand on any part of it. The windows weren't set right in their openings; the place would be drafty in the winter no matter how much the woodstove inside roared. A fat sow rooted around in the mud in one of the pens, and a calf and its mother lowed from inside the barn. Above the door to the cabin, a hastily made sign proclaimed GROCRYS.

So they couldn't spell. That wasn't a hanging offense. The unease crawling down my spine was fear of another confrontation. I had to get over that.

A wagon rested to the right of the cabin, though whether it would actually move wasn't certain. The wheels were mismatched and missing spokes, and several boards were gone from its frame. It looked more like it had crawled there and died than someone had parked it.

A man sat on the front stairs, a large book open on his knees. He traced the words with a finger as he went, mouthing them silently to himself as he scribbled notes on a piece of paper. From the look of the book, it was a Bible. When I was twenty feet away, he glanced up at me and closed the book with the paper inside, setting it down and standing. Tall, blond, and lanky, with a mustache that stopped at the sides of his mouth and eyes that were a bit too close together, he wore rough woven pants, a white shirt, and suspenders that he'd taken off his shoulders.

He raised a hand to greet me, smiling, but then laughed in a high titter that didn't fit his broad shoulders and handsome face. It was the sort of laugh that made me wonder if he was entirely sane, though I chided myself for the thought as soon as it came. This business with George Longcor and my worries for Father were making me find villains everywhere I looked, and I was one to talk.

I cleared my throat. "E-excuse me, sir. My name is Warren Bullock, and I'm looking for a friend of mine who disappeared a few weeks ago. You might have heard of him. George Longcor? He was traveling with a baby, so I think he'd be easy to remember. Maybe he stopped here for supplies or directions?"

The man stared at me, his brow furrowed. "You always ride a plow horse as if it were somethin' worth ridin'?"

I glanced down at Surrey, feeling somehow defensive of him. Other people had made snide remarks in passing about my horse. "He's the most reliable creature I've ever seen," I said. "I'll take him over something flashier, easy."

He gave a noncommittal grunt. "Looking for a place to stay?" His speaking voice didn't match up with that laugh. Maybe he'd just been…clearing his throat? There was an accent there, but I couldn't identify it.

"I wouldn't mind," I said slowly, surprised at the change in subject. People either yelled at me or told me they didn't know anything. They didn't ask if I wanted to stay the night. "You know of anything in the area?"

"We got a pallet in the front room we rent out." He walked up to me and offered his hand. I forced myself to lean down and shake it; I'd gotten more used to the gesture in the past few days. His palm was clammy. Perhaps he'd just come in from the fields. Judging by the amount of tilled earth to my left, they hadn't made much of a dent on their 160 acres so far. "I'm John. Gebhardt," he said.

German—the accent was unmistakable now. I knew a German family back in Lamar. The wife made an excellent dish with apples, even if I couldn't ever remember its name. This didn't strike me as the sort of place where I might get a fine dish like that, but you never could be sure. "You live here alone?" I asked, eyeing the house. The porch was in poor repair, the windows lacked shutters, and there was a strong smell of boiled cabbage in the air.

"Nah," he said, and that tittering laugh burst out of his mouth again, high and piercing. You could likely hear it from a hundred yards away. "Kate and I are here with Ma and Pa, of course."

Behind him, the door opened, and a man's outline appeared silhouetted in the frame. He was wiping his hands with a towel. He stepped forward into the light, revealing an older man with a slight stoop, though he seemed to move well enough. He had a flat face with broad features. Silver hair slicked back away from his forehead, and his mouth seemed set in a permanent frown that even a thick full beard couldn't hide. He stared at me without saying a word.

"M-my name's Warren Bullock," I said into the silence, looking forward to the time I could be done with all this, one way or another. Lamar was only a hundred miles away, but it felt like a thousand at the moment. I didn't know how to talk to strangers. How to tell when I was supposed to start or when they actually stopped. Conversations like this made me feel like I'd gone out in public without my trousers, and that was under the best of circumstances.

"This is Pa Bender," John said. "His English ain't too good, so he don't speak much around strangers."

"Komm rein, Johannes," the man said. His voice sounded like grating rocks. "Zeit zum essen."

"Supper," John said. "Fifty cents for a meal. Two dollars for a meal and the pallet."

The sun was well on its way to setting, and Independence was still at least twenty miles away. How many of the other people who disappeared had been in this same predicament? It was tempting to keep pushing on, but I'd sworn I wouldn't put myself in danger. If it were just John and his father, that would be one thing, but the sound of someone else clattering dishes came from behind the old man.

Staying with a family had to be safer than risking facing whoever was making everyone disappear from the area.

"I'd love a place to spend the night," I said, getting off Surrey.

John smiled again, then ruined it with that laugh once more. If he kept that up the whole evening, perhaps I'd be better off just sleeping on the prairie and taking my chances.

His father had already disappeared inside. John showed me where to set Surrey up for the night, then told me to come in when I was ready.

It took me a while to get Surrey rubbed down and situated. The barn wasn't a place I'd want to put any animals in during the winter, with holes large enough to fit my hand between the boards. The calf and its mother stood in one of the stalls, idly chewing on some hay. Two horses, old and bony, stood in the third and fourth stalls. They nickered at me, and I threw some hay into their stalls, though the more humane thing to do might have been to shoot them.

As soon as I stepped through the cabin's doorway, my doubts exploded into a low-level panic. The windows were small, and even then, they seemed to let in less light than they ought to. Most people oriented their houses to get as much sun as possible. The

Benders hadn't learned that before they built the place, apparently. It was as if I'd stepped into the night, and I had to let my eyes adjust for a moment before I could inspect my surroundings.

It was all one room, with the back third separated from the front by a sheet of dirty canvas with a flap toward the wall where people could go from one side to the other. The side by the entrance held a table with four mismatched chairs, two cupboards, a sink, a hutch, and a wood-fired oven range. A mound of dirty dishes sat beside the sink, flies buzzing idly above the caked-on meat and gravy. Against the wall by the door, a pile of flattened straw with a blanket thrown over it implied tonight's sleeping arrangements.

I didn't want to *touch* anything in the room, let alone lie down in that pile of straw tonight. I wouldn't have let Surrey sleep in such conditions. Torn between turning and running away from this as fast as I could, and staying at the one place I'd decided ahead of time would be safe, I froze in the doorway and did nothing.

Pa Bender sat at the table, already well into a bowl of stew, his eyes focused on it so hard, he might've been worrying it would escape. I might as well have not even come in, for all the attention he gave me. An old woman stood by the stove, ladling another bowl full. She was short and heavyset, with her gray hair done up in a neat bun. She wore a blue calico dress with a tiny floral pattern, though it was so worn, the blue was coming up on gray.

Her eyes might have flicked to me for a moment, but when I really looked at her, she pretended not to see me.

"Have a seat," John said, pulling out a chair and waving me forward.

If I'd been hungry outside, the smell inside did away with that in short order. Something was *off* about the room, as if I'd find a large patch of mold growing on one of the walls. A strong scent of lye cut through the odor, though not enough to hide it completely. "You didn't know I was coming. I don't want to put your mother through the ordeal of making more food." I still hadn't stepped fully into the room.

She continued to ignore me, walking over to the cupboard and taking out a couple of cans. John and I watched her open them, then dump them both into the stewpot on the stove.

"See?" John said, giggling again. "Plenty for all." He gestured to the seat next to the divider between the rooms.

I scrambled to come up with a reason—any reason—why I'd have to sleep in the barn tonight. A contagious disease. I was a light sleeper. I snored. I might murder them all in their sleep. But nothing seemed like it would work for what I needed, and I stood there with a forced grin on my face until a fourth person walked into the room, emerging from behind the canvas curtain.

My heart began to thud in my chest.

CHAPTER SIX

"Day and night he traveled the route between Osage Mission and Independence, seeking to solve the mystery."
—Jacksonville Republican
(Alabama), May 24, 1873

S HE WAS A FEW YEARS older than I, lithe and confident, with high cheekbones and long brown hair with hints of red. Her skin seemed to have escaped the harsh sun of Kansas summers. She was buttoning her dress, though for a moment I caught a glimpse of skin down to her breastbone. I stared in shock—too stunned to do the right thing and drop my eyes—until she was finished.

She laughed when she saw me, showing a mouth with perfect white teeth. "They're just a couple of buttons. It's not as if I paraded in here naked."

"This is my sister, Kate," John said. "Kate, this is Warren. He'll be spending the night with us, or he will if ever decides to come in the house and sit down." That got another titter out of him. Was it some sort of nervous tic? Whatever it was, I'd better get used to it if I was going to be here long at all.

For as dark as the room had felt moments before, having Kate enter made it almost feel normal. Her dress was so pale to almost be white, with a red ribbon around the waist. She smiled easily, and—better yet—had a wonderful laugh. "What brings you to the middle of nowhere, Warren?" she asked, taking the seat next to the stove. Her accent was much slighter. I stumbled forward and took a chair next to hers. Ma plopped a bowl of stew in front of me. It was watery, with large chunks that might have been meat mixed in with what had to be carrots and potatoes.

I looked back up at Kate, staring at her. For once, the thoughts barging into my head had nothing to do with violence, but still managed to make me just as uncomfortable.

She laughed. "Is there something between my teeth?"

I snapped back to attention, the words coming out by rote. "I'm looking for a friend of mine. George Longcor? He was traveling through here a few weeks ago, his baby girl in tow. They never showed up in Osage Mission."

"Oh yes," Kate said, the smile dipping from her face, but not disappearing completely. "You're the second person to come through on the search. I heard about that poor man. Were the two of you close?"

"Outlaws," John cut in, not letting me respond. "I told everybody around here I seen them across the river. They shot at me by Drum Creek a month ago."

"You saw them?" I asked, thoughts of Kate's long hair and dimple disappearing for a moment, though the memory of those buttons...

"They tried to kill me. I was lucky to escape with my life. Bloodthirsty devils. It ain't safe to go there alone. We told the other one the same thing, didn't we?"

Kate nodded. "He didn't listen."

I tensed. "An older man, with a fast horse, a full beard, and a slight limp?"

"He a friend?" John asked.

"He's my father," I answered. All thoughts of George vanished. "How long ago was he here?"

Kate frowned, then turned to her mother. "Wie lange ist es, seit der ältere Mann hier war? Den der die Kinder gesucht hat."

Her mother ignored whatever had been said. Kate looked at me. "Nine days, maybe? He came in the afternoon, but he didn't stay."

Nine days! Even more time made up. My earlier optimism returned.

"Where did he go?" I asked, trying to keep my voice calm.

"We took him to Drum Creek," John said. "To show him where the bandits live. Then he went off to find them. He didn't come back."

"Drum Creek?" I asked. "Is that far from here?"

"Just two miles east," John said. "I could show you in the morning, if you want. Too dark now to see much." Again the tittering. "Unless you want to see the inside of a grave."

"But don't the outlaws all come up from the south? From Indian Territory?"

John shrugged. "I don't know where they come from. I didn't ask them as they were shooting."

Everyone else at the table was eating their stew. Ma was staring at me as hard as Pa was staring at his bowl. I picked up my spoon and did my best not to see what it was I was about to put in my mouth. If the rest of the family was eating it regularly and hadn't died, it couldn't be that bad.

After the first mouthful, I decided that dying from the meal might actually be a mercy, if it meant I didn't have to finish the stew. But then Kate smiled at me—at *me!*—encouragingly, and I found myself smiling back and eating another spoonful, fool that I was.

The meal went on in much the same fashion. John prattled about anything that came into his mind, though Kate made up for it with her smiles. It made me wonder more than once how in the world a family such as this one could have produced a woman like that. Could those really be her parents?

Stranger still, she seemed to have taken a liking to me very quickly. Her foot tapped against mine a few too many times for it to be purely by chance. When she made contact with me, I didn't get the same jolt of discomfort I got when anyone else came too close. At one point she stood from the table and walked over to the counter to get a glass of water. As she walked by me, she passed close enough for her hips to brush my arm. I was thankful the lighting wasn't any better.

You could shoot her in the middle of the night. Kill the family while they sleep. Smother her with a—

I shook my head to clear it. It had been a while since the Voice had come on so strongly, and I did my best to force it from my mind. Kate helped.

Every time I looked over at her, her lips curved in a slight smile, as if she and I were sharing a secret. After she nudged me with her foot a fourth time and then threw me that little half grin, I had to struggle to keep from smiling myself.

You could slice her throat with a sharp knife. Rivulets of blood, all spilling down the front of her dress.

The thought was enough to make me want to search for weapons, just to be safe. I pushed the urge down. The last thing I needed was to make Kate see how odd I could be.

It wasn't that I'd never had much contact with girls. We got along fine enough back in Lamar, but they all knew me as the one who was so particular. I was the "youngest Bullock son," and my brothers and family had all built that title into something important.

Here in Kansas, I didn't have any of that baggage. Kate saw me and didn't think of anything other than a new man visiting her home. Maybe she longed to get away from here as much as I would have. Could I blame her for being perhaps a bit more forward than was proper?

And would I complain about it?

Of course not.

But then the meal was over, and somehow amid all of that, I'd finished my bowl and even eaten a second. My stomach hadn't given up on me yet, though the butterflies I'd thought were coming from Kate's advances might actually be from indigestion, at least in part.

After supper was cleared, Kate asked me if I didn't mind helping her with the dishes. John laughed like a hyena at that, staring at me with his mouth slightly open and a big smile painted across his face. So it was clear I wasn't the only one to see what was happening. Still, no one was objecting. I went over to the sink with Kate and helped her with the chore, standing a fair bit closer to her than was necessary.

Kate told me about her time in Kansas. How her parents had come over to America from Germany when she and John were still little. How harsh the winters could be out on the forefront of civilization. I commiserated with her, telling her in turn of my family's constant moving. Iowa. Missouri. California. How my brothers never seemed to be able to stay in one place longer than a few years. Father's years as a lawman. "It's in our blood, I guess."

"I think there's more to that than most people think," Kate said.

"Blood makes all of us do things we don't even realize at times. It's where I got my gift, I'm sure."

"Your gift?" I took another plate from her and dried it.

"You've heard of spiritualism? Second sight?"

I placed the dish down far more gently than it needed, trying to weigh my words before I spoke. "Is that something you go in for?"

She laughed. "I admire the effort to keep the skepticism from your voice, but don't worry. It's nothing I haven't heard before. Many people don't believe, but it doesn't matter in the end because I know what I know. I might be able to help you, actually. If you have anything of Mr. Longcor's or your Father's? I could use it as a focus and see what the spirits say."

I fumbled at my pockets for a moment, my mind somehow assuming I had something—*anything*—of George's to give to her. I wanted to be closer to her. To have her not just notice me but respect me. Even look up to me. But I had nothing, and a few moments later, I had to admit as much.

Her smile slipped, but only for a second. "Well, not to worry. Often the other side wants to contact us as much as we want to contact them."

My stomach slipped. "You think they're dead then?"

She laughed. "I wasn't saying I'd ask your father or Mr. Longcor. The spirits can see things we cannot, however."

And just as quickly as it had fled, my skepticism returned. Was I really going to buy into all this hokum just for a pretty pair of eyes and a finely curved waist? And what if she was only having a joke at my expense? Which was likelier: that I was suddenly viewed by a beautiful woman as a catch, or that this was a routine Kate tried with all their visitors? Something she and John and the rest of them could laugh about when I was gone.

"That's okay," I said. "I don't think I'm that far desperate just yet that I need to try anything too extreme."

Now the smile really did leave Kate's face. "Yes, well, I have to be seeing to some chores elsewhere."

She left the room, leaving me staring after her like a lost puppy. I realized then that not only was I mooning after a stranger, but I'd been roped into doing work at the place I was paying to stay. Still, I didn't quite know how to get out of it, and I ended up not only cleaning and drying the dishes but putting them away after I was done.

At least the room would be that much neater. I had to sleep there tonight, after all.

The horizon was a brilliant orange when I was finished with the dishes, and I stood in the middle of the room, looking from the canvas to the door to John and back again, wondering what I was supposed to do next. I cleared my throat. John sat at the table reading the Bible, scribbling notes once more as he went. He certainly seemed to obsess over it.

Ma sat at the table, working on mending a pair of pants, while Pa whittled something that looked like a melting dog, his knife reflecting the firelight. The room was quiet except for the scraping of his blade, the turning of John's pages, the slow crackle of the fire, and Ma clearing her throat now and then.

Kate didn't make another appearance, and I kept wondering if I could have handled the situation better. Still, I'd set out on this journey to find my father, not a bride.

Perhaps a half hour later, she finally emerged from behind the curtain. My heart jumped, and I stumbled to my feet. I tried to think of something to say, but she strode through the room and out the door without so much as glancing my direction. John watched her go and then looked to his parents. Ma jerked her head once, and he closed the Bible and hurried after his sister.

Which left me standing in the middle of the room, staring at Ma and Pa Bender and wondering what I was supposed to do now. They made no moves, just returned my gaze. What were they thinking?

They're old. You could grip her by the neck and wring your hands, just like Mother killing a chicken back at the farm.

Enough. I'd been silent for too long already. If I didn't say something, who knew where my thoughts would end up? "Have you lived here long?"

"Vielleicht ist er bescheuert," Ma said, her eyes on me.

"Excuse me?" I asked. "I'm sorry, I don't—"

"Keine Frage," Pa answered. "Und jetzt müssen wir auf ihn aufpassen."

"Wie immer," Ma said back.

"I don't speak German," I said again, quieter now, as it seemed clear they were well aware of that and didn't care.

Ma strode over to a hamper of washed clothes and began to fold, while Pa fetched a box of tools from behind the curtain and set about working on one of the doors to the hutch. It was as if Kate's departure was some sort of signal they could work on new projects.

I debated offering to help, but neither of them looked my way, and speaking more would only make me feel awkward all over again. So I took a seat at the table again and stared at my hands.

This was ridiculous. Father was in trouble, and I sat around too frightened to even try a conversation?

I looked up from my hands. "How long have you lived here?"

Neither of them so much as blinked. If I'd tried to fold clothes the way Ma Bender was, Mother would have made me start all over again. It wasn't so much "folding" as it was "organized wadding." Ma's hands moved in jerky motions, and she scowled at each new piece. Was she upset I was there?

"I need to pay, don't I?" I asked, thinking perhaps they assumed I would try to ride off without settling my debts.

The two said something to each other in German again, but I might as well have not been in the room. I stopped even trying to decipher what they were saying.

"I'll just go for a walk then," I said, standing.

Pa leaped up from his work and rushed to stand in front of the door, chattering away in a gruff voice, then pointing at me, at the door, and then slicing his finger across his throat. Perhaps he meant to warn me it was dangerous outside, but it could just as easily have been him threatening to kill me if I tried to leave.

"It's not safe?" I asked.

He nodded once. "Not safe." He returned to his repairs.

One glance at his technique said volumes about the Benders and their odds of actually succeeding on the frontier. When he tested his fix of the crooked door, it closed even worse than it did before. He barked what might have been a curse and then hammered at the end of the wood, trying to force it into place.

What would have inspired a family like this—so clearly inexperienced with actual life on a farm—to travel across the country or the world and try their hand at it here? Their fields weren't well tended, their horses were practically bones, and the odds of their orchard living long enough to bear any fruit were slim at best. For a moment, I thought of what I might do to help, if Kate really felt the way she…

Nonsense. As soon as Kate got to know me better, she'd be as scared of me as anyone else. And what did I want to do in Kansas? Just because I liked to put things in order didn't mean I needed to do the same thing to the Benders, even if I felt sorry for them.

"I could fix that door," I said, standing again.

Ma sighed, exasperated. She glanced over at Pa and barked something that clearly sounded like an order. When he didn't respond, she repeated it again, louder.

He nodded absently, searching through the toolbox for something else.

"It wouldn't be that hard," I said. "I could just—"

Ma pointed over at the cupboard, then at the curtained area of the room, then at me, snapping off German with each movement.

Pa closed his eyes, took a deep breath, and stood. "She wants give you kuchen."

"What?"

"Kuchen. Cake. You." He grabbed me by the arm, and the Voice snarled in response. I managed to keep it in check, even as he dragged me over to the table.

"Sit," he ordered, pointing at the chair right next to the curtain. It was covered in greasy reddish-brown stains, with what might have been mold spots dotting the fabric. I'd have sooner thrust my hand in the fire than get anywhere near something like that. I swung my arms from side to side. "I'd rather stand, I think. All that riding today."

"Sit," he said again, jerking my arm down.

I sat, pulling the chair as far forward from the curtain as it would go, then turning myself and perching on the edge of the chair.

He grimaced, looked over at his wife, and said something else in that guttural tongue. He sounded angry, even if his face didn't quite match up with the tone.

While Ma Bender responded harshly, Pa paid her no mind and

headed behind the curtain. I inched the chair farther away from those stains.

Ma kicked at the basket of laundry, spilling it onto the floor. She hurried to me, grabbed me by the shoulders, and pushed me back toward the curtain. She patted the table three times. "Sit. Kuchen," she said and tried a smile on me. Her teeth were yellowed, with large gaps between each of them at the gumline. I wished she'd just kept her mouth shut.

"I'm not hungry," I said.

She turned my chair so it faced the table, then walked to the far side of the table and pushed it in my direction, forcing me to back up until I was almost pressed against the burlap.

Lunge for the toolbox. Take the screwdriver and hammer it into her temple.

I could either resist the Voice or resist the Benders. I didn't have it in me to do both. I leaned as far forward as I could, but I didn't move my chair again.

While Ma puttered through the cabinets for whatever diseased cake she was planning on giving me, Pa banged around behind the curtain. What was he doing back there?

If he had a knife, he could plunge it through the curtain into your back. You need to kill him.

I ignored the thought. Just because I was wicked didn't mean everyone else was. He'd been working on fixing the door. He was probably looking for something else he needed to give it another try.

Instead of a piece of cake, Ma found a gas lantern and lit it, turning it up as high as it would go. I squinted in the new light that cast my shadow onto the sheet behind me. Why was I going along with this? Why didn't I have the nerve to just tell people no? Probably because I worried that if I started there, I had no idea where I'd end up.

Pa had gotten quiet, and Ma stared at me in the bright light, as if transfixed by my face. I'd seen rabbits make much the same expression back when I was hunting. Was she afraid of her husband? Afraid of me? Perhaps there was something strangers could see by looking at me. Some kind of physical sign of what I was like inside.

Ma leaned forward, her tongue darting out to lick dry lips.

"Are you quite well?" I asked, even though nothing about this felt right. If I spoke German and knew what they'd been saying, perhaps it would all make sense. Or it might have been some sort of cultural difference.

And where was Pa? It was far too quiet. Too easy to imagine him creeping up behind the burlap, staring at my shadow cast on it by the lantern.

He's going to kill you. Slit your throat. You need to attack!

I felt pulled between my imagination and the Voice. If I didn't—

The front door opened, and Kate walked in with a smile on her face. She took in the room with a glance, and the smile disappeared. She was over to me in three steps, grabbing me by the shirt and pulling me away from the table. We tumbled to the floor in a heap.

Pa Bender came out from behind the curtain, wiping his hands on a piece of oily cloth. John peeked his head in through the front door. "Everything okay?" he asked, tittering.

I stared from Kate to her mother and then back again. "She was just wanting to give me a piece of cake."

The four of them broke out into quick German, all speaking over each other. Kate bounded to her feet, her face flushed, and she gestured behind her at the door several times, then at me. John laughed a few times but only made a stray remark now and then. Pa's responses were short and curt, as he stood by the curtain with his arms folded. Ma was the one who yelled back at Kate, the two of them practically screaming at each other.

At last Ma whirled and grabbed the basket of clothes before pushing past her husband and disappearing behind the burlap curtain. Pa followed her. John laughed again, high and long. "Never a dull moment," he said, then went outside.

Kate stood in the middle of the room, breathing heavily, her hair somewhat frazzled. I realized I was still on the floor, having been too stunned to think of standing. I corrected that now. "What was that about?" I asked.

It took her thirty seconds to calm down and answer. "I've told her not to be alone with our guests before."

My eyebrows raised. "You were worried I'd hurt her?" Was it that obvious how dangerous I was?

"No. Yes. It—it's more complicated than that. I didn't want to tell you, but…she forgets herself at times. She fancies herself a good baker, and she was, before. But now she gets confused while she's working. Last month, she added arsenic to a pot of tea she'd been brewing. I don't know why. Maybe she thought it was sugar. But if I hadn't been here and seen it, I don't know what would have happened."

I stared in horror at the curtain. "So you think she might have poisoned me?"

Kate held up her hands, her voice pleading. "Not on purpose. She means well, though people here in Kansas think she's nothing but mean. It isn't our fault you all can't hear anything but anger when we speak German. Ma just wants things to be back to the way they were, and she won't admit they're getting worse, instead. I'm sorry. I shouldn't have left you here. I'm the one who's supposed to keep an eye on her."

"Your father didn't seem too concerned to leave me here with her," I said.

"He doesn't want to admit it any more than she does. Please, let's forget it, can we? I won't charge you for the room, and maybe you can try to not mention this to others?"

I found myself reassuring her. If anyone could understand someone fighting with themselves to do good, it was me. Did her explanation entirely match with what I'd seen happen? If I spoke the language, or were a better judge of body language, maybe I could tell, but as it was, I was more confused than anything else.

"I think I'd like to turn in," I said at last.

"Yes," Kate said. "Of course. The bed's just over there. We'll get out of your way."

I hesitated once again, staring down at the pallet. Would it really be safer in the house? The Benders had left the room. I could slip out unnoticed. It wouldn't take long to saddle Surrey and head off somewhere without strangers who made my skin itch.

Except John said he'd been shot at, and he'd offered to take me to where it had happened. I couldn't shy away from difficult things, not if I was going to be of use to Father.

I compromised by staying fully clothed, lying down on the pallet, and facing the wall while hoping I'd fall asleep quickly.

Instead, the violent thoughts took over, one after another. Blood. Body parts. Screams. Knives flashing in the dark. It was worse than it had been since I'd left Lamar, probably because I wasn't just sleeping alone, but with other people, in a house full of any number of weapons.

Would they mind if I got up and looked around the place, just to get a general idea? How would I be able to sleep if I didn't? I ran through all the different places I'd have to search. Even without rifling through drawers or cupboards, I could think of several objects that might prove too tempting to me in a weak moment. The fire poker was the most attractive, and the Voice had a wonderful time going through the different things I could do with it.

Somehow, I managed to stay lying down and still.

It took the Benders an age to finally bed down for the night, forcing me to listen to every footstep and murmured conversation— all in German—even if they didn't emerge from behind the canvas.

I lay in the crude bed, tossing and turning and wondering again why I hadn't just slept outside. It wasn't as if every traveler in the area went missing, and a little risk might have been worth avoiding this poor excuse for a sleeping arrangement. No matter which way I tried, some piece of straw or edge of *something* was there to jab me in the back, and I couldn't decide how best to handle my head. The straw kept getting close to my mouth, leaving me at a low level of panic.

John and Kate chatted back and forth on the other side of the curtain, peppered with John's tittering laughs. Ma and Pa said nothing other than short syllables now and then.

Light from their lanterns cast a glow through the canvas, bathing my side of the cabin in strange shadows. Above me, the roof seemed pockmarked with strange holes, as if someone had hammered thick nails into the beams and then pried them out one by one. That, or used it for target practice. Perhaps the wood had been used when they built the place.

At some point, I slipped into an uneasy sleep, my dreams filled with strange cackling and a presence always behind me, lurking. Threatening. The air was thick, pressing me down into the straw. I woke drenched in sweat, my blanket a tangled mess that had snared my right leg. I went and opened a window, hoping the air outside might somehow cool me, though I didn't even get a breeze out of the effort.

When I turned to go back to my pallet, a face appeared in the canvas opening leading to the Benders' side of the cabin. A shadow with deep eyes and a snarling mouth, its brows, nose, and lips traced by moonlight for a moment before it ducked back into the darkness.

I froze, wondering if I'd just been seeing things. I hadn't heard any movement from beyond the canvas. Now that I listened, I was fairly sure I could make out two sets of snores coming from that direction. Just soft enough to be noticed, but constant and steady.

It had to have been my imagination. A result of the horrid sleep, the nature of my journey, and the high heat. But I couldn't bring myself to lie down again for at least five minutes. I stood there, staring at that opening and waiting for the face to reappear. If I were to lie down, how would I know if it crept back out again? And what if it were to do something more than creep?

It hadn't been any of the Benders. Far too hideous for Kate or John, and it had moved too quickly for it to have been one of their parents.

After reminding myself again and again that it was late and I was too old to let little flights of fancy be ruling my actions like this, I lay back down, though I moved so I could see the opening.

During the day, I would have laughed at my mind for conjuring impossible situations, but now—in the middle of the night? I pictured a demon creeping through the darkness, silently inching this way and that as it positioned itself to attack. At any moment, it might spring, its claws outstretched and its mouth wide, full of an impossible number of fangs.

At some point, I fell back asleep.

Voices woke me once more. This time, I'd fallen so fast into dreams that waking only came in stages. I heard the voices, but I didn't understand them. I lay there listening, the words washing over me.

"—uns helfen, andere aufmerksamer zu machen."

"Aber es könnte genauso gut zu viel von der falschen Sorte ziehen."

"In jedem Fall müssen wir uns entscheiden und es hinter uns bringen."

John's tittering cut through the air, and my eyes snapped open, my hand gripping for something—anything—I might use to defend myself. For that single instant, all worry of becoming too violent evaporated from my mind, and I wanted nothing more than a revolver.

It was still dark, with no hint of dawn and no light in the cabin. The window let in enough of the moon for me to see Kate and John standing in the opening of the canvas. Kate must have seen my eyes open, because she came to crouch next to my bed immediately.

"I'm so sorry about that," she said, her face close to mine. "It's just we've been listening to that awful beast make that noise for the past thirty minutes, and we didn't know whether it would make more sense to walk through here and go give it some water or whatever it is that's making it make such a fuss, or to leave you be and hope it just quiets on its own."

"Beast?" I asked, my mind still thick. With Kate's face so close to mine, her eyes intense and her mouth right in front of my face, it was hard for me to focus on anything else. Had I really wanted to get a gun? What was happening to me?

"The pig!" she whispered. "Hasn't it been waking you up?"

"I was asleep," I managed to get out.

Kate turned back to her brother. "See? I told you we should have just stayed quiet."

To my left, another shape emerged from the darkness. I jerked back, startled, as it seemed the monster had slipped from the shadows, ready to spring on me. And then it was shoving past John, and I recognized it for Pa's figure.

"He's been in here the whole time?" I asked.

"He slipped in to get a glass of water," Kate said. "His throat can get so parched at night when it's like this, and he knows the cabin well enough to move so softly, you'd never hear him. The door squeaks, though. Something awful, and always at the wrong time. But I've kept you up enough as it is. You're anxious as a rabbit. I'd hate for something to happen to you. Why, someone might be coming here in search of you next, and wouldn't that be awful?"

Her words washed over me, but every time I tried to pay attention to the flow, I got distracted by Kate's hand on my arm or the way her lips moved. I cleared my throat and drew back my arm. It wasn't proper, even if it did feel wonderful. "Can't be too careful," I said at last.

She smiled and leaned even closer. For a moment, I thought she intended to kiss me, but then I realized she'd just repositioned herself so she could stand more easily. "Stay safe, Warren. Tomorrow, we'll go out and see if we can't help you on your quest."

Kate and John left the room without waiting for me to respond.

I didn't fall asleep again. Each time my eyes grew heavy, I remembered that face in the dark and the way Pa had crept through the room like a drifting shadow. Father wouldn't have let an old man, a wizened woman, a pretty face, and a simpleton intimidate him, but I wasn't Father.

The Voice kept whispering what the Benders could do to me if I let my guard down. It kept encouraging me to strike first. What sort of a Bullock was I, anyway? One so ill-equipped to even tell the difference between real danger and pure fancy? No one was going to club me over the head while I slept. What would be the point? I had no money. I was no threat. I wasn't worth the effort it would take.

So, instead of listening to the Voice or my worries, I stayed in bed, my hands in tight fists as I waited for the dawn to come.

CHAPTER SEVEN

"Into this horrible hole was plunged the unfortunate victims whom they murdered in daylight. The hammers used for breaking the skulls were such as are used by stonebreakers on our streets, and the handles are about twenty inches long."

—The Times-Picayune
(New Orleans, Louisiana), May 16, 1873

I WAS ALL TOO READY TO leave that house as soon as I'd rubbed my eyes clear in the morning. Outside, I took a few deep breaths and swung my arms in circles, as if, by moving them quickly, I might get rid of whatever gunk the bed had left on me. The air was already warming, promising another hot day ahead. The sow sat in the pen across from the door, snuffling angrily as it stared at me. At home, that was the sign our pigs wanted food, so I poked my head back into the house and looked for the slop bucket where I'd put the table scraps from last night.

Instead, I saw Kate standing by the table with her foot up on a chair, bent down to tie the laces. Her leg was bare from the knee down, her ankle finely turned and her skin pale white.

"Warren!" she said, smiling. "You look like you've never seen a leg before. You've got two of your own, you know."

I blinked rapidly, blushed, then turned to face outside again. "I'm sorry. I—I know I shouldn't—that is to say, I—"

"Calm down," she said, close enough now to drape an arm across my shoulder. "I don't mind you seeing. People worry too much about things like that. It isn't as if you kissed me."

That last bit was practically whispered in my ear, sending a shock all the way down my spine and into my toes. I stepped forward, away from her reach, if for nothing more than to be able to think clearly. This sort of behavior was unlike anything I'd ever encountered before. But then again, I hadn't *been* anywhere before. Not by myself. How was I to know how people behaved at home, other than my family and the neighbors around me?

Mother had always insisted true women never let a man see their ankles, and Kate had skipped right past that and gone straight to her calf. That, paired with the amount of skin she'd revealed yesterday when she'd been buttoning her blouse, was enough to spin any man's mind.

Instead of turning to talk to her or wait for her explanation, I went to the barn and saw to Surrey.

Horses did what you expected them to. Horses were

dependable. And I'd never had images of Surrey's fetlocks flash into my head unannounced. Kate's legs were almost as bad as the Voice.

You could chop them off, one at a time. Two lifeless limbs, just like a leg of beef at the butcher's.

By the time I was back outside, Kate had gone away, leaving John to see to the animals.

"Kate surprised you this morning, I hear," John said, smiling as he laughed like a high-pitched jackass. "She likes to do that now and then, just to keep strangers on their toes. She don't mean nothing by it."

I forced a laugh and what I hoped was a passable smile. "Of course not. I was just surprised, is all."

"Drum Creek is four miles northwest of here," he said. "We should make it in plenty of time, and if we don't find what you're looking for, you can head down south and ask in Cherryvale before going farther west to Independence."

His German accent seemed to come and go, depending on who was around us. I walked Surrey over to stand by the sty, next to John. "You were really shot at?"

He nodded. "They were whooping like savages. I didn't hang around to ask questions. I turned and ran as fast as I could. You know what they do, ne?"

I frowned and shook my head.

"They come up on you when you ain't paying attention. Club

you over the back of the head and slit your throat. Even though anyone knows slitting a throat don't always work."

"Excuse me?"

"Throats. They don't slice easy, unless you got a good sharp knife. You ever tried cutting a raw steak with a dull knife? Imagine doing that, but the steak is thrashing around at the same time. Even if you clubbed the man over the head, you'd still have to get through tendons and into the windpipe."

Do it now. Grab a knife and carve into his flesh, Slice it into strips.

"Don't listen to him," Kate said, walking up behind us. "He likes to make people uncomfortable."

John took the statement as if it had been a huge insult. "All I say is if it were somebody living, awake, I wouldn't go for his throat. So much blood, and you can't be sure you cut the right thing if you're short on time. Better to take the knife and—"

I cleared my throat. His words were making the Voice far too happy. "You've put a lot of thought into this."

"Of course," John said, then laughed. "I need to be ready in case someone tries to slit mine, ne? And they don't stop there. Not these villains. They put the body just so, positioning the right arm across the chest. It's a ritual of some sort. Black magic."

It was the bit about black magic that pushed me over the edge, going from thinking there might be a chance this was serious to anger at someone wasting my time. "I don't think this has anything to do with black magic," I said. "And if you think making fun of the situation is worth your while, I'll head on by myself."

Better to be free of this family, anyway. For a moment, the thought crossed my mind: What if it were one of them? John seemed to know far too much about attacking a body. Could he be sneaking out at night? Or Pa Bender, perhaps? The old man had been in my room last night, and I hadn't even known he was there. The slow gait and silent treatment could be an act.

But just as soon as I'd had the thought, I let it go. No one would be able to murder as many people as had disappeared and keep it quiet with a family around. What would you do with the bloody clothes? How would you explain your absences? No, the Benders might make me uncomfortable—everyone but Kate, at least—but they weren't killers.

Killing wasn't a family business, and besides: They didn't seem evil. Just very odd.

We were underway in not too much more time. John led us, cutting across fields as he chattered over his shoulder about any number of things I couldn't quite hear, punctuated always by that tittering laugh. Kate cocked her eyebrow at me and rode close enough for us to talk more intimately.

For once, she didn't try to do anything to make me blush or feel uncomfortable. Instead, we talked about what she thought about life out here in Kansas and how things were with her family.

How was it that only a few days away from home could make

me feel like a completely different person? There was still enough of me to feel like me: talking to or touching most people still shot stabs of anxiety down my arms. The Voice was still there, and I still had to follow my rules or risk giving in to all those violent dreams, but no one knew that about me. If Father or Newton were to see me now, would they even recognize me? I had a fresh chance to become a new Warren with each person I met.

What if I just never listened to the Voice? What if I got to the point where I could just ignore it? Just seal that part of me off, like walling up the catacombs in *The Cask of Amontillado*. Would that ever be possible?

Around Kate, I felt like I was the best Warren yet. And I felt guilty because what sort of demon thought about women while his father was in trouble?

"This is all just so…confining," Kate said. "Like the foolish clothes they make women wear. Why should I have to put on layer after layer, while men can parade around without their shirts, and no one says a thing? Perhaps if I were in one of the real cities— New York or Philadelphia—then all these silly fashion hoops would make more sense. But out here in the middle of nowhere? You might as well worry about what to put on the cow."

"I think women are a fair bit different than cattle," I said.

"You know what I mean. You've been places. California and back? That's seeing the world, or at least a slice of it."

It was best not to remind her that I'd done it at the tail end of a wagon train, following orders the whole way. "I don't see what pushing so hard for change will do, though. Other than make people think you're too forward."

"But I don't care what people think about me. Not here, at any rate. A real spiritualist is looked up to in the world. People come from miles around just to see them at work. The Fox sisters were under fourteen when they first made contact with their murdered peddler. They've gone on to give séances to hundreds. They've been to *Europe*. But no one's ever going to notice me here. Not unless I do something fantastical, and not as long as I've got a family as bizarre as the one I've got."

I tried to say something to reassure her, but I stumbled over my words. Ahead of us, John was pointing at something and going on at length about it, even if all I could really make out were his laughs. Sweat was already pouring down my back, and for a moment, I wondered what it must be like for Kate. Women really did wear more layers than men.

"So why don't you run away?" I asked at last. "Go somewhere that's more to your liking?"

"Because unaccompanied women of a certain age attract the wrong sort of attention. If I were with someone else, under different circumstances…"

She trailed off, and I struggled to think of the right thing to say. She couldn't be talking about me, could she? I wasn't the sort of man a woman like her would look twice at. But before I could stammer out some sort of response, John turned around and headed back to us in a half crouch. I used that as an excuse to say nothing.

"Get down," he whispered. "Do you want to get shot? We can't know if they're watching."

I hurried off my horse, searching the line of trees that had appeared on the horizon for any signs of outlaws, even as I recognized I wouldn't know what to look for if there were any. Father had tried to teach me as much as he could on our trip back from California, but that had been several years ago now, and I hadn't had cause to need any of it since then.

The three of us approached the trees at a slow walk. John had his head ducked low, and Kate kept her horse between her and the trees, so I tried to follow suit. A faint breeze rustled the leaves and fields, and grasshoppers flew to the air in alarm with each step, their wings clattering in the quiet.

I'd felt out of sorts now and then since I'd left home, but this was the first time I'd felt I was walking into what might be real danger. I always worked so hard to avoid violence. Getting shot at by outlaws had been far from my mind when I'd first headed out.

A bullet out here, far from real help, killed you more likely than not. If it didn't hit anything vital straight off, the wound could get infected, and then the best-case scenario might be losing a limb.

Shoot a man through the jaw, and his whole face can peel open. Take your gun and—

I bit the inside of my cheek and crouched lower, cursing myself for cowardice even as I couldn't stop from doing it.

"Was it here?" I whispered to John.

"What?"

"Was it here they shot at you?"

He nodded once. "I was heading to the creek to give my horse a drink, and right out of nowhere, three or four shots at once. Bullets kicking up dirt and grass, and me with my heart pounding out of my chest."

We were close enough now to see through the trees on either side of the bank. Unless the outlaws had decided to hide in the branches on the off chance of someone coming by, no one was there.

The three of us waited a beat longer, then stood and breathed easier. I chided myself for letting my imagination run wild as it had.

We forded the creek, taking care with our horses on the steep banks. John and Kate both dropped into the water, dunking themselves completely and laughing at how cool it felt.

Club them over the head, and they'd float facedown, spinning in the water as they made their way downstream.

I blinked and tried to refocus. Even though the thought of getting so wet would normally make me cringe, I was hot enough now to follow Kate's lead into the water.

Dripping wet, we searched the opposite bank for any sign of activity: campfires, horse tracks, or any discarded items. We came across a child's doll that caught our interest for a while, its cloth skin weathered with the wind and rain, its button eyes staring blankly at the sky. Whatever child had lost it, they'd left no other sign.

As we went, my mind kept getting drawn back to Kate, like a dog gnawing a bone. The more I thought about it, the more I sympathized with her situation. Yes, she might be throwing herself at me, but in her circumstances, that might make the most sense. What did I know about what life was like as a woman? Having a random stranger fall for her might well be her best route out of Kansas. Her family was certainly odd enough, between their bizarre actions in the night and her parents' closemouthed attitude.

It wasn't the sort of thought I just threw out. Back home, any woman close to my age already knew all about me. My quirks were common knowledge, and people liked to laugh about them behind my back. Addie never missed the chance to remind me of it and how humiliating it was to be my sister.

But I was different here. Knowing someone like Kate could look at me and even consider for a moment I might be able to help her made me sit up straighter. If I had a fresh start with someone, maybe they could learn about me on my own terms, not from stories around town.

"I'm sorry," Kate said to me after an hour of searching. "There just doesn't seem to be anything here."

After the first half hour or so, I'd thought to try putting some of what Father had taught me about tracking to use. I knew just how much a trained tracker could tell from what seemed like very little information. Out in the beating sun that morning, I couldn't find any evidence anyone had been here in at least the past week. No freshly broken branches. No horse tracks. No rumpled grass from someone sitting.

This was the closest I'd come yet to finding an actual clue leading me to Father, and it turned out to look just like any other stretch of riverbank. The disappointment made me feel hollow inside.

We'd dried out some from our dunking, and Kate's braid was only somewhat worse for wear. Surrey and the other horses were hitched by the river, and I had more than a few scratches from rooting around in the underbrush.

"It was a long shot anyway," I said. "But I'm getting closer. I'll find him."

John only laughed, though I was getting used to the sound by now, so it didn't grate on me in quite the same way.

Kate looked at the horizon. "There's a storm coming."

I checked, expecting to see thunderclouds. The sky was overcast but didn't seem particularly ominous. "Why do you say that?"

"I can feel it. I know you're not a believer, but it's true. It's going to be a bad one. A killing storm."

"You mean you feel it in your joints?" Father could do that sometimes, before.

Kate took a deep breath, considering her words. "I know you said you didn't believe in it last night, but it's true. I can sense things other people can't. Talk to spirits. See the future. And right now, they're telling me the worst storm in years is headed straight for us."

She paused for a moment, then turned to me. "No. Straight for *you*."

I didn't know what to say, so I said nothing.

Kate flicked her eyes to the sky and then back to me. "Fine. Ignore that if you want, though you'll wish you hadn't soon enough. But I really think I could find something out for you about your father or Mr. Longcor, if you'd let me. With my gift?"

Spiritualism again. Now that I'd had a whole morning to interact with her, it wasn't as easy to brush the thought aside. And what harm could it do anyway? At worst, it could be some more nonsense about an unseen storm. "I don't know that I want to wait for it to be night again," I said.

She smiled and tilted her head to the side. "Who said it has to be night?"

"Isn't that always when these sorts of things are done? So you can, I don't know, talk to the other side more easily?"

"Maybe for the pretenders. It's easier to hide wires and tricks when people can't see as well. But spirits don't disappear when the sun comes up. They can talk to me now just as easily as they can twelve hours later. Though it's harder to hear them when I'm around an unbeliever. Do you think you could swallow your skepticism long enough to try? If it hasn't worked in a half hour, it won't work at all, but at least you'll know then."

I considered it for a moment longer. Who was I afraid of looking foolish in front of? It was just the three of us, and she seemed so confident about it. So at last I nodded.

"Sure. What could it hurt?"

CHAPTER EIGHT

"Prof. Miss KATIE BENDER Can heal all sorts of Diseases; can cure Blindness, Fits, Deafness, and all such diseases, also Deaf and Dumbness. Residency, 14 miles East of Independence, on the road from Independence to Osage Mission, one and one half miles South East of Norahead Station."

Katie Bender, June 18, 1872

IT TOOK SOME TIME FOR Kate to find a suitable place: underneath a towering cottonwood that had to be at least a hundred years old. Its branches hung out over the creek, throwing the whole area into shade. The prairie grass grew more thinly there, and it would be cooler.

Kate pressed her lips together in determination. She'd rolled up the sleeves of her blouse and walked around the area, picking up any stray twigs and leaves.

"The fewer distractions around, the better," she explained.

"And most spirits prefer a clean environment. Have you ever done anything like this before?"

"I've only read about it in books," I said.

John tittered. "You're in for a treat then. Nobody talks to them like Kate."

She ignored him, sitting with her legs folded to the side, gesturing for us to follow. "There are a few rules, and I need to make sure you know how important it is that you follow them. We will hold hands, and you must. Not. Let. Go. We have strength in numbers so long as we are connected, but as soon as that link is broken, all protection is gone."

"What would we need protection from?" I asked.

"We're trying to find out about a group of outlaws who may have very well killed many people," she said, her voice solemn. "And we're doing it in a place they've been active. There's a fair chance one of the victims will be the one to respond to our summons. Spirits who left this world through violence can sometimes want to inflict that same violence on as many people as possible."

"So…we might get hit by invisible fists?"

"Don't think about it," she said. "They feed on emotions. Fear. Jealousy. Love. Anger. That's why we must all be calm before we begin. Our minds clear. Our purpose united. I've found it works best if we're all focused on the same question. In this case, we want to know where your father has gone. Keep that at the front of your mind, and don't let anything else take its place."

This was much more involved than what I had expected. Father had always spoken dismissively of spiritualists, and I'd never read anything to dispute that opinion. They were charlatans and swindlers. But what was Kate going to get out of this? I wasn't paying her. She hadn't even asked for anything in return.

"Some of what you'll see might surprise you," she continued. "Don't be frightened. You have to keep those feelings in check, or they can run the whole effort off the rails. I might sound... different, depending on what sort of spirit I come in contact with. As long as you keep cool and don't break the circle, everything will be fine."

"What happens if I break the circle?"

"If you're having second thoughts, I don't want to risk it," Kate said.

John laughed.

How did we get to the point where they were the ones trying to persuade me to stop this? I didn't want to let John make me feel like that, so I sat down. "I'm ready."

Kate and John sat across from each other, in front of me, the three of us forming points of a triangle. Kate held her hands out to either side of her, and I was all too ready to take one. Her palms were smooth, her fingers delicate, and she gave me a slight squeeze back that prickled the hairs on my neck. But then John held his hand out, and some of the magic went away. His hands were blocky, rough, and sweaty.

"We begin by clearing our minds of everything but our one purpose. Nicholas Bullock, and nothing else. Close your eyes. Take regular, even breaths. In. Out. In. Out. Feel the world around you. The wind in the trees. The grass beneath us. The sound of the creek passing by. Feel your connection to it all—your spot in this world that only you can fill. Be at peace. Calm. Determined. And breathe."

For the first while, I felt more self-conscious than anything else. What would my brothers say if they were to see me now? Wyatt would be laughing over the story for years. Our family wasn't the séance type. We only went to church occasionally, and only when Mother insisted long enough. But I'd decided to try this, and when I tried something, I didn't like going halfway.

To my left, a mouse or a bird rustled through the leaves, causing the branches to shake in fits. Then it was silent again.

What would it be like if we really could contact a spirit or a ghost? Meeting a person, you never knew if they were telling you the truth or not. Why did everyone always assume that changed as soon as you died? If this were true, I didn't see why there was any reason to assume we could—

Focus. Clear my head. Think on Father. Breathe.

A rustling came from my right now, closer. From the sound of it, perhaps a groundhog. The animals we'd scared off with our searching were finding their courage once more. But for all the noises around us, I only noticed now that there were no actual animal sounds. No birdcalls. No grasshoppers. Though a few flies had found us, buzzing around my head. The mosquitos would follow soon enough, and in my experience, some of the ones in Kansas could carry off small children.

Kate squeezed my hand again. "Focus," she said. "Don't think about focusing. Just focus."

Right. Reach out to the universe. Be at peace. I could do that for five minutes, couldn't I?

Slowly, the world seemed to fade away. The sound of my breathing drowned out everything else, until all I was focused on was that steady beat. It was as if I could hear my heart getting slower and slower.

Kate's hand tightened on mine a little more. "I feel…" She trailed off, then started again. "Something's coming."

I'd expected to be skeptical. I hadn't thought for a moment I'd be afraid, yet it felt like someone was peering over my shoulder, their face perched just out of sight if I were to open my eyes. I tried to cope with the fear the way I always did: picking it apart in my mind, never mind the warnings Kate had given. She must do that with everyone. If you told someone not to think about something, all that did was make them think about it. For all I knew, it was a common trick of swindlers.

But I was a man of books. I shouldn't fall for cheap manipulation. So why did it feel like something was gnawing outward from my stomach? A mixture of nausea and dread washed over me, enough to make me want to pull my hands back to my side, stand, and run for cover.

I managed to keep from breaking the circle, but I opened my eyes in spite of Kate's commands. With the band of outlaws somewhere nearby, we could be sitting here helplessly, just asking to be attacked. It would explain that feeling of being watched.

Except, when I glanced over my shoulder, no one was there. I checked the other one, just in case, but with the same result. No masked men crawling up to slit our throats. Nothing to be seen for miles other than the fields and the flies. There were more of them now: at least five or six, no doubt drawn to our scent.

"Who are you?" Kate asked, her face wrenched in concentration. "I sense…pain. Are you our friend? Are you Nicholas? Do you recognize Warren? Is that why you're here?"

Father wasn't dead. I couldn't even consider it, not if I wanted to still have hope enough to move forward. I half expected some ghostly outline to appear in between us, our own Jacob Marley come to give us guidance. Had it grown darker in the shade? The sun no doubt had gone behind a cloud. I shivered. Had the temperature dropped as well?

"No," Kate said. "You're not Nicholas. Why are you here? Why do you—"

Her hand clamped down on mine so hard, I screamed. Her wrists *twisted*, pulling my hand around at a painful angle. I had to move my elbow out to the side or risk having my wrist snapped, and still she clenched onto my hand with a strength I wouldn't have expected even from a full-grown man. John cried out as well, his eyes wide with surprise and fear as he tried to contort himself into a position that was under less strain.

"You're hurting me, Kate," I said, the nerves clear in my voice. I knew it sounded whiny, but I—

"Kate isn't here." The words came from Kate's mouth, but it was a harsh whisper laced with a rasp. It sounded…*reptilian*, more than anything. She opened her eyes, and they were nothing but pure white, though with her face turned toward me, it was clear where she was focused.

She tilted her head down and slowly smiled, though it grew and widened until it was more of a snarl than anything else. "You should let go of our hand," the voice said, speaking with more of a twang to its words than Kate ever had. "We might be more forgiving, if you do."

Kate twisted her hands even further, reaching an angle I would have thought was impossible, nearly snapping my wrist. I had to fight back as hard as I could to get to a position that was barely tenable.

If she wanted me to let go of her hands so much, why was she gripping so tightly, her fingers digging into my skin like claws? I wanted to tear myself away from her. *Don't break the circle.* But this couldn't be real. Things like this didn't happen. It was a swindle of some sort. Mirrors.

Except this wasn't in a shadowed back room. The sun was still shining somewhere, even if it felt like the whole area had been cast in darkness. As much as I wanted to believe this was fake, I was more scared of what would happen if I let go of Kate's hand, her warnings echoing in my ears.

John began to scream, long high-pitched shrieks that repeated again and again as he stared at his sister, spittle running down his chin. He lunged backward, his feet scrabbling at the grass for purchase.

I yanked back on his arm. "We can't run," I snapped. "Stop panicking." Even then my mind raced around in circles, desperate for an explanation of what was happening.

With a final yell, he slumped forward, unconscious or dead.

"What is it you seek?" The voice whispered through Kate again.

"Nothing," I said. "Go away. I didn't—"

She closed her eyes and breathed in slowly through her nose, as if savoring a scent in the area. "Lie again, and I will punish you." Her eyes snapped open, still totally white. "What is it you seek?"

"M-m-my father," I said. "I'm looking for him and my friend—"

"George was never your friend. You've never even met him. What is it you seek?"

My jaw dropped, and a pit opened in my heart. The hope that this might somehow be a sham grew even dimmer. With those blank white eyes and sneering smile, Kate seemed more a drowned specter, back to wreak vengeance.

She dug in even tighter with her fingers, her nails spasming inward in a quick jerk. Tiny crescents of blood appeared around each finger as she dug those nails into my skin. My hand felt like fire.

"I just want my father," I called out. "I want him home safe. I want to prove to myself what kind of person I am, once and for all. I don't want to be wicked anymore."

Her laugh sounded like a blade being sharpened on a whetstone. The wind whipped at the trees above us, but her voice still cut through the noise, as if she were speaking directly into my head. "Safety? It doesn't exist in the world. George didn't get peace, and your father never will now either."

"Do you know where they are?"

"Dead," Kate said. "George is rotting in a grave along with his whelp, and your father joined them a week ago. Food for crawling things. But they're not alone. There are others in that grave with them. Ten or more, and ten times that scattered here and there, floating facedown in the rivers or with empty sockets staring up at the sky as the ravens feast."

Dead? No. This couldn't be real. It had to be a lie. "Where?" I asked, my lips dry as bone.

Blood trickled from the corner of Kate's mouth, running down her chin and dripping to her dress. She tilted her head to the side, staring at me in what seemed to be confusion. "First, a price."

"A p-price?" Any moment, my wrist would snap in two, and I'd lose my grip. Whatever it was that had taken over Kate would lunge forward, its jaws stretching for my face. "What price?"

"An oath, on your life. If I tell you, you will go now. You will not stop until they are dead. Each and every one."

"What are you talking about?"

"Every murder has a murderer. They run for safety while you waste your time lying to yourself and others. You don't need to find George. You need to find *them*."

"I'm not going to kill them," I said. "Not unless I have to."

The thing laughed at me again, drops of blood flying from its mouth. "Tell yourself whatever lies you need to—only promise you will go and go now." It dug its nails farther into my hands.

"Yes," I said, panting with exertion. "Right away."

It stared at me for so long, I thought something had happened. If it hadn't been for the blood that continued to drip from its chin and the struggle it was just to hold on to its hand, I would have thought time itself had stopped. "Search Indian Territory. Go west. Ride quickly."

Its head lolled back, lifeless, and Kate's body slumped toward me. The iron grip that had been digging into my left hand disappeared, but I still sat there, wide-eyed and gasping. I didn't want to believe I'd seen what just happened. It would be easier to jump into the creek and never come out again than to admit it.

To my right, John began to stir, his limbs twitching sporadically.

I had promised to do something, hadn't I? Why did my mind feel so blank?

"What happened?" John asked, sitting up. He had somehow

managed to hit his head in the middle of everything; a trickle of blood seeped down the left side of his face. He had thrown up at some point as well.

I cleared my throat. "Your s-sister. She—she—"

His eyes focused once again, and he rushed to Kate's side, cradling her head in his hands and gently turning her over onto her back. "It's never come on her that hard before." His voice was soft. Awed. Around us, the sun had come back from its hiding place, and birds were singing in the trees again. He looked up at me. "Did she tell you anything?"

"It—*she*—said George and my father were murdered and that the ones responsible were heading to Indian Territory. I had to promise I'd go after them right away."

"Then what are you doing sitting here?" John asked. He laughed, but the titter was much more nervous and appropriate for once.

"Kate," I said. Why was I sweating now, when moments before my teeth had chattered? "I wanted to make sure—"

John stared down at his sister again. "I don't know what that thing was that got hold of her, and I don't think I want to. But I know as sure as sunshine if you don't do what you promised to the letter, we'll be in much more trouble than we want to think about. I'll take care of my sister. You get on that farm horse of yours and start trotting off toward Independence, and don't come back until you've done everything you swore to do."

I patted myself down, as if I'd forgotten something on the

kitchen table at home or was searching for an item I couldn't think of. My mind spun in circles, going nowhere.

"Go!" John yelled, snapping me back into it and pointing off to the horizon.

I nodded once and, with a final glance to Kate, hurried off to Surrey. I didn't want to believe any of this. In the span of a few short minutes, my world had been upended. Father dead? Voices from the beyond? I felt cut loose and abandoned, falling into an abyss toward an inescapable doom below. At that moment, I would have traded everything I owned—even my soul, if I had one—for just a shred of hope.

But none was in sight.

CHAPTER NINE

"Upon the back of his head and to the left, and obliquely from his right ear, a terrible blow had been given with a hammer. The skull had been driven into therein, and from the battered and broken crevices a dull stream of blood had oozed, plastering his hair with a kind of clammy paste and running down upon his shoulders."

—The Poultney Journal
(Vermont), May 23, 1873

SURREY'S MOUTH WAS FOAMING AND chest heaving before I was calm enough to think rationally. I couldn't gallop my horse the whole way. He'd be dead long before I got to Independence. So I pulled him to a stop, got off, and walked alongside him at a fast pace, my mind still running through the things I had witnessed.

The farther I got from Kate and John, the more I wanted to question what exactly had happened. It was just past noon, and the world went on the same as it always had. Clouds had rolled in while we'd been trying to reach the beyond, and they hung low in the sky now, hovering over my head like an axe about to fall.

The air, meanwhile, was just as oppressive, sweltering and thick with moisture. A few prairie dogs and rabbits scrambled out of my way as I rode by, but even they seemed to move with a sluggish sense of concern. Sweat trickled down my back and forehead. My stomach growled, and I realized I hadn't eaten lunch. I fished around in one of my saddlebags for some jerky, then chewed on it as I continued to think.

More than anything, I wanted that séance to have been fake. Before I'd set out on this journey, I would have laughed at anyone foolish enough to even try one. Seances were nothing more than scams designed to steal money from the simpleminded. But how could *that* have been fake?

The wounds on my hand from her fingernails were only just crusting over. She'd had *blood* drooling from her mouth. John would have to be an excellent actor to make himself seem as terrified as he'd been.

I tried to talk myself out of it, going over in my mind what I would have told someone else if they'd come to me with that kind of story. She could have had a stronger grip than I'd suspected. Strong enough to break the skin with her fingernails? I tried doing the same thing to myself, but I'd cut my nails close enough that it never would have worked, no matter how strong I was.

Blood from her mouth? Perhaps if she'd bitten down hard on her tongue, that would have bled enough to cause that, but she'd be talking with a lisp for the next few weeks. Could she have hidden some sort of packets in her mouth that she bit down on instead? She hadn't sounded like she'd had anything in there.

And what about how cold it had gotten? How the sun had dimmed, the wind thrashing at the trees?

The mind did strange things when it was under stress. Could that explain any of it?

After all was said and done, there was a significant difference between living through something and having someone tell you about it after the fact. From the comfort of a living room or over a nice supper, so much of the fear trickled away from the story. But no matter how many times I tried to convince myself otherwise, I couldn't forget the raw emotion of what I'd been through.

Besides, what would be the point of Kate faking that? I hadn't given the Benders any extra money because of the séance, and unless someone wanted to say an entire family was going around killing people, sending me off to Indian Territory did nothing to help the Benders.

But perhaps I was dismissing that notion too lightly.

So I dwelled on the question, ridiculous as it might have seemed at first. Could the Benders be the ones doing the killing? A scatter-brained young man, a gnarled grandfather, a surly grandmother, and a young woman desperate to get away from all of them?

I might as well begin suspecting my own mother.

The tall prairie grass scraped at my hands as I walked. The jerky dried out my mouth, and I took a drink from my canteen. It helped to picture my father walking next to me, probing me with questions about my logic. I wasn't sure what I'd experienced back there with Kate, but I knew it had scared me more than anything I'd ever seen. But would it be so bad to investigate Indian Territory? Yes, it was dangerous, but I couldn't shy away from danger. Not with Father in trouble. And wouldn't the territory be the perfect place for outlaws to hide? I'd get down there, ask around, and then continue following the trail wherever it might lead.

I was tired of overthinking; it was time for me to make a choice and live with whatever came from it.

Your father is dead. Rotting in the earth, never to be found, but you could find his killers. Find them. Bind them. Flay them alive, the skin—

I clenched my jaw and pushed those thoughts back. I could choose to believe in some spirit or believe my father might still be alive. It wasn't a hard choice to make. For today, my choice was to head toward Indian Territory as fast as I could.

Which was when I realized in my haste to set out, I'd just gone off in the direction John had pointed, not questioning for a moment if it was the right one.

I pulled Surrey to a halt, reaching into my saddlebags for my compass, cursing myself for being so brainless. It could mean hours wasted just because I—

My compass wasn't there.

My bags were as neatly stowed as they'd been the last time I'd looked, everything folded and placed just so, and the slot for my compass was as empty as a missing tooth. I checked through everything, just to be sure, my stomach sick with the realization. Around me, the prairie rolled endlessly in every direction. No houses, no sign of smoke, no fence posts. With the heavy cloud cover, and without a compass, there was no way for me to know which way Independence lay or where I should head to find the nearest road. I took a few deep breaths. Yes, I was lost. But my saddlebags were full of jerky and cornmeal to make some johnnycakes. I had the rifle, and wasn't I the one who had reassured Newton I knew plenty about living on the trail?

What did I know about the area? I got my map from my pack and stared at it, chewing on the inside of my lip. This was Kansas, not Indian Territory, and I was only a few hours from the Osage Mission Trail, if I could just figure out which way it was. No matter which direction I went, I'd come across a landmark eventually, but until I oriented myself, the map was useless.

If somehow I was heading north . . .

I'd come to a railroad line, but it might be a week or more of travel.

Father had taught me how to follow a trail. How hard could it be to follow my own? Although that would lead me back to John and Kate and whatever it was I had experienced, and my stomach tensed just thinking about it.

The important thing was to not be going around in circles. If there really was an angry spirit willing me onward, I couldn't afford to waste a second.

There were hours to go before nightfall. Setting up camp and doing nothing made no sense, not when three of the four directions would lead me to safety in a few short hours. I'd already been heading this way for a while, so it made the most sense to continue and do my best to reassure myself it was the right decision.

When I'd traveled on roads before, I'd been surprised at just how rough they'd seemed. Little more than well-traveled paths, really. What I hadn't realized was how much easier they'd made the journey. When you stared out over the prairie, it looked like nothing more than a big, wide expanse of grass and sky, with a few trees and bushes added here and there at times to break the monotony. It would be easy to assume you could ride blindfolded in any direction you wanted and never have to worry about tripping on an obstacle.

But the tall grasses hid surprises time and again. Gullies appeared almost out of nowhere, deep enough for someone to walk through and never be seen from above. There were prairie dog holes scattered in clumps; each one could break a horse's leg if you weren't careful. And here, off the main trail, there was more wildlife as well. The Osage Mission Trail hadn't been that busy, but it had been enough to tame the country to a degree I only noticed now that I was off it.

There was no natural border between Missouri and Kansas. No real reason for the countryside to look significantly different on one side or the other. But Missouri had been a state for decades, serving as a launching point for countless pioneers heading west. All those people had brought money with them and left with wagons, oxen, horses, and supplies. It meant Missouri had time to develop.

Kansas, on the other hand, was barely into its infancy as a state, really. Yes, it had been accepted into the union more than ten years ago, but the war had taken up the bulk of the country's attention for much of that, between the actual battles and then the time it took to recover. Before that, Kansas had been a hotbed of unrest, with slaveholders and abolitionists pouring into the area to try and sway it one way or the other.

Back in Missouri, there were plenty of people who would say Kansas was more a part of Massachusetts than it was anything else, since so many abolitionists had moved to the place and started families. Then again, I'd heard of plenty of people from Missouri doing the same thing fifteen years ago, in hopes that they could elect enough people to make the state legalize slavery.

None of that seemed to matter once you were out in the prairie, all alone. It was easy for me to imagine I was the only person to have ever walked this way before, even though I knew the Osage had been here long before any American had shown up.

An hour later, I still hadn't seen another soul or a sign of a road or a trail, and the cloud cover hadn't lightened a shade. Wherever the sun was, it was setting; I couldn't see as far as I had earlier in the day. If it got too dark and I continued, I was liable to fall right into one of those gullies. Better to spend some time looking for a safe spot now, then resume my journey in the morning. I'd get to some water and boil it so I could drink it safely.

I remembered Father warning me of how many things could go wrong on the road. "You think things through three times before you do anything," he'd said. "When you're in the wild, think 'em at least two more before you do anything rash." Back then he'd always smiled and said boys were more full of rash than anything else, until they turned eighteen.

All the more reason to take my time and keep my wits about me.

The clouds couldn't stay there forever, no matter what Kate had said about a storm to end all storms. People couldn't know the future, and if they got lucky now and then, that didn't mean anything special.

Now that I checked on the clouds, I saw the horizon was getting ominously dark. I could think of few things I wanted less than to have to spend the night out alone in the rain, though with the way the day had been going, it probably lay in store for me. It wouldn't take the storm of the century to ruin my evening. Maybe I'd get lucky and the storm would push off in a different direction.

I continued until I came to the banks of a steep gully with a stream flowing along it. There was enough space on either side of it for me to camp, and I led Surrey down its banks and then along the water until I came to a spot that was fairly level.

When I'd traveled to California and back with Father and the wagon company, making camp had always been something other people decided on. They'd tell me that's where we'd be sleeping, and that had been good enough for me. It felt strange now to make the decision on my own. I might not have traveled alone, but I'd been on the trail enough to know just what could go wrong. Snakes. Wolves. Panthers. Flash floods. Any number of emergencies Father had described to me over the years jumped to mind.

I told myself I was being silly. If it started to rain in the night, then I'd worry about getting back to high ground. *I should have plenty of warning.* I proceeded to get off Surrey and get the place set up for the night.

A half hour later, I was feeling quite proud of myself. I'd collected a pile of dry wood that would be more than enough for me to cook my supper on, and I had a blanket set up on a pile of leaves even Father would have to admit looked comfortable. I might be far away from civilization, but all those nights on the trail hadn't left me completely helpless.

The only thing that had gone wrong was a small mishap with my matches and the stream. I tried using them wet, but they were too soggy to get any friction. Not a problem. Father had shown me how to use flint and steel, and I'd brought both.

It shouldn't have been that hard. You couldn't travel west and then east again with wagon companies and not have a good idea of the basics, but I'd only actually done it four or five times, and that had been years ago. I had more than enough dry grass for kindling. The sun had baked the area before the clouds came over. But no matter how many times I tried with my flint, the spark just wouldn't catch.

After what must have been two hours of attempts, I threw the flint into the bushes and plopped myself down on the blanket.

You're a failure. A pretender. Useless.

Where had everything gone wrong? Things in Osage Mission had been different than I'd expected, but I'd adjusted. Ever since the Benders, something had changed. I felt continually off-balance; things that I'd taken for granted for as long as I lived were suddenly in question.

The worst part about it all was that when I'd left, I'd actually felt hopeful for the first time in years. Like Poe's Dupin in "The Murders in the Rue Morgue," I'd use my brain to follow clues and save my father, and then I'd stop worrying what I was and *know* what I was. Instead, it had been more like jostling my way through a crowd. I might have a general idea of where I wanted to go, but I kept getting hit off course and going where other people sent me.

A *séance*? Had I really lost my head and run off just because of a few gusts of wind and some blood? Kate must have bitten her tongue. It was the only thing that made sense. And her brother had played the part perfectly. As for why, it could be for nothing more than to make fun of the stranger from Missouri. It wouldn't be the first time I'd been made the butt of a joke.

When I found my way to Indian Territory, I'd take charge of the investigation again. I'd come up with a plan and follow it through. I'd—

A booming roll of thunder interrupted my thoughts. Surrey nickered and shuffled restlessly to my left. I scrambled up the bank, now shadowed in darkness. On the horizon, lightning streaked through the clouds, splashing them with purple streaks. Thunder rumbled in front of the storm, deep and bone shaking. The sky had turned a shade of dark green I'd never seen before.

My heart rate sped up, pounding in my chest, even as I tried to reason myself out of this. So much for hoping the storm would miss me, though at least it hadn't started raining. Yet. The air filled with a sickly-sweet scent that often came with lightning. It always reminded me of strawberries.

I did my best not to think of Kate's warning, because if that had been true, then didn't it imply the séance had been true as well?

I'd been through some bad storms when we'd traveled to California and back, and I knew just how much worse a storm was when there weren't four walls around you and a roof overhead. Back then, I'd been happy to have the wagon cover, the whole family huddled together around a lantern, the wind clawing and tearing at the fabric, searching desperately for a way in.

Tonight, I didn't even have that thin protection. The campsite I'd been so proud of was good for sleeping and a campfire (if I could have made one), but terrible for real shelter. Different options flashed through my mind. I could lead Surrey down the stream, searching for a spot on the banks where perhaps the water had eaten into the ground, but I didn't know where this stream came from. If a wall of water came barreling down it in a flash flood, I'd be lucky to stay alive. Those carried so much debris in that first surge, you might as well get hit by a moving brick wall.

So perhaps it would be safer to abandon the gully and go out into the open. Searching for a tree for cover would be a terrible idea in a lightning storm. There were few enough of them that it would just be asking to get struck.

But what else could I do?

Lightning flashed above me, a jagged snake shooting through the sky. Whatever I was going to do, I had to do it now.

I hurried over to Surrey before struggling with him as I got the bridle over his head and strapped my saddle on.

His eyes were wide with fright, and he kept trying to rear up, straining at the lead with every burst of lightning or clap of thunder. I managed to calm him enough to get up the banks, and then he was all too ready to follow me anywhere other than where we were.

I wished I had someone I could follow like that.

The sky grew darker as the clouds blocked out any bit of light that might have still been present. It got to the point that I could only see when the lightning flashed, though it began to flash so often, the sky was steadily illuminated.

Rain pelted down from above: big hard drops that slapped against my face. Within moments, the rain had increased to a nonstop flow, until it sounded like I was standing in the middle of a waterfall. My clothes were so wet, I might as well have jumped in a lake.

The downpour calmed Surrey somewhat, probably because the roar of the rain helped drown out some of the thunder. Above us, lightning flashed almost constantly, some of it stabbing into the ground in brilliant white, other bolts moving sideways through the storm, turning the clouds a burning purple. I'd never seen anything like it, and I stopped and stared, my mouth slack.

Until something hard stung my cheek. And my hand. And then hail was falling all around me, white balls bouncing up from the prairie, some of them as large as my thumb. I whipped my coat off and threw it over my head, making sure to be next to Surrey to protect him somewhat too.

It continued for minutes or hours. I lost track. My hands became covered in welts, and Surrey kept shifting uneasily, still trusting me, but seeming to question the decision. My breath came in quick gasps, and I felt faint. Now wasn't the time to panic, but the Voice reminded me of the cow I'd found in the field after it had been struck by lightning: Its legs splayed in the air. Its flesh covered in a zigzag open wound, black around the edges.

This was the worst storm I'd experienced in my life. I'd never been in anything close to its power, and here I was in the middle of the prairie. The hail came and went in spurts, and each time it lessened, I continued searching for someplace to lie low. Surrey and I came to another gully, but water roared through it, a mass of writhing brown chaos filled with tree branches and even a wagon wheel at one point.

The thunder was so constant now, it felt like one continuous sound. The hail was so thick, it looked like it had snowed, pressing down at the prairie grass. Rain came down in buckets, as if someone were hovering over me, pouring one after the other.

A gust of wind tore at my jacket, shoving me toward the storm.

Lightning flickered in front of me again, and in that brief instant, I got a glimpse of something in the sky: a long thick hand reaching out of the clouds above to plunge into the soil beneath. My stomach dropped, and I stopped, staring in front of me, willing the lightning to come back so I could get a second look.

Another bolt struck almost next to me, turning the night air white before a clap of thunder smashed down so loudly, it hurt my ears. Surrey reared in surprise and terror, ripping the reins from my hand and galloping into the darkness, carrying my saddlebags with him. I took off in pursuit, but I knew it was hopeless. There was no way I'd be able to catch a panicked horse. The best I could do was cross my fingers he wouldn't run too far and that I'd be able to find him once the storm was through.

Lightning flashed in front of me again, and again, and then a third time, enough to show without any doubt what was coming my way: a giant swirling funnel of fury. It was hard to tell how close it was, but the base of it looked at least a quarter of a mile wide. The center was too dark for the lightning to shine through, but the edges of it were a flurry of flying branches, leaves, and rocks.

I'd heard about tornadoes before, of course. You couldn't live in the Midwest for long without running into someone who'd seen them. When one was in the area, you ran for the storm cellar and locked the doors behind you.

What were you supposed to do when the nearest storm cellar was miles away?

Lightning struck behind me, illuminating the tornado from the front, revealing a series of round clouds at its top, repeated in several layers, towering up into the sky.

The twister was closer than it had been before.

If I'd had half a brain, I would have saddled Surrey properly and ridden off with him. Maybe then, I'd be able to do something other than just hope for the best. On horseback, I might have had a better chance of outrunning this *thing* in front of me.

Above everything else came one clear thought: *Kate was right.*

And if she'd been right about this, then—

The lightning above the storm picked up, bouncing back and forth over the tornado in an almost-constant stream of electricity, casting the whole prairie in a flickering eerie blue light. It was as if the tornado itself were about to turn into a bolt. With that much light, I was able to tell the vortex was coming straight for me. The air filled with the smell of fresh-cut wood and plowed earth.

Around me, the rain stopped at once.

My head felt like someone was pushing on both of my ears, hard.

I turned to the right and began running as fast as I could. Anything was better than nothing, and it might make the difference between living and dying. The wind tore at my clothing and buffeted me a foot to the right before I could get my balance again.

It sounded like a train from hell bearing down on me, the air filled with an overpowering roar. My lungs ached from how hard I'd been running, each breath a fierce pain as my chest heaved.

Newton had been right. I never should have come on this journey. Why did I ever think I was up to being anything more than a failure or a murderer?

A tree branch sailed overhead, only lit for a moment by the lightning before it whipped past me, scraping at my face as it flew. I had to spit to get the blowing grit out of my mouth, but I didn't even dare take the time to put a handkerchief up to block the dirt.

I pictured myself ripped from the ground and tossed hundreds of feet into the air, rushing up to meet the lightning before falling to the earth, charred and lifeless. Was this some sort of hex from the evil spirit? It was violent enough—and soon enough after my experience this morning—to make me wonder.

But in the end, it didn't matter. I forced my legs to keep

pumping. A limb as thick as my thigh soared past, and then an entire bush, bobbing through the air in a tangled mass. Something hard crashed into my left side, and I fell before scrambling back to my feet.

This was too close. I wouldn't even need to get sucked up by the tornado to get—

My feet lost purchase with the ground, and I was lifted into the air, tumbling head over feet this way and that. My skin was scratched and hit by a thousand different objects: rocks, twigs— even the carcass of a prairie dog at one point. I had never felt so completely helpless before. There was nothing I could do.

For one moment, lightning flashed while I was turned the right way. The ground was at least twenty feet below me and getting farther off.

Something hard collided with the back of my head, and everything went dark.

CHAPTER TEN

"I need not tell you that the whole countryside is convulsed with horror and indignation, and burns with a flame of revenge that can only be quenched with blood."

—Star Tribune
(Minneapolis, Minnesota), May 15, 1873

━━━━━━━━

I HADN'T EXPECTED TO WAKE, AND when consciousness returned, I almost wished it hadn't. My body was a patchwork of bruises and aches and scabbed scrapes. My jacket had been ripped away, and my shirt had a gash in it six inches long. Everything was still damp; shivers ran through me from time to time. When I tried to sit up, the entire prairie spun, and I bent to the side and tried to vomit. Nothing came out.

Lying back down seemed like a much better idea, so I stayed in the dirt, staring at a sky with delicate white clouds and the occasional bird zipping by. The light breeze might as well have been a slight puff of air, compared to what I'd lived through last night.

How had I lived through it? The memory of that storm—its sheer violence and size—made me go lightheaded again. How had Kate known? Or had she just felt it in her bones the same way old men in Lamar could tell you when a storm was coming?

There had to be a rational explanation.

I might not have been able to sit up yet, but I experimented with moving my arms and legs and hands and feet, just to see what real damage had been done. Jolts of pain shot through my left thigh, enough to bring tears to my eyes. Broken, or just badly injured? I lifted my head to look.

A chunk of wood as thick as my thumb jutted out from the front of my thigh. How had I not noticed that as soon as I was conscious again? I didn't think it had gone through anything important, but it had gone through enough. My pants were soaked red around the wound, but it seemed like the bleeding had stopped during the night. It would start up again when I walked on it, though. If I *could* walk on it. I'd have to take the wood out and bandage my leg before I'd be able to know. Assuming I knew how to bandage it correctly.

Better to just lie here a spell longer. There were plenty of other questions to think about.

What had happened to Surrey? Was he lost on the prairie somewhere, or dead, or had he gotten to safety? For his sake, I hoped he was alive and well, but without him, how was I going to get back to civilization? I couldn't walk. I'd had my saddlebags tied to him. Would they have been ripped off in the storm, or had my horse gotten far enough away that they'd stayed firm?

Right then, I would have shaken a thousand hands if I could have just known at the end of it all, I'd be back on my journey and no worse for wear. I'd have hugged a stranger, even.

Time to try sitting up again.

The world still spun, but I wasn't overwhelmed by nausea, and I managed to get all the way up, my left leg protesting the movement.

I found myself in the middle of what looked like a freshly plowed field—or at least a field with all the grass and plants ripped out from it. Branches, leaves, and rocks lay strewn about as if tossed by a giant that had been playing with them until he grew bored. Ten feet in front of me, a dead hare lay slumped in a pile, its blank stare meeting mine as if to say it could have been worse.

A dead hare meant food for today, assuming I could figure out a way to cook it. I wasn't quite to the raw-meat stage of my adventure yet.

But first, the wound.

I grabbed on to the branch, or whatever it had been, in my leg, but I hesitated before drawing it out. Better to be prepared. I took off my shirt and ripped it into sections, trying to make them as long as possible. That taken care of, I took hold of the branch once more. Even touching it shot pain through my whole leg.

Don't think about it. Just hold on and pull. I was a Bullock, and it was time I acted the part.

· 138 ·

You're a failure, and you always will be.

In my head, it was going to be easy. It hadn't gone all the way through my leg, after all. How deep could it be? Pulling it as hard as I did, I discovered all too well. The wood wasn't smooth like an arrow. It was rippled and jagged, and I must have torn more of my leg pulling it out than had been torn as it went in. I could *feel* the bumps and jags moving inside me as I removed it. Tears ran down my cheeks, and I screamed as loudly as I could. My vision went dark around the edges, but I didn't pass out.

Instead, I sat there breathing heavily for what might have been thirty seconds. I was bleeding again, and I had to take care of the wound. I inspected the chunk of wood I'd removed. Three inches of its end were covered in blood. The tip was a ragged bit of splinters. I had no idea if some of the wood had come off inside me, but I also didn't know what to do about it if it had. I wasn't a doctor. I moved my leg some, trying to see if it felt like anything else big was in there, but it hurt so badly, I had no idea if I'd be able to tell.

So I hitched my pants down and wrapped the leg with the strips from my shirt, keeping the pressure tight. The first few layers bled through right away, but after I was finished, it seemed like the bandage was keeping the blood where it was supposed to be.

Who was I fooling? I was fumbling in the dark, hoping for the best. If I didn't find someone who knew what they were doing—soon—I was likely facing infection and a chance of death soon after. Every minute I sat taking my time was a minute less I had to search for someone who could help me.

I shambled to my feet, or at least tried to. My left leg buckled as soon as it had any pressure on it. Walking wasn't going to be possible without a crutch of some kind.

Luckily, there were more than enough branches to sort through and find something that would work. Most of them were too short or flimsy or crooked, but after shuffling around on the ground for a half hour, I found one that even had a place where I could rest my armpit.

I spent some time trimming stray twigs and offshoots from it, the work distracting me from all the other problems I faced. Once finished, I used the crutch to pull myself to my feet. As long as I kept all the weight off my left leg, the pain was manageable. The crutch was a little too tall, but I'd worry about that later. More troublesome was the fact my mind didn't seem to want to do what I told it to. I'd find myself staring off into the distance when I should have just been working on that crutch, and my eyes didn't want to focus on anything too close to me. My head started to hurt, and I rubbed my temples to try to make it go away.

Time. That's what I needed. I'd feel better the more time went by.

Standing, I surveyed the area, hoping I might see some sign of Surrey, but worried it would be nothing more than my horse's dead body. Instead, I saw wreckage in every direction. Tree branches— tree *trunks*—scattered like kindling. Really, it was a miracle I'd come out of this alive and with just a single puncture wound. It smelled like a lumber camp. Fifty yards away, a dark line had been etched into the earth. I hobbled over and stared down at a trench three feet deep. It ran in either direction for as far as I could see, weaving back and forth but always continuing.

My brothers would never believe me if I told them this story.

They'd never hear it if I didn't manage to get back alive.

It had taken a few minutes just to walk those fifty yards. It wasn't going to get any easier. I stared at the sun. Easy enough to tell which way was east now, though what I didn't know was which direction would get me safe the quickest. If I could get healed up, I could get back to finding Father. It all depended on which way I'd been headed yesterday. If I'd been going west the whole time, then I had to be close to the railway line at the least. But if I'd been going north or south, it might be better to head east now and get back on the Osage Mission Trail.

The decision that had seemed important yesterday was even more vital now.

You're going to die a failure. Proof you were never worthy of the Bullock name.

Now that I couldn't hurt anyone else, the Voice seemed set on making me as miserable as possible.

I scanned the area, hoping to find any shred of a clue as to which direction would be best. Nothing stood out, but I knew this single decision could likely be the difference between living and dying. What had I done wrong that my life should come down to a shot in the dark? Worrying about it wouldn't help. In the end, I decided to go east. If I'd been heading north or south yesterday, then the trail couldn't be that far away.

After an hour of travel, my armpit was raw, and my back had developed a knot from the awkwardness of my gait. The light hurt my eyes, and I kept getting distracted by simple things. I'd tried to throw up again twice, though if that was from the pain or the blow I'd taken on the head, I didn't know. I sat, panting, and reconsidered my options. I'd left the destruction from the tornado behind me quite early, as it had wandered off more to the south than I was heading. Here the prairie looked no different than it had yesterday. A rattlesnake peeked out from its den ten feet to my right.

I still carried the dead hare I'd found in the morning, though I tossed it to the side now. In my confusion of the morning, I'd forgotten to gut the animal, and I didn't want to risk eating spoiled meat. My stomach rumbled in protest. If Father were here, he'd no doubt be able to scrounge together a full meal just from the plants that surrounded me. I should have paid more attention to him all those times. It had just seemed easy, so I'd never thought about it.

Time to stand again. Dwelling on my situation wasn't going to help. Besides, it wasn't as if I were in the middle of the desert. I'd keep walking, and I'd come across someone.

After that, the hours bled into one another. Walking settled into a routine: take a step, plant the crutch, and shift to take another step, over and over. The sun rose high into the sky and then seemed to hover there for far too long. Thankfully, I'd worked the fields often enough that my skin was used to it, but there was a big difference between a regular day of work and what I was going through now.

My stomach was a tight knot of pain that I tried to ignore. Water hadn't been an issue yet. I'd come across two small streams and had just drunk without boiling it. If I lived long enough to get sick, it would be a good problem to have. Navigating the prairie was a much bigger issue. It had been one thing to travel up and down the hidden streambeds and gullies when I was healthy and riding Surrey. Now each one required a painful descent and difficult climb. When I could, I walked around them, even if it added some time onto my journey.

Step, crutch, step, crutch, step, crutch.

Did the wound feel like it was getting hotter? That had to be my imagination. How long would it take for an infection to set in? Surely at least a few days.

I kept thinking of all the things I'd lost in the storm. When Surrey had run off, he'd taken with him my food, my rifle, my money, and my clothes. Even if I managed to find help, where would that leave me?

And what about Father?

The sun was halfway to the horizon by the time I hurled my crutch down and collapsed on the ground, aching, nauseous, and hopeless. There'd been no sign of any settlements. No smoke. No fences. No roads. My left armpit was an open sore, and my leg felt like so much dead weight.

I lay down and stared at the sky. How long could I go without food? A week? Two? I tried to remind myself I had time, but then I shifted my pants down to check on my leg. The blood had completely seeped through the bandage, turning the top half a ruddy red. It didn't feel wet, so it must have stopped bleeding at some point, but I ought to be changing the bandage and washing the wound if I wanted to have a shot at avoiding infection.

But what would I use as a bandage? I couldn't walk across the prairie naked. I shouldn't have used my whole shirt the first time. I'd keep that in mind the next time I was wounded by a tornado, miles away from anyone.

I knew I wasn't helping myself by getting discouraged, but it wasn't like a pump I could just stop working. It took some time to convince myself to start walking again. In the end, I decided I might not have a good idea how to survive in the wilderness, but I'd do my best to be as tenacious as possible.

So I kept walking well past sunset. I had no gear to set up. No food to cook. No way to make a fire, and it wasn't cold enough to need one anyway, though I thought differently as I tried to pass the night without a shirt on.

When I did stop, I lay down and fell asleep in moments. My dreams were a mixture of the things I'd just lived through: storms and blood and a woman's laughter somewhere in the distance. I woke just as tired as I'd been when I'd first lain down.

The next day passed much like the first, though I got an earlier start. I had to take more breaks, when my arm felt like it just couldn't keep going or my leg started to hurt too much. I passed the time by picking a spot on the horizon and seeing how long it took me to get that far.

Much longer than I would have liked.

And still there was no sign of another human. There were rabbits and snakes and deer, antelope, eagles, foxes, raccoons, and turtles. I even saw an elk at one point. The larger animals reminded me there were other creatures that might be far less friendly if they were to find me in this state: coyotes or panthers, or even a buffalo herd.

By the time the sun was setting again, my mind had been stuck on listing off types of animals for the past hour or so, going over the names again and again. A part of me knew that wasn't normal behavior, but a larger part just didn't care.

Sitting down, I took stock of my condition. My left armpit was bleeding slowly from the scraped skin. Losing my shirt hadn't done that wound any favors. When I examined my leg, the bandage seemed even darker. The skin around the edges was hot to the touch and a fierce red. It didn't take a doctor to connect the signs of infection with the way my mind had been behaving and how my body had begun to shake now that I'd taken a pause. The evening air felt like it was coming down straight from the tundra.

I was feverish, and if it got much worse, I'd get too weak to walk. From there, I might as well find a ditch and roll into it for a grave.

Stopping would be a mistake. The infection would only grow. I needed to make it as far as I could to have any hope for finding help, so I struggled back to my feet and resumed my limping march.

Step. Crutch. Step. Crutch. Step. Crutch.

A man in our wagon train to California had gotten a leg wound once. The "doctor" who had been with us had been forced to amputate. I could still remember the man's screams as they'd carved into him, the sound the saw had made as its teeth scraped through skin and down into the bone. How long had it taken his wound to get that bad? I couldn't recall, though I knew it had started to smell well before, like a burnt cake with far too much sugar.

I thought I saw Father at one point, riding past me. He stared down from his horse and shook his head, then continued on without a word. I passed Mother as well, sobbing by the side of the road. Newton, James, Virgil, Wyatt, and Morgan—even Adelia. None of them missed a chance to tell me how hopeless I was and how foolish I'd been to come on this journey at all.

Night fell. The moon hung in the sky like a billiard ball waiting for the next shot. The wind blew over my skin, giving me goose pimples, though I kept sweating anyway. My muscles felt like I'd been working all week on the farm without a break, and there were these areas on my neck beneath my chin that flared with pain every time I moved wrong. In the distance, coyotes howled, but I paid them no mind.

Had to keep walking.

My eyelids had weights hanging from them, and it was all I could do to keep them open. Why was I still walking? I couldn't remember, except I knew I'd thought it was important. But now I wanted to stop. To sleep for at least a few hours. I'd have to feel better after I slept, right? Because my eyes wanted to close so badly. In the end, I made a compromise: I'd walk with my eyes shut.

For the first few yards, it seemed to work fine, and I felt very pleased with myself. Until I slumped forward, falling asleep in midstride and slamming into the ground face-first before I could catch myself.

I lay there, staring at the faint stars the moon hadn't washed out. Was I supposed to get back up? I couldn't seem to remember. "I'll do it in the morning, Father," I said, then drifted off into oblivion.

CHAPTER ELEVEN

"The work of searching the premises still goes on, and what may yet be developed none can tell, but the people are prepared for anything. In an old Bible which was found in the house, and on the family record page, was written in German the following memoranda: 'Big slaughter day, Jan. eighth (8).' And another which read 'Hell departed.'"

—The Democratic Press
(Ravenna, Ohio), May 22, 1873

FOR THE SECOND TIME IN as many days, I woke up surprised to be waking at all. My mind still felt fuzzy, and my vision was blurred when I first opened my eyes, but it edged into focus, and as it did, I noticed other details around me.

A clock ticking, for one thing. Not in my room—the sound came from behind a closed door. The scent of freshly baked bread. The feel of clean sheets on my skin.

That reminded me of my leg, and everything else snapped

together. The memory of the storm. The wound. My long walk trying to get help. Someone must have found me because here I was in a neat bedroom of a house that showed signs of refinement: Crown molding along the edges of the ceiling. Hand-carved trim around the door, which was a fine six-panel model. Oak. A braided rug on the floor, at least six feet long. And the floor itself, wide pumpkin pine planks.

It was a house someone had put time and effort into. That, or money, but the finishing on everything led me away from that thought. The carving on the trim was too uneven for a factory, and the rug was good, but not store quality. All that made me feel calmer. Anyone willing to take the kind of time it took to do all these things—on top of whatever other work they had—was a person I felt comfortable around.

I peeled back the covers to inspect my leg. The monstrosity of a bandage I'd slapped together was gone, replaced by a clean winding of cotton tied off as neatly as at a hospital. It throbbed some, now that I was paying attention to it. The skin around the bandage was no longer an angry red, however. I wasn't sure how long I'd been unconscious, but it must have been at least a few days. I didn't remember anything of them. One moment I'd been hobbling across the prairie, and the next I was here.

Voices came from outside the door: a man's low rumble and a woman's lighter tone. I pulled myself out of bed, fighting a wave of dizziness. The sooner I found out where I was and how much time had gone by, the quicker I could start planning.

But willpower could only do so much, it seemed. I teetered out of bed and took two wobbly steps toward the door before I fell in a heap. My leg might have been recovering, but it still didn't want any weight on it.

The floor vibrated as someone stepped toward the room from the main part of the house. A rap came at the door. "Everything all right in there?"

"Yes," I said, then glanced down at myself, half naked and sprawled on the floor. Would I even be able to get back into bed? But did I want a stranger helping me? For once, it was an easy choice. I cleared my throat. "Actually, no. Could you come help me?"

The door opened, and a man peeked around it. He had bright eyes and a neatly trimmed, pointed beard. Dressed simply in homespun pants, an off-white shirt, and suspenders, he seemed to be in his forties. He smiled when he saw me. "Thought you could handle it already, did you?"

"My leg didn't want to work with me."

"I expect not, considering what had been done to it before I found you."

He helped me back into my bed and got me situated. Even that small amount of effort left me winded. His wife came in, wearing a simple blue dress with sleeves to her wrists and a hem to the floor. She'd put her hair up into a neat bun, though a few locks had escaped. She held a tray filled with supper: bean soup, thick slabs of fresh bread, butter, milk, and even a few slices of cheese.

"Glad to see you awake," she said. Her voice matched the brightness of her husband's. "I was beginning to worry your horse might break in here if he didn't hear from you in the next day or two. Please eat."

"My horse?" I accepted the tray gratefully and dug in. With the smell of that soup and bread, my appetite had come back with a vengeance.

The man spoke. "My name's Leroy Dick. I'm the trustee for this county, so I don't want you thinking you owe me anything for what we've done. Just part of keeping the place in order, though I wouldn't mind knowing how you came to be where you were."

"My horse?" I asked again, worried I had misheard them. If Surrey were somehow alive and not lost...

"I've never seen anything like it," Leroy said. "Three days ago I was out in the field, cleaning up after that big storm that blew by. Off from the west came a riderless horse, still loaded with packs and a rifle, though all of it was soaked through, and the packs looked like they'd been thrown on in a hurry. At first I was worried it was another case of a missing person, but the horse walked right up to me, nudged me with its nose, and turned to head back where it had come from. There was no doubt it wanted me to follow.

"I got my own mount as fast as I could and headed off in pursuit. After the first couple of miles, I thought I must have been silly to be following a strange horse that far, almost as if it were a person. But I kept at it—I'd gone that long, might as well see it through. And then, after five miles, the horse stopped by some sort of pile on the ground. That pile turned out to be you. What happened—you fall off after taking ill?"

I shook my head, my mouth too full to answer at first. The soup was seasoned just right, heavy on the pepper. "Surrey—that's my horse—ran off in the middle of the tornado. I thought I'd lost him for good."

Leroy's eyebrows rose. "Tornado? That might explain why the doctor found those splinters buried in your leg. Seems like you might have a story and a half to tell." He nodded to his wife, who left the room, closing the door behind her.

I paused before I launched into what had happened. How was I supposed to know who to trust and who not to? But then I realized I was worrying about a man who had literally saved my life and that there was such a thing as being too distrustful. So, over the course of an hour (and a second helping of that soup—and then a third), I told him everything, almost. Hearing about the disappearances, coming to the area, staying with the Benders. I left out anything about the Voice and much of what happened during the séance, however. There was a limit to trust, after all, and I didn't want him to know what a monster he'd taken in.

Leroy grunted here and there at appropriate places, and he asked a few clarifying questions, but for the most part, he just let me talk. I didn't sense any sort of judgment. No comments about foolish actions I'd taken or other decisions I should have made.

His acceptance made me feel even more at ease, as if I'd just come in from a harsh winter storm to sit by the fire and warm up before heading out into it again. He leaned forward when I described the tornado, his eyebrows raised and his mouth slightly open.

"A story and a half indeed," he said once I was finished. "It's a shame you didn't come to me first when you got to the county. I could have spared you that incident with the Benders and given you a better place to stay while I was at it."

"You wouldn't have gone to them at all?"

He tilted his head from side to side indecisively. "I'd have had you steer clear of them altogether. They're a singular bunch, but Labette County is full of singular people. The frontier attracts that kind like a magnet, the good and the bad."

His wife came back into the room, bringing in a slice of blackberry pie with whipped cream. "It isn't fresh, of course. But I made some yesterday for when we had company over, and there was some left."

I accepted it gratefully, feeling somewhat guilty for taking so much charity. Father would have never allowed it. I did make a resolution to take my time with the pie, though. Someone had to show the Dicks that people from Missouri had at least a sprinkling of manners. Then I realized I'd been around the couple the entire time without thinking once of checking the room for weapons. The Voice hadn't said a peep yet.

While they sleep at night, you could grab an axe and swing it down on his skull, cracking through the bone as it—

There it was, right on cue. I tried to push it from my mind, biting the inside of my cheek to get my focus back.

"How many people have been moving into the area?" I asked Leroy after his wife had ducked out again.

"Too many to count, it feels like. There's some that move in and even move out before I ever get to know them. One family—the Ingalls, I think their name was—came in with their wagon, built and furnished a cabin, planted crops, and then were gone before they even had time to harvest them. Scared off by the Osage, I guess. Of course, that was going on four years ago now. Fewer folks up and move out as easy, now that the Osage made their sale official."

"When did the Benders come to the area?"

"Three years ago, give or take. They were more particular with their stake than most. Wanted it on a thoroughfare so they could run their inn and grocery store, though a sorrier inn and grocer's, I've never seen. Nothing but canned garbage you could buy in a city and a pallet full of bugs and molding straw."

"The Osage Mission Trail isn't exactly packed with people."

He snorted a laugh. "Not to someone used to farther east, no doubt. But it's as close to a thoroughfare as we get right now."

"With all these…disappearances, what have people been saying?"

Now Leroy grimaced. He had an easy way about him that

made me trust him as if I'd known him for years. "We've had all manner of guesses for that. I brought together a meeting a while back, and most everyone around came together to talk about it. We need people coming here and bringing their wallets with them. But right now, the only thing everyone hears about is how many people go missing once they get here. That's not the sort of thing that makes you too popular.

"Personally, I think it's some of them villains over in Ladore. The town's far too wild, and word is more than a few of them are wanted for murder anyway. A place like that attracts its own sort, and I'm not talking about just the singular kind now."

"Have you looked into it at all?"

Some of the light went out of his eyes, and he shook his head. "I'm supposed to be the one keeping the peace around here, more or less. I've led searches up and down the county, but we haven't found anything. My own cousin Hank's gone missing, so it's personal for me just as much as almost anyone. You're not the first person Kate's made her offer to contact the great beyond to find out, you know. She asked me twice, though I told her the same "no" each time. Something's not right about that girl, and not just because she shoves herself at any male fifteen years or older."

A wave of shame washed over me. No one wants to feel like they've been made a fool of, and now I wondered if that wasn't what Kate had been doing all along. "You don't believe she has any real powers?" I sounded like a fool even asking the question, but the memory of the blood streaming down her chin was far too recent. "No one's talked about anything that seemed…more than a show?"

"No one's even let her try, near as I can find out. Not for want of her offering, though. The girl's got a fair number of odd ideas. For one thing, she likes to prance around naked at night, from what I've been told."

"Not while I was there, she didn't."

"Yes, well she did when Hank was, and he wasn't the sort to make that kind of thing up. Never quite had the head for that amount of imagination, and he's not the only one to say it. There's a reason almost all the people who stay at the Bender Inn are men, after all."

"So what should I do about my father?" At that moment, I wanted more than anything for someone else to step in and take control of the whole effort. I'd thought I could do it on my own, but if the past Warren knew what the current Warren knew, there's no way he would have made the same mistake.

"I wish I could tell you," Leroy said. "I haven't seen your father, and I haven't seen Mr. Longcor either. I remember what it was like, not yet twenty and thinking I could solve all the problems of the world if I just had half a chance. But you get older, and you start to realize the folks you're so frustrated with now were frustrated the same as you were back then. Problems don't disappear with nothing more than grit and determination."

He walked to the window and peered out through the white

curtains. "What should you do? If it weren't your father, I'd tell you to move on with your life. You're going to have enough trouble of your own without the need to try to solve someone else's. Pick a trade, find a girl, settle down. Why, you could come out here to start a farm of your own if it suited you. We could use more of the kind of people who want to help others instead of just themselves."

I cleared my throat. "If I'd only come out here to search for George and his daughter, I'd—"

"I know. I can't say what I'd do if my pa went missing, but it sure wouldn't be nothing. Only thing is, I have nothing to tell you as far as your next steps. Well, other than rest. You're not going to be any use to anyone the way you are now. Why, when I came across you, you didn't even have a hat anymore. I've got an old one you can use and some clothes to go with it."

———

The Dicks were more than generous with their hospitality, letting me stay on another three days until my leg felt fine enough to walk on without much difficulty. And no matter how much I wanted to be off on the trail again, I knew pushing things too quickly would slow me down in the long run.

The days of rest helped. My leg hurt less, and I started walking on it a few minutes at a time to begin with, then more as it grew stronger. Leroy's old clothes were a bit tight across the shoulders and hips, but they worked, and they were a complete outfit: pants, shirt, jacket, chaps, and a gray hat to top everything off. I looked like Wyatt in them and wondered what my brother was doing right then. *You shouldn't be the one on this journey. Any one of your brothers would have done much better than you.* If Newton had known how likely it was Father was in real danger, would he have insisted on coming in spite of everything?

I spent several hours each day with Surrey, brushing him down and doting on him. For all people had made fun of my choice of horse, that choice had been the thing that had saved my life, and I wasn't going to forget it. He got plenty of apples and oats, and he seemed pleased to take a rest after so much traveling.

The days passed. I helped Leroy with some of the chores around his farm: Chopping wood. Mending some of his harnesses. Fixing a broken door on the barn. When it came time for me to leave, I realized I'd hardly worried about germs the whole time I'd been there. (Well, not enough that the Dicks noticed, at least.) I didn't even shy away from Mrs. Dick's embrace when it came time to leave.

You could crush her head with a rock. A few hard blows and it would cave in.

"Have you decided what you'll do?" Leroy asked me.

"I'm going back to the Benders. John said he'd seen bandits, but I've got my doubts."

Leroy nodded. "Keep your rifle handy, no matter where you go. I don't want to be hearing about you disappearing next. You got a revolver?"

My insides clenched up. "No."

"You'll be needing one. I've got an old Remington you can have. Anyone trying to stop this madness is someone I want to help."

I didn't know what to say, and so I said nothing as he disappeared into a back room and came back with a revolver and fully stocked belt. "I used it during the war, and I converted it to a cartridge a few years ago. Much easier to reload."

"I can't take this," I managed to blurt out.

He only smiled. "You see me again, you give it back. In the meantime, I have a feeling it'll do a whole lot more good in your hand than it will in my trunk."

If Father really was…if he'd been killed, then perhaps the Voice could serve a purpose after all. I didn't let myself think too far down that path.

I took the revolver, though I couldn't force myself to buckle the belt on just yet.

No matter what I'd been told about the Benders, I had to check in one last time with Kate. To look her in the eye and ask her about what we'd experienced by that creek. To ask John about the bandits and test his story.

Something didn't line up with that family, and I had to know what it was before I moved on.

And so Surrey and I headed off to the Bender cabin, one more time.

CHAPTER TWELVE

"Every horse-stealing operation, highway robbery, assassination, or burglary now occurring in Kansas is laid to the Benders."

—The Galveston Daily News
(Texas), June 18, 1873

———————

MY JOURNEY WENT WITHOUT INCIDENT until the house itself came into view. It was a scorcher of a day, right in line with the sort of weather we'd been having ever since I'd woken up from the storm.

Whatever the people of this area had been doing, God had first sent a fierce gale and then followed it up with its opposite. It felt like I was riding through a desert more than a prairie.

The traveling gave me time to worry. What would it be like to confront the Benders again? What would Kate say to me? What would I say to her? Arguing was dangerous for someone like me. Sometimes it felt like the only thing standing between me and a bloodbath was my ability to keep my temper in check. It might have died down the past few days, but the Voice was always there, whispering in my ear about how easy it would be to end any argument quickly.

Perhaps a hundred yards from the house, a gust of wind carried a strange sound: a high-pitched whine mixed with a pant that made me stop Surrey. My stomach *twisted* when I heard that noise. Had it been human? I tried to tell myself it had been the squeak of a rusty axle or door hinge, but it had sounded desperate. Pained.

Sweat poured down my face, and I got out my handkerchief again to wipe most of it off. Ahead of me, the Bender homestead was quiet, the air shimmering with the heat of the sun. No one walking around the house, no John out on the front porch reading the Bible. The noise had vanished after a few seconds. Could it have just been the wind whistling through the field?

You should get your rifle. You might need to protect yourself.

For once, was the Voice being reasonable? Or was it just trying to lull me into listening to it?

I grabbed the rifle from my saddle scabbard and checked the chamber, making sure the rounds were still ready. I hadn't been taking care of it the way Father had taught me, and I worried it might not be as accurate as it should be. As long as I wasn't shooting at a distance, it should be enough. There might not be anything ahead, but I couldn't assume that. It wasn't the revolver; I wasn't completely abandoning my principles. I tucked the stock against my side, then nudged Surrey back to a slow walk, straining my ears for any repeat of that sound.

Fifty yards, and the noise returned. Quick but deep breathing, mixed with a wheeze I'd only heard from my grandfather on his deathbed. I raised the rifle and cocked it, keeping my finger off the trigger. Something was definitely not right at the Benders'. Had they been attacked by bandits after all?

Just because I hadn't liked the look of the family didn't mean I wished them any harm. Leroy's words about them were still fresh in my mind, and the thought of hurting Kate made me want to start searching rooms for weapons again.

I was close enough now to pinpoint the source of the noise: coming from the pigsty in front of the barn. The large sow was on her side, her body heaving in distress as she struggled to breathe. "Is anyone there?"

The wind snatched at my voice and tore it away. I cleared my throat and spoke louder. "I'm armed, but I don't want to hurt anyone. If you're here, come out and talk."

The door to the house stayed closed, the windows shuttered. Only then did I make the connection: Who in their right mind would keep the windows closed on a day like this? What exactly did I think the danger could be? Outlaws who decided to lock themselves into a stuffy house, hoping on the off chance someone would be fool enough to ride by?

I chided myself for being so yellow, then uncocked my rifle and dismounted, walking over to the sty to get a better look.

The sow was suffering from the heat. Her trough was empty, the mud cracked. She lay there staring at nothing, her mouth opening and closing convulsively as she gasped and wheezed. That alone was enough to tell me something had gone horribly wrong. Even if you didn't care for animals, a pig like this was an investment. No one would leave her in this condition.

I put the rifle back in its scabbard and hurried over to the water pump by the barn. Halfway there, an overpowering stench washed over me. A mixture of ammonia, feces, and rotting meat, all of it so strong, I gagged as soon as it reached me. We'd had enough decaying rats in our walls for me to know what death smelled like, but this was ten times worse.

Covering my mouth with my handkerchief, I sluiced some water into a bucket and hurried it over to the sow, pouring some of it over her and setting the half-full bucket next to her on the ground. She gasped and struggled to her feet, then lost herself in the water. She'd need food as well, but first I had to find out what had happened in the barn.

I tried to steel myself for whatever it was I might discover. The Bender family, perhaps, victims of an outlaw raid? Whatever it was, this had to be connected with the disappearances. Didn't it?

The barn had been barred shut, and I paused with my hand on

the handle. Inside, it sounded like a beehive had been let loose. I took a breath, held it, and opened the door.

A swarm of flies burst out, weaving and churning through the air like a specter. I squinted my eyes shut and felt the rush of wind as all those insects swirled around me, ramming against my skin, getting caught in my hair. I wanted to run, but I stayed still, waiting for the flood to die down. The smell had gotten five times worse with the door open. I turned to the side and retched onto the ground before wiping my face and swatting at the flies that still buzzed around me.

In the middle of the barn, an animal of some sort lay sprawled across the floor, the flies coating its skin making it look like its hide was writhing, black and rotten. Empty eye sockets stared at me, and a mealworm wriggled out from the one on the left before plopping on the ground. It took me a moment to realize this *thing* was a calf; it had been tied up and abandoned to starve to death or die of thirst. I turned and fled from the building, wanting to get as far from the sight of those blank eyes as I could.

Away from the barn, I sat on the ground and gasped for breath, trying to calm myself. If I couldn't even face the horrors of a dead calf, how would I be able to stand up to whatever might be waiting for me in that cabin? But if that's what had been waiting in the barn, what could have happened to the Benders?

My mind scrambled, trying to make sense of everything and hoping to come to any other conclusion but the obvious: someone had come and killed the Benders. No decent human being could simply abandon animals in this state, knowing they would die such an awful death. I might not have liked all the Benders, but surely Kate would have spoken up for the beasts. She seemed like a woman who got her way.

Which meant that whatever had befallen the other people who'd been disappearing had also happened to this entire family.

I stood and brushed myself off, trying to regain some composure. Whoever had done whatever was done here, they were long gone by now. The sooner I was in the cabin, the sooner I could move from guesswork to making real conclusions. There might be clues about who had done this.

Four corpses weren't going to spring up and surround me, even if the image of that rotting calf still burned in my mind. Its lips peeled back, its...

No. Forget the calf and move to the cabin.

Though I'd told myself it would be safe, I held my rifle out in front of me in both hands, as if it were some sort of magical staff that would protect me.

I strode to the cabin, climbed the front steps, and kicked in the door. An envelope drifted to the ground, knocked out from the doorframe where it had been pinned. The shoddily made lock burst with the force, and I rushed into the room, my rifle leveled and ready to fire.

But no one was there to greet me, alive or dead. No Benders.

No bodies. No smell—or at least nothing like the smell that had been in the barn, which still seemed to be stuck in my nose. Instead, the empty room looked as if the Benders had just gotten up from a meal and walked off, never to return. Four dishes of stew, rotting and covered in flies, sat on the table. Light drifted in through the door and cracks in the shutters, dust motes swirling as I walked farther in to check behind the curtain partition. No one there either, though the smell got worse for a moment, perhaps as the bad stew made itself known.

None of this added up. There were plenty of valuable items still in the house. A clock, books, silverware, and more. Even the family Bible remained, though that would have been dearer to the Benders than anyone else. The family wouldn't have left everything, but bandits wouldn't have either.

I stepped back outside, wanting to escape the stuffy atmosphere and go where I could think.

Why was so much still here?

Except, as I considered it, not everything was.

The horses were gone, as was the wagon. There hadn't been much in the way of clothes in the cabin either. Bandits wouldn't have left all these items, nor would any decent family worried about its possessions.

But a family that was scared? That was running away from something or someone?

One of two possibilities unfolded in my mind. In the first,

the Benders fled from someone bent on killing them, driving off into the night, leaving almost all their belongings behind. For a moment, I even considered the evil spirit Kate had channeled, before dismissing it. I wasn't going to complicate matters by bringing the occult into this.

The other option was that the Benders themselves had been the ones at the root of all the disappearances. The four of them might have decided they were in danger of getting caught, scrambling to gather what they could before hurrying out into the prairie. Kate might have engineered the entire séance to convince me to leave as soon as possible. That lined up with what I'd seen. People who were too frantic to think of simple things like untying a calf or letting the sow go free.

They needed to be found, either to be saved or to be brought to justice, but I had to know what I was getting myself into first. There had to be a way of knowing, some sort of evidence that would make this all make sense.

I headed back into the cabin, then opened the shutters to let as much light in as possible. If the Benders were the culprits, then they knew what had happened to my father.

I began making my way through the home's contents, moving dishes and cans and books and trash, sifting through it all for anything that might give me a clue. Nothing stood out from the rest. I checked underneath the cabinets and dresser, then pulled out each drawer to see if anything had been hidden or left behind by accident.

What was I looking for? A letter from them admitting to having killed someone? A body shoved under the floorboards?

You're a failure. A disgrace to the Bullock name.

There was nothing else of note in the main part of the cabin, so I headed back behind the curtain, where the family's living area had been. The smell there was musty and...*off.* Was the air from the barn being blown back here directly? It smelled like rotting meat, once again. I opened the shutters, hoping to air most of it out.

It was more cramped back here, the space taken up by another straw mattress and a woodstove. The family must have all huddled together on the same bed. It didn't take nearly as long to search. Three hammers had been shoved back beneath the stove: two with clawed backs and a third homemade sledgehammer with a short handle. There'd been stories of corpses appearing with their heads smashed and their throats slit. Were these what the Benders had used to attack their victims?

It wasn't a signed confession, but I was getting closer.

When I extended my search to the outside, I came across the envelope that had fallen to the ground when I'd barged in. The wind had taken it halfway to the pigpen. I picked it up and tore it open.

It contained only a slip of paper with a string of numbers on it.

0126092956281711

0101290802020410

7504121364031804

6403180501022304

07032026

I stared at it in confusion, turning it over as if there might have been an explanation on the back of the note. Nothing. It was almost as if someone had been practicing their numbers, one after the other in no order at all. It seemed like something John might do, just to waste time. Or a code of some sort? Who would have sent something like that to the Benders? I was sure it meant something, but how would I ever know?

Whatever this was, it wasn't an answer, so I shoved it into my back pocket. I needed something I could figure out right away.

I rummaged through the pigsty, then swallowed my disgust and checked the barn again. Through the swarm of flies, the dead calf seemed to laugh at my struggles, its mouth drawn back in a permanent smile that showed far too many teeth. And still I found nothing.

When Newton had asked me why I had a chance of succeeding where others had failed, I'd told him I was better with the details. What I hadn't said was that the Voice might make me able to understand the monsters who'd done this.

If I listened to it.

For years, I'd been shoving it away. Suppressing it. Convinced it would turn me into a murderer. But I'd take any chance at finding Father, so I went back to the front stoop, sat down, and turned things over to the Voice.

If I'd killed all these people, what would I have done next?

Escape. But not in a rush. No. Plan it out. Get away so you can kill again. Feel the hammer in your hand as it makes the first blow. The tug against the knife as you draw it across throats. The blood's warmth cascading over your hands. Take the body and—

And what? For all the people who'd disappeared, very few bodies had been found. To go this long without being detected, I'd need a place to hide the corpses.

I stood and entered the cabin, paying attention to the smells more than the sights now. I'd thought the place needed an airing, but the stench of rotting meat still lingered in the back room. I clomped on the floorboards, listening for any difference—a hollow echo that might indicate a basement or a muffled thump that could be from a hidden chamber.

Over by the Benders' straw pallet, my stomp caused something to jostle. Part of the floor rose, then fell again.

I threw the pallet to the side, digging through the straw to reach the wood beneath. I found hinges: a trapdoor. Tucked into the cracks on the opposite side of those hinges, I found a leather strap. I pulled it out and started to lift the door open, but then the strap caught my eye.

It was too narrow for something that was supposed to be a handle. Some fine tooling had been etched into its surface. When I tilted it to the light, a name appeared.

LONGCOR.

My knees buckled, and I dropped to the floor.

With that single word, everything snapped into focus. The Benders had *known*. When I'd come to the family, they'd known exactly what had happened to everyone. What they had done to them. And I'd looked them in the eye and believed them when they lied about it. What sort of a fool was I, to be duped that easily by a group of people who'd made me uncomfortable right from the beginning?

Instead of pressing them, I'd let Kate's high cheekbones and auburn hair convince me my instincts were wrong. And now they'd escaped, and with them, any real hope of finding Father or bringing them to justice. They'd had weeks to get away already. I never should have come out here in the first place. If Wyatt or Morgan or any one of my other brothers had come, they wouldn't have ridden off on a fool's errand. People took them seriously.

I was a joke.

And Father? Unless he'd somehow managed to get away, his corpse might be lying in the hidden room beneath me, waiting for me to find it.

You could smash their heads in with a pipe. Jab a rusty knife into their eyes, over and over. Shoot each one of the—

No. I clenched my jaw, opening and closing my hands into fists. There'd be time enough to decide what to do with the Benders if I ever found them, and the Voice might play a part in that. But for now, I still had work to do. Any number of people would have been better suited to catch the Benders, but I was the only one who'd come looking. And I might not have the best skill set, but I had the time, and I had the determination.

I stood, grabbed the leather handle, and lifted the trapdoor open.

Immediately the smell in the room grew worse than it had been in the barn, even: an overwhelming scent of decay that reminded me of how my brothers had described a battlefield a few days after the conflict. I stumbled back, then forced myself to peer down into the cellar, picturing a pile of rotting bodies stacked one on top of the other. For a moment, the thought crystallized even further: a woman, sightless and limp, crushed by a mound of other corpses.

It was pitch-black down there. Anything—or anyone—might have been waiting for me.

I rummaged through the cabin, searching for a lantern but only coming up with a pile of rags and an almost-empty bottle of whiskey. I stuffed the rags into the neck of the bottle, turned it upside down to get them good and soaked, and then lit the rags on fire. The flames immediately snapped at me, and I flinched back, letting the bottle fall into the cellar, where it shattered on rock.

Peering down into the depths, the guttering firelight revealed a bloodstained sandstone floor. Or at least I assumed it was blood. So much of the floor had been covered, you might have thought it was painted a rusty brown. The smell was better suited to a slaughterhouse, but if there had been bodies there, they'd been moved.

Or they'd been buried beneath the stone.

Was there a part of the cellar I couldn't see? A place behind a false wall, perhaps? Only one way to find out, though the thought of actually descending into that pit twisted my stomach. I tried to keep Father in mind. This was for him.

I set my rifle on the floor to free up my hands, then climbed into the cellar, my pulse pounding in my ears as I swung to the side to avoid the burning wreckage of the bottle. I slipped as I was going down, falling into a heap instead of pausing to give myself time to grab my rifle.

Not that I needed to worry. The cellar was as empty as it had first appeared. The dirt walls had fallen in here and there, coating some of the sandstone in caked-on earth. If someone had been buried beneath the stone, it had been a while before. I ran my hands over the walls, searching for anything I might be missing.

Nothing but earth.

Once again, my search had been useless. The only hope I had for making things right lay in finding the Benders. And when I found them, I'd—

Boot steps sounded above me in the cabin, entering the kitchen. I gasped and stomped at the fire as best I could. I clawed at the walls and took out handfuls of dirt, throwing them on top of the flames to finally get them to go out. If I could have, I would have lunged up and closed the trapdoor, but there was no way I'd be able to do that quietly.

And my rifle was still above me in the cabin.

The boots moved back and forth in the kitchen. Could it be one of the Benders or one of their accomplices? I pressed myself against the cellar walls.

The boots clomped into the back room, knocking dust down beneath the rafters above me.

I scrambled to think of something I could do to protect myself. Throw dirt up at their face, then jump and try to swipe at their legs to knock them down, or—

Above me, a man spoke. "Whoever's down there, you come up nice and slow unless you want a bullet right between the eyes."

Who was I fooling? "I'm unarmed," I called out.

"Come out. Now."

I caught hold of the edge of the trapdoor and lifted myself out, coming face-to-face with the barrel of a revolver as soon as my head cleared the cellar. The open window behind his head left his face in shadow, and I stayed frozen there until he uncocked the gun and holstered it.

"Warren?"

"Yes?"

"Sorry, I'm not thinking straight at the moment." He stepped forward and offered me a hand up. I accepted, and once I was standing, I recognized Leroy Dick and began to breathe easier. He'd been happy and easygoing at his home, but there wasn't a trace of warmth and cheeriness on his face now.

"Where are the Benders, and what on God's good earth is that smell?"

"I was trying to figure that out myself."

"I know I was the one who assured you there was no way the family could be behind all this. I'm still not convinced they are, but that cellar you're standing in is doing an awfully good job of changing my mind."

I nodded, wishing I were outside or anywhere other than where I was. "I was just looking for any signs of where they might have headed, and I found this cellar. The smell's awful, but it's empty. Do you think they…buried bodies beneath the slab?"

Leroy took a lantern and held it down into the cellar. It wasn't large—perhaps ten feet square and about seven feet deep. "Only one way to really know, isn't there? But if we're going to dig this place up, we're going to need help."

CHAPTER THIRTEEN

"One of the blackest of all black crimes ever spread upon the records of man's worse than inhumanity to man is known to the reading public of this country, and perhaps other countries, as the Bender tragedy of Kansas."

—The Memphis Reveille
(Memphis, Missouri), December 7, 1876

―――――――

A FEW HOURS LATER, IT FELT like the entire county had shown up to search the Benders' homestead. Leroy had gone to some of the neighbors and talked to the men, and from there word had spread. Something was happening at the Bender farm, and everyone wanted a chance to see what it was.

I didn't recognize any of them, of course, and none of them recognized me, which earned me more than a few side-glances and some outright stares. I tried to handle it all without getting flustered, though I blushed on more than one occasion, and the

Voice whispered constantly into my brain—vision after vision of bloody attacks, each grislier than the last.

I didn't bother trying to dismiss the thoughts. The old Warren had failed. A new approach would be necessary.

Someone brought a team of horses and a plow. Another person brought the fixings for coffee, apparently planning on a long night. There were at least fifty men there—far too many to help with excavating the cellar. Leroy took charge, sending some of the men to search the nearby rivers and tasking still others with digging up the floor of the barn as well, reasoning the rotting calf might have been left there to keep people from looking too carefully at the spot.

I stayed with the group that would focus on the cellar. I'd been down there, and I wanted to be the first to see if our suspicions were correct.

The only problem was that we didn't have enough space to work. The hole had to be made big enough to get the slab out, and to do that, we'd need to disassemble the entire cabin. With so many men, we began to get to work on that until someone cleared his throat.

"Wouldn't it be easier to just move the cabin out of the way?"

We all stopped, staring at the man—a thin, bony thirty-year-old with a patchy beard. Then we turned to the base of the cabin, where the logs sat right on the prairie with nothing holding them there. So, instead of taking apart the cabin, we lifted it a corner at a time and placed them on rough-hewn logs. Then it was just a matter of attaching the horses to the building and pulling. The entire cabin slid across the field, slowly revealing the pit of a cellar, which brought the smell out into the open. Several men who hadn't been inside yet cursed, but the rest of us just got shovels and began to dig.

I was down there with the rest of them, carving into the cellar walls to get it wide enough for the slab to be hauled out. Could corpses lie underneath me even now? I tried not to think about it, but everyone around me was muttering the same thing. I heard five different names mentioned: George Longcor and his baby, of course, but also Ben Brown, a Mr. McCrotty, Henry McKenzie, and Johnny Boyle. Others speculated about just how many strangers might have disappeared that no one knew about.

No one talked about Father.

To hear some of them speak, as soon as this slab was broken open and removed, a hundred bodies would come crawling out of the ground.

I kept digging, keeping my thoughts to myself, though my hands got so sweaty, it was hard to grip my shovel. This many people around me made me want to run for a quiet spot on the farm, and the thought of Father and what might actually be beneath me—and the prospects of having to touch it and dig through it—was enough to make me question my resolve.

But not stop.

At last we had the cellar open enough to move forward.

Someone brought a metal spike and sledgehammer, and in less than a minute, the stone was broken in three places. The stench of death grew even stronger. One of the men walked off to the side and threw up, and the rest of them grimaced and swore.

We hitched horses to the slab pieces and dragged them up a makeshift ramp we'd excavated. The sun was setting, casting long shadows across the land. The heat from earlier in the day was gone, replaced by a wind that made my sweat-soaked back prickle with each gust. Silence descended on the entire group as we stepped back from the hole and let the horses do their work.

Torches cast an unsteady light down into the pit, but it was enough to show not a single bone or shred of clothing. Just tamped dark earth that stank enough to make your eyes water.

Leroy held back some of the men who moved forward to start digging. He looked at me and said, "You're the one who started this, son. You should be the one to do it, if you want."

I pressed my lips together but stepped forward and jumped into the hole. The earth gave a moist thump as I landed, and I half expected to see blood welling up around my boots. Something about being down there felt *right*, in a way that sent chills down my back. The Voice thought this was lovely.

Find them. Make them pay. Draw it out slowly. Cut them apart, one piece at a time.

As soon as my shovel sliced into the dirt, a new wave of smell washed over me. It was as if I'd dug into a giant rotting steak instead of simple dirt. The crowd around the edge of the pit gasped and stepped back. I stood there for a moment, my handkerchief pressed against my mouth in a futile effort to lessen the stench.

In the end, I tied the cloth around my face and resumed digging. With each shovelful, I expected to finally see evidence of death beyond the smell—a severed hand or a crumbling skeleton. But no matter how much I dug, nothing came to light.

Eventually, Leroy called down to me to rest and let others take over. He'd come to the same conclusion I had, it seemed. The bodies weren't going to be found in that pit. Perhaps the smell came from blood that had congealed under the rock. Or maybe the place was just cursed, haunted by the spirits of the people who'd been murdered. Standing in the guttering torchlight, I thought anything seemed possible. In any case, I accepted the hand up and stepped off to the side to try and recover my thoughts.

I stared at the activity until my feet wouldn't let me stay there any longer. I'd made a good showing at being normal, but now I needed a few minutes by myself. I was horrified by the scene, but at the same time, I felt drawn to it, as if this were where I belonged. Taking one of the torches, I went for a walk around the property.

Seen from afar, the place looked like a mound of activity, as if an ant colony had discovered fire, working late into the night. One cluster of men worked on the cellar, and another was busy digging into the barn. A few smaller groups were focused on the sty or rummaging through the items from the cabin.

All the work had left me parched, so I walked to the table the women had set up next to the sty. Leroy's wife, Helen, was pouring drinks for anyone who came by, and some of the other women had a pot of soup simmering over a fire. If you ignored the reason we were all here, you might have been able to convince yourself this was a town festival of some sort.

"Have they found anything yet?" Helen asked, holding out a tin cup.

I took it gratefully and tossed it down, not even tasting whatever it was. My mouth felt so dry, it was a miracle I could swallow at all, though the liquid helped. "Nothing," I said, handing the cup back.

She refilled it. "I just can't believe the Benders of all people. That is, they were never the nicest folk on the prairie, but a *family*? It has to have been the parents. Shifty-eyed and squirrelly, the both of them."

"There might still be a different explanation," I said, not really believing it.

Helen snorted. "That's taking charity a little too far, if you ask me. They might as well have left a handwritten note admitting it. I never did trust them. Germans. Talking so you can't understand it. If they were here right now…"

Her eyes flicked to the men and back. There wasn't much doubt about what she meant with that ominous statement.

"If they were here, we'd see some justice," I said, punctuating the words.

She nodded once, her gaze steady.

I'd stayed with Helen for the past several days. She'd always been nothing but warm, kind, and funny. The perfect picture of a housewife, and she reminded me more than a little of my own mother. To have her already saying things like that made my insides squirm.

Was everyone just a thin veneer away from evil?

Wasn't it right to kill, if the person needed killing?

I shook my head clear. The Voice might be good at coming up with ways to get revenge, but I needed the other part of me right now. The analytical Warren. Turning my back to the whole scene, I walked over to the orchard for some quiet. I picked the spot for several reasons: first among them being the fact everyone else was ignoring it. But more than that, the orchard bothered me almost as much as anything else on the homestead so far.

Orchards were things that took years to develop. A person who planted an orchard did it knowing it would be five to ten years before it really began to pay off. To me, they were almost like a promise with the land. Why would a family like the Benders— ready to abandon everything at a moment's notice—choose to start their life here by planting an orchard?

Not that it was thriving, of course. The trees were small stubby things, with trunks little wider than my wrist. Each had a scattering of branches poking out toward the night sky, but they all could have used a fair bit more water to flourish, not to mention a good pruning.

Again: Why plant an orchard and then refuse to take care of it? Some of the others in the group tonight would no doubt have called me simpleminded to be worrying about such a thing right then, but to me, it was a detail that stuck out and demanded an explanation.

I walked up and down the area, holding my torch close to some of the trees as I passed. Most of them were apple, though I was fairly sure a few were pear. Despite how scraggly the trees appeared, one of the Benders must have been trying to take care of them. The field had been plowed recently, the earth turned to ensure nothing else began to take root in the area other than the trees, letting the fruit get all the nourishment it could out of the ground.

But as I walked, some areas felt unnaturally low; the ground had sunk. I'd go to take a step, and the step was deeper than it should have been, as if I'd missed a stair tread, though not as extreme.

Having worked on my fair share of plowed fields, I knew that wasn't normal.

Intrigued, I stepped to the side of the field and held my torch lower, casting the light across the field instead of on top of it. It wasn't precise, but several pools of shadow appeared: long oval-shaped depressions in the ground. At least four or five.

I had my suspicions now, but I didn't want to bring other people in on it until I was more certain. Instead, I headed over to my saddlebags and took the ramrod out of my rifle. Leroy noticed me and followed me over to the orchard.

"Did you find something?" he asked in a hushed voice, his eyes intent.

"Not sure. Do those look like graves to you?" I pointed to the different pools of shadow I'd seen.

Leroy squinted, then rubbed his eyes. "Your eyes work better than mine do. All I see is dark."

I walked over to the first depression I'd noticed and stuck the ramrod into the earth, wiggling it back and forth as I pressed down, navigating it through the soil, deeper and deeper. As my hand got closer to the earth, I questioned myself. These could all just be natural low spots or places where the Benders hadn't—

The end of the rod caught on something beneath the surface. I jiggled it for a moment, thinking it might be a small rock, but it wouldn't give. So I pushed harder. The vibrations in the rod didn't feel like I'd expect them to feel if they'd hit a stone. It was more like pushing against a piece of…steak.

With a final push, whatever was under the ground gave way. The rod shot forward about six inches, then stopped again.

I stared up at Leroy, who was watching all this with his mouth open. "Is it?" he asked.

There was only one way to find out. I removed the rod from the ground. As soon as it was free, a stench came with it: rotting eggs, feces, and molding meat. The torchlight revealed the rod had brought out something caught on the end: a clump of something gray that didn't seem like anything until I noticed the hair follicles on it.

After seeing so many horrors today, I would have thought my stomach would be immune to anything else. I would have been wrong. When Leroy and I recovered—standing twenty feet away from the orchard now—we exchanged glances for a moment, both of us taking deep breaths of fresh night air. Even here, I still thought I could catch wind of the scent, as if it were something physical that had crawled up my nose and settled in for a long stay.

"You wanted to find them, son," Leroy said. "Looks like you have."

CHAPTER FOURTEEN

*"They kept a sort of wayside inn, and whoever entered
to seek shelter in their quarters never saw the light of
day again."*

—Calhoun Times (Georgia),
August 8, 1880

———————

I F THINGS HAD FELT LIKE a whirlwind before, they only got
more intense now. Leroy called out to the different groups,
and everyone dropped whatever task they'd been working on to
descend on the orchard with a slew of shovels. In a quarter of an
hour, six different depressions had been identified, and a group of
men dug into the soil over each. Less than five minutes after that,
one of the men yelled out and stumbled backward from a hole over
to the side of the orchard. The rest of the team there moved away
from it as well.

I could smell the reek from ten yards away. There were plenty
who elbowed their way forward to get a better look, but even the

thought of that many bodies pressed in around me was enough to make me clench and unclench my fists. Instead, I listened to the cries of disgust and anger, along with a swarm of mutters.

One of them—an older man with a slightly stooped back and a thick beard—let out a stream of what I thought was German, a constant spout of words that just kept going under his breath. He was talking to himself, perhaps cursing the Benders, but it drew curious looks and one or two glares.

Others closer to me drowned him out as he stalked off.

"—even tell it's human, from the state it's in."

"—worse than Appomattox was, when I—"

"If I ever get my hands on them Benders, they won't—"

I let the words wash over me. My knees buckled, and I plopped down in the middle of the dirt without another word.

Until now, I'd thought I was prepared for whatever my investigations might uncover. I'd read more than a few books about detective work, and I'd seen Father, Wyatt, and the others work on different cases over the years as well. But until I smelled that grave, it had all been academic. In that one breath, I'd recognized how real it all was. That smell had once been a human, living, crying, and hoping, just like me. If it hadn't been for the Benders, they would have gone on doing that. Instead, they'd been tossed into a grave and forgotten.

That was just a single corpse. How many others could there be? And what if Father was among them?

My hands trembled when I held them in front of me, and it felt like someone had tilted the ground, making everything I did feel unbalanced.

The evening grew later, and the body count kept getting higher. With each one, I steeled myself, ready to look down into the grave and recognize something. The clothing. The face. Could I even handle facing that, with the rest of my family miles away?

But each time, it was another stranger. In a way, that made it worse because it raised my hopes. Father was one of the most capable men I knew. He'd gone after outlaws, survived gunfights, and fought in wars. Would it be too much to hope he'd have been able to see the Benders for what they were, even if I hadn't?

At some point, I got over my reluctance and threw myself back into the work, hoping I might forget some of the horrors by focusing on the jobs that needed doing. I dug into the earth. I walked up and down the field in a row of men, our torches high as we searched for other depressions. I held a rope as one man descended into the farm's well.

They found a victim there too.

With each discovery, the mood of the crowd grew darker. The Benders had been consistent with the way they'd killed. Each corpse had its head smashed in and its throat cut. The doctor from town was in the throng, and he inspected each body as it came to light.

"I expect it was a hammer blow of some sort to the back of the head," he said. "Club them when their backs were turned, then slit their throats while they were stunned. You said there was a trapdoor in their house, didn't you? If they'd struck them as they slept or perhaps as they ate, it wouldn't have been much effort to open the door, cut their neck, and then toss them in to bleed out. That would explain the stains and stench in the pit as well."

My knuckles whitened on my shovel's handle. To do that a single time was already abhorrent. To do it again and again, to strangers? The Benders weren't people. They were monsters. Did *things* like that even deserve the honor of a courtroom? This was one time when I might not have protested much if the mob had caught the Benders and taken them to the nearest tree.

Was that the Voice, or was that me? It was harder to tell right now, with my thoughts turning more violent and my desire to keep them in check dwindling. These bodies were what would happen if I ever gave in to the Voice, but didn't justice demand something similar be done to the murderers, in return?

That sentiment was echoed all around me, and rightfully so. These weren't faceless victims to many of the people there tonight. They were cousins. Friends. Neighbors who had disappeared.

Please, not Father.

By this point, someone had found a bottle of cheap perfume and passed it around. If you put enough on a handkerchief and tied it around your face, you had a fair shot of convincing your nose the stench was only half as bad.

We'd found at least five bodies so far. With one grave, it was hard to tell because there were too many arms and legs to be only one person. Most of the corpses were still unidentified, though not for lack of trying. In one case, the body had decayed so much that the head came right off when they tried to lift it out of the pit. Leroy had recognized his cousin Hank by the clothes and color of hair.

When the sixth came to light, it caused another flurry of whispers, another press of bodies as everyone crowded round, trying to see who it might be or if there were any other clues. I was at the front of the crowd, with a clear view of everything.

They'd found the torso first, and they dug carefully toward the head, dusting away the dirt to try and get what details they could from the rotting corpse. It wasn't a pretty sight, but it was one we'd grown more used to with repetition. Brown hair. What might have been a strong jawline. A workman's clothes. Really, it was much the same as all the other bodies we'd found. They'd tried to lift one of the earlier victims out of the grave without totally digging it out first.

It had broken in half as they pulled. They hadn't tried that again.

So this time, they unearthed the whole body, working their way down to the man's knees and then his feet. There was a small blanket or bundle of clothes bunched up by his thighs, as if it had been tossed there before he'd been buried. The German man who'd been swearing before reached down to move it out of the way, but when he tugged on the light-yellow fabric, it revealed a tiny hand encased in a mitten.

Not a bundle of clothes then. A baby.

The man stumbled back, falling to the ground, giving everyone a clear view of George Longcor's eighteen-month-old baby, dead.

The sight was met with absolute silence. The crackling from the torches and the whicker of horses seemed to have become unbearably loud. Crickets chirped all around us, and it felt wrong. As if something like this—an awful crime brought to light—ought to have more of an impact on the world around it.

I stared at the body of the man I'd met multiple times over the years. The same man who'd bought me a piece of licorice every time he visited. You'd be hard pressed to tell it was him now. His flesh had shriveled and decayed, his head lolling to the side, his empty eye sockets staring into nothing,

Someone whispered something to his neighbor, and the spell was broken. The news spread like a lightning bolt through the crowd, a sea of gasps that spread out from the grave in a matter of seconds.

The doctor hurried into the grave, swatting away the hands of others who tried to help. He lifted the baby out of the dirt and laid her reverently on the ground beside the opening, brushing her face clear. I had to turn away after catching a glimpse of her pale features.

"She wasn't killed like the others," the doctor said at last.

"We can see that," Leroy said, the anger in his voice clear. "What did kill her? What sort of monster would—"

The doctor cleared his throat and cut back in. "Judging from the lack of wounds or broken bones, I'd say she was put in there… still breathing."

You might have thought that pronouncement would make everyone quiet down even more, if such a thing were possible. Instead, it spawned a low chorus of murmurs.

I pictured the baby struggling and crying at her dead father's feet, Pa Bender standing above the pair, glaring down as he tossed in the first shovelful of dirt, John pitching in to help. The way the poor thing's voice would muffle and then—

I had a hard time swallowing. A pit had lodged in my throat. I gripped the shovel in my hand and wanted more than anything to find someone I could hit. Some way to get back at such a terrible action. It would have been more humane to leave the baby out for the coyotes or to simply—

My mind didn't let me finish the thought. I was stuck in a loop, thinking in circles as I tried to make sense of it all and couldn't. For some evil, you didn't wait for the courts or the constable. Some things had to be stopped as soon as possible.

If I'd had the Benders in front of me right then, I would have gotten my rifle and pulled the trigger and never had a heartbeat of guilt or regret. For once, the Voice and I were in complete agreement.

What had started as whispers and low curses had turned into shouts of rage. A man twenty feet to my left was crouched on the ground, sobbing. Several women screamed in fright. One of them took an axe and stomped over to the orchard, laying into one of the apple trees as if it bore some of the guilt.

It shouldn't have been possible that something like this could come to light, and all we could do was feel bad about it. It didn't help that I felt partly to blame. I'd stayed with this family for a night. I felt like a fool, but that had to be something the townsfolk felt far more sharply.

And then one last corpse was unearthed.

By then, another body barely registered a change in the people's mood. Some went and stared. Others stayed back, talking in small groups, their rage bubbling higher and higher.

I didn't want to go look. I'd made it this far without discovering Father. Why did that have to change now?

As soon as I edged up to the grave, I didn't need to see the face to know who it was.

I recognized Father's coat. Good thick leather. On the lower right corner of the front was the stain from the time I'd spilled grape juice on it when I was five. When I was eight, I used to wear the coat at night, pretending I was him.

My eyes were drawn to his face like a magnet. I didn't want to see it. I knew it would be better if I didn't, but I looked anyway. I had one quick glimpse of his full beard masking rotten, sunken cheeks, the skin mottled gray and purple, the eyes—

I collapsed on the ground, sobs finally breaking out of me in one burst after another. I grabbed on to the grass and clenched it between my fists, as if somehow that might ground me. Scene after scene flashed through my head. Planting in the fields with him. Building a stone wall. Fishing. Time on the trail. Hugging him after he came home from a long trip.

All of it, gone, with no hope of it coming back. For a spell, I could think of nothing else.

But then:

They did this to you. They deserve to pay. Break their skulls. Slit their necks. Watch the blood flow down and pool at their feet.

The Voice threw picture after picture at me. Things I could do to the Benders. And I didn't resist them at all. I wanted those feelings. Wanted that rage. Around me, more people had turned to destruction. The Bender house was being practically ripped apart as items were thrown out of the doors and windows. I hurried to join them, desperate to find something—anything—I could do to somehow feel better. I wasn't thinking about evidence or investigations. I wanted revenge.

And then someone was saying something about the Benders having a German neighbor, and wasn't he always friendly to them and how could there be two German families nearby without the one knowing the other? And that German wasn't just a house over—he was right in the crowd and had been down with the graves and the bodies, like the Benders had shown up to laugh at everyone behind their hands while the town was in a frenzy about the killings.

It didn't take longer than ten seconds for that thought to go from a whisper to a roar to the German in question being grabbed by ten pairs of hands and propelled through the crowd and over toward the table where the women had been serving food.

We weren't a hundred individuals anymore. We had somehow come together to act as one very loud, and very angry, person.

"How long did you know the Benders were murdering these people?" we asked in a sea of voices.

The German—it didn't matter what his name was or where he'd come from or why he'd been here—stuttered out something that might have been an answer but certainly wasn't anything approaching what we wanted to hear. We shoved him back and forth around the circle, his face white and blood trailing down the corner of his mouth.

"Why didn't you tell us earlier?"

And once more he was too slow to answer, and this time he was punched once and then a second time. With the second blow, he fell to the ground, and I lost sight of him for a moment as we pressed forward. He might have been trampled for all I cared. He might not have been Pa Bender, but he was close enough for now. Near enough to take a little of the bitter taste out of my mouth.

We pulled him back to his feet and herded him toward the cabin. He had to be shown. Had to face what he'd let happen. Standing by and doing nothing was just as bad as holding the knife—or near enough.

Someone brought forward a rope, and it was passed from hand

to hand toward the front of us, and as the rough feel of the hemp passed through my hands, for a moment a different image came to me. A tree and a crowd and the silence that followed as the body kicked for air. The shame I'd felt for being unable to stop the lynching.

Father had been there too.

And that thought was enough to resonate inside me to the point that I could think clearly again. Because I knew how disappointed Father would be with me if I did this. Went along with a lynching, no matter how angry I felt.

Justice and the Bullocks were supposed to be one and the same.

"Wait!" I called out, blinking and holding out my arms as if I might somehow push back the tide that was surging all around me. "We can't do this!"

My voice was lost in the chaos. Now that I was no longer in tune with the mob, I could barely move, with elbows and arms digging into me on all sides. Perhaps if I managed to push my way to the side, I might be able to break free and run around the group to the cabin, where I could yell through a window or—

When I tried my half-formed plan, the crowd pushed back, lifting my feet clear off the ground. For a few terrifying moments, I feared I'd be thrown to the ground and crushed beneath the sea of angry people. My feet touched down again, and instead of trying to move against the mob, I moved with it, shoving and elbowing along with them. The memory of the lynching weeks before must have given my arms more strength, for I managed to force my way up to the front and even through the front door.

Just in time to see the noose jammed over the German's head and the rope pulled taut as it lifted him into the air.

The mob roared in satisfaction but kept shouting questions from all sides.

"Where did they go?"

"Why did they do it?"

"How much money did they pay you?"

He couldn't answer, of course. They hadn't tied his hands, so he clutched at the rope and pulled, trying to get room to breathe. The mob had given the man a small circle of space. His legs kicked, occasionally finding purchase on a shoulder or a stomach or a head. His chest expanded long enough to tell me he was at least being somewhat successful.

I tried to push again, but the people here were the biggest and the strongest. The first attempt landed me on the floor, and the second time I tried, a man put his fist around my neck and hollered something about waiting my turn.

"Stop!" I called out again when I was able to. My voice was hoarse and weak. "We don't know he did anything. Stop!"

This time, a few people noticed me, one long enough to punch me squarely in the face. My nose erupted with blood and pain, and my vision went dark for three seconds. I shook my head clear.

Somehow, the rope had loosened enough to let the German fall back to the cabin's floor. He lay there gasping, his face still flushed with blood.

"We can't do this!" I called out again.

But they could. And they did. The German went up into the air a second time, swinging from the main beam of the cabin, back and forth as he came close enough for some to strike at him with axe handles or fists. It went on for what felt like forever, his eyes bulging and his face so dark, it was purple.

Again, someone let him drop to the ground. Now he lay there, struggling more feebly, unable to answer any of the shouted questions.

Until he was lifted a third time. He had no more struggle left in him. His legs barely moved. He tried to hold on to the rope, but his shoulders slumped not five seconds after going into the air. The mob kept him there for another eternity, and then they let the body fall to the floor and rushed out of the house, still yelling for all they were worth.

I sat on the floor, letting them surge around me. When I'd gone out with my father, I'd finished the scene full of righteous fury, angry and disgusted that humans could resort to something like this.

Now I was only disappointed, crushed that all my efforts to ignore the Voice had been swept away like a twig in a torrent. I knew how close I'd come to cheering along with the rest of them. To feeling like the death was justified. I'd wanted the man—a total stranger I knew nothing about—killed. I'd lunged for him myself.

Yes, I'd realized what I'd almost done, but by then it was too late to stop it. And hadn't I been the one to start this search in the first place? Hadn't my dogged persistence led to the discovery of the bodies and everything that had followed?

The old part of me wanted to throw away my rifle, go back home, and start checking for weapons again. Those hammers in the cabin—were they still there? I wasn't safe around them.

But that old part had been shoved to the side. Had the Voice taken over? I found myself not really caring. I didn't want just anyone dead.

But the Benders? They needed killing.

Needed it more than the poor dead German on the floor in front of me.

I should have—could have—done more to save him, but I was a failure even at that. Why did I think things would be any different if I were to chase after the Benders? This wasn't a world that cared about things like that, people dying. Did the German have a wife? A son? Did it matter?

I hated myself for failing Father. For being so reluctant to come after him. For even debating going in the first place. But no matter how much I wanted the Benders to suffer for what they'd done, I also knew I'd never be able to make them pay.

What had I done right since I'd left home? Anything? The whole journey had been cursed from the beginning, with me blundering from one mistake into the next. Sure, I'd helped find the victims, but finding these bodies did nothing for the dead, and it had only cost another man his life.

I'd never been particularly religious, but this was close enough to a sign from the heavens that God—if He existed—wanted me to go home and give up.

I was a lost cause.

And then the German gasped for breath, his back spasming and his eyes opening.

I didn't believe it at first, but then I found strength to hurry over and crouch next to him, taking the rope from his neck and fumbling for a cloth to wipe his face and a cup that I might use to get him some water.

As I did so, my mind scrambled to process what I'd just seen. If I'd thought that dead body was a sign to go home, what was this? I'd been in that room for at least a few minutes. The German hadn't breathed the whole time.

And now he was sitting up and holding his head?

What sort of a sign was that?

I peeked my head out the door and looked around. The mob had broken up, its anger spent as they scattered to their homes. The night was dark again. They must have hurried to vanish so quickly. Still, I ushered the German to the side of the room when I brought back the water. "You'll be better off hiding for the next few days if you can," I murmured to him.

He drank the water and stayed quiet, staring at nothing.

My mind kept churning. This same mob was going to try to follow the Benders. Leroy would do his best to lead them, but they were past thinking, and I couldn't rely on them to be anywhere near successful. The Benders had at least a few weeks' head start. They wouldn't be found through numbers. It would take someone to follow their trail with logic and patience.

Someone like me.

If the German could die and come back to life, then even a failure like me could turn things around.

Yes, I'd failed Father, but that didn't mean I had to let him go unavenged.

CHAPTER FIFTEEN

"It is considered certain that a little girl was thrown alive into the grave with her father, as no marks of violence was found on her body."

—Daily Eastern Argus
(Portland, Maine), May 13, 1873

B ACK WHEN I'D STARTED THIS journey, I would have thought the best course of action was just that: action. If I wanted to catch the Benders, I'd run out and jump on Surrey and race off to try to catch up. But if the past few weeks had taught me anything, it was that simply heading out to do *something* might feel good, but it was often the exact wrong thing to do.

The Benders had a week head start on all of us. That wasn't the sort of distance you clawed back through a fast gallop. If I wanted to have a chance at catching them, I was going to have to do at least as much thinking as I did chasing.

I gave myself fifteen minutes after the German had run off.

Time to sit and try to calm my mind so I could think clearly, though I found myself chewing on the inside of my lip. Father was dead. Nothing I did now would change it, but if I kept my head level, I'd be that much likelier to catch his killers.

And then I began to pick apart the problem.

If I were going to be chasing after the Benders, I'd be one of many. With the sort of crimes they'd committed, there would likely be a bounty on their heads soon, but even if there weren't, news would spread about the killings, and there'd be no shortage of people trying to track them down for revenge. Father wasn't the only one they'd killed, after all. If I wanted to find them first, I had to be smarter than the rest of them.

I stayed up late into the night, my brain churning through everything I'd seen during the day, trying to make sense of which details I should pay attention to and which I could safely ignore.

All the victims (other than George's baby girl) had been men. With how attractive Kate was, that didn't seem hard to understand. She was the bait, but what were they after? The killings seemed too methodical to be something done just out of bloodthirst. They were all strangers to the family, so that ruled out grudges or personal malice. As near as I could tell, the only remaining reason would have been money. They could have stolen whatever the men had on them, as well as their horses, wagons, and other belongings.

Except there hadn't been any large treasure trove of stolen goods. The Benders hadn't been caught selling wagons or used rifles or horses. Then again, with Indian Territory just a short ride away, there would have been any number of outlaw colonies to visit where no one would think twice about buying boots with a blood-stain or two. Either the Benders had been sending one of their own off to cash in, or someone else had been coming to do it for them.

But finding out what they were doing with the money only helped if it got me one step closer to finding the Benders. If I were in their shoes, what would I have done?

Assuming they'd been spooked and left the house in a hurry—which the state of the cabin implied—they would have piled whatever they could in their wagon and made their escape. Where would I run to? Somewhere unfamiliar?

A family that killed so many people without being caught, and also managed to dispose of all the stolen property, was a family that worked with a plan. They would have thought something out ahead of time and then put that plan into action when they needed to.

It's what I would have done, and I was just as monstrous. I might not have liked the kinship I felt with them, but it was something I had to face and get what use I could from it.

That theory matched up with the fact their wagon and their horses had been gone when I got there. On the other hand, with a wagon like that and horses like those, they couldn't have been planning on riding very far or fast. With all the money they must have accumulated, surely they would have been ready to buy a train ticket, and there were only so many towns where the trains stopped.

The first step wasn't to search for the Benders then. It was to search for their wagon and horses. Either they'd abandoned them somewhere, or they'd sold them to someone. Whichever it was, that would be the signpost for where I should go next.

I congratulated myself on this bit of logic, right up until I realized how little benefit it really offered me. There was an entire world out there for the Benders to hide in. Even if I were to find their wagon, and even if someone there were to remember which way the Benders had gone, I'd still need to know where they'd gone next, and that wasn't the sort of information I could rely on random strangers to know.

No, it would be far better to have some sort of clue. The Bender farm would be crawling with people again in the morning, but for now, I had the place to myself. Then again, staring around at the condition of the farm didn't inspire much confidence that there would be anything left to search out. The house itself had literally moved places, and all their belongings were scattered in a pile outside, some of them hacked apart by the mob. Was there any chance someone had missed something in all that and that it was in a condition for me to actually find it and use it now?

That line of thinking was just my brain trying to talk me out of some hard work. Instead, I grabbed a lantern and began sifting.

The night was almost as muggy as the day had been, but a breeze blew in now and then from the west, and that was enough to keep things tolerable. Everyone had hurried off at once, leaving behind tables, shovels, pickaxes, plates, bags, and more scattered around the farm, many of them dropped wherever their owner had been when they'd all lost their minds. They'd be back in the morning in force, but for now, the area was dark. The mob had taken their torches with them, and my one lantern cast a weak light in a pool on the ground around me, painting everything in dark shadows that made even the most common broom look sinister.

I wasn't going to find anything in the piles of things the townsfolk had brought with them. Instead, I picked my way over to the mounded wreckage of the Benders' belongings. The straw mattresses had been ripped apart and scattered on the ground in handfuls. Chairs, cabinets, chests, and bags sat in the most random of spots, most of them on their sides or leaning drunkenly from missing legs.

Based on what had been in the home when I'd first arrived, it seemed a few neighbors had already helped themselves to some of the remaining valuables the Benders had left behind. There were no dishes to speak of anymore—none in one piece, at any rate—and most of the odds and ends were gone. The Bible had been left behind. I leafed through it and found some notes of the Bender family history. Thinking perhaps that might come in useful at some point, I found room for the book in one of my saddlebags.

Other than that, what exactly was I hoping to find? A map with a dotted line and an X at the end of it? A handwritten note saying, "Meet up in St. Louis"? Definitely not, but could there be something that showed where they'd been before? A keepsake from a different city? A letter from a loved one that might give me an idea of a place they would be more likely to hide? When I'd searched the cabin before, I'd been focused on finding what might have happened, not where they might have gone.

I sifted through the contents of a drawer that had spilled out across the plain. Some unmatched utensils, a whisk, a ball of twine, three half-burnt tallow candles, and some torn rags. If I were a genius detective, perhaps I'd take one look at the items and piece together the entire life story of the Benders, but right then it looked like nothing more than garbage.

Things didn't improve from there. Most of the time, I couldn't even tell if what I inspected came from the Benders or from someone in the horde of people who'd been everywhere today. I set aside each item that seemed like it might have some larger meaning, and by the end of two hours, I had ticket stubs to Saint Louis, Chicago, Philadelphia, and New York City, as well as seven different receipts for various foodstuffs, a map of New Orleans, a drawing of something that might've been a hat and might've been Maine, and several notes that had been so hurriedly scrawled that I wasn't sure what they said. My best guess was Bible verses, but I didn't know the Bible well enough to know for sure. Was there a book of Jonathan?

The energy I'd felt a few hours ago had completely drained away, and I struggled to keep my eyes open. I kept finding myself sitting down, supposedly sifting through papers but really just nodding off or staring into the darkness in the direction of my father's grave. Each time I chided myself, trying to remember that in a few short hours, the farm would be crawling with people again. I doubted any of them would be half as methodical as I was being now, and after they all descended on the place, odds were there would be nothing left worth finding.

Assuming there was anything left now.

I'd rest for just a few minutes, then attack the problem anew. Just lie down and close my eyes and give myself time to decompress.

The sounds of the evening filled the air. Crickets. Wind across the grass. I was sitting in the middle of the prairie, open to the elements. *Anyone could come along and find me. I should take the time to set up a proper camp, but that would involve effort.*

To my right, something rustled, a *shifting* sort of a noise. Earth falling on top of itself. An animal?

I opened my eyes and stared in that direction. Father's body was that way. Would someone think they could sneak back in the middle of the night and check if the bodies had any valuables left on them?

If Father were in my shoes, he'd go check. The victims deserved that much.

I hauled myself to my feet and stumbled over toward the orchard, my legs feeling like millstones. The lantern gave up against the night, casting a pool of light that barely made it a few feet in any direction. The trees loomed up, and I was in the middle of the graveyard.

One by one, I peered into the holes, trying to remember which one held Father, but my mind wouldn't focus. Someone had draped each of them with cloth of different patterns. White, striped, gingham. The thought of raising the sheets and staring down at those corpses was too much for me. I'd count the bodies instead. As long as I got to seven graves, I'd know it was enough.

At the fourth, I paused, trying to make sense of what I was seeing.

It was empty.

I glanced around, not sure what I was looking for. The grave robber I'd feared? A coyote that had crept in to drag off a body? My rifle was back with the rest of my belongings, and I still hadn't taken the Remington Leroy had given me out of the bag where I'd stashed it.

If a pack of coyotes attacked me now, I'd—

Something moved again, the sound of steps carrying across the plain. It wasn't far—maybe twenty feet—but it was big, and it was headed toward me.

"Go away!" I hollered, then whooped a few times, intent on scaring the coyote off.

The noise came closer.

The light from my lantern shied away from whatever it was,

and it stayed as no more than a dark shadow in the night as it came nearer. Ten feet. Five.

As if someone had lifted a curtain, it came into focus all at once: Father shambling toward me, his shoulders tilted at an awkward angle, his head lolled to the right, dangling by a strip of skin and muscle, his empty eye sockets staring into mine as he raised his hands and—

I screamed and sat up, waving around to ward off whoever might be there. After a few moments, I realized I wasn't standing by the grave at all. I was still sitting where I'd decided to take a rest.

It had been a nightmare.

Once I'd calmed down some, I forced myself to stand again and do another circuit of the wreckage of the Benders' furniture. Anything to keep busy instead of thinking of that grave again. I sifted through the items. Three broken chairs that were little more than splinters. The sink had been thrown to the ground so violently, the wood had cracked down the middle. I used my toe to poke through the straw from the bedding, not really expecting to find anything. I didn't.

The drawers from the hutch were both upside down, one on top of the other, their contents scattered across the area. Not that it mattered, unless the Benders were somehow conveying messages using whisks and—

My torchlight cast a shadow on one of the gaping holes in the hutch, where the drawers usually sat. The wood didn't quite line up the right way, and a corner of...*something* was peeking out from the seam of the wood. When I crouched next to it, I saw the wood there had cracked open, revealing the corner of a small slip of paper.

I searched around for a hammer or a chisel or stick—anything that would help me pry the wood farther apart. Finding nothing, I gripped both sides of the hutch and tried wrenching it open. It gave a little—enough for me to see there were more papers in that compartment.

My heart pounded with anticipation. I kicked at the hutch again and again until the wood completely splintered, and twenty or thirty small pages came fluttering into the open.

I spent a moment grabbing all of them, making sure none had gone flying away. When they were more or less in order, I held my torch up to be able to examine one of them.

They were covered in numbers, one after the other.

2451310629020307282512O7

0311230403112305570207291

050421

I sat on the ground, staring at the page in confusion. It was the same as the slip of paper in the envelope I'd found yesterday. Clearly they meant something, but what? A moment's glance confirmed the same sort of code had been used on all the other pages in the compartment.

So close to an actual clue, but so hard to make sense of it. What sort of code only used numbers?

My mind wasn't at its clearest, having gone through the trauma of the long day, and it being the middle of the night now, but there was no way I'd be able to sleep without at least trying to solve the puzzle.

Could it be letters of the alphabet? I took the first slip and tried to parse it. Two could be *B*, four would be *D*—no, that didn't work. What if it was twenty-four, which would mean *Y*, and then it would have to be five, because there were only twenty-six letters, which would make *E. YE.* One could be *A*, and three would be *C. YEAC?*

Not one and three then. Thirteen? *M*—and then it would be ten, because there could be no zero. *J—YEMJ?*

That didn't make any sense at all. Besides, without having an idea which letters went with which numbers, it would be impossible to get a clear answer quickly. Could it be done? Possibly, but it didn't feel right.

I rubbed my eyes and tried to focus on the numbers again, but by this point, my body didn't want to keep up with my will. I'd think more clearly with some sleep, and these pages weren't going anywhere. I checked once more to be sure I hadn't missed any, then tucked all of them into one of my saddlebags and set up camp a hundred yards away from the Bender farm.

Far away from Father's grave.

Even there, I still felt uncomfortable being so close to the grisly surprises the day had offered. When I lay down, I kept my rifle next to me. My days of resisting the Voice were over, at least until I'd caught the Benders.

I fell asleep within moments of lying down. My dreams did not improve.

CHAPTER SIXTEEN

"On Sunday, two special trains were run to the scene of the murders. One went from Independence and the other from Coffeyville. They brought down fully 1,000 sight-seers, who went about peering into the holes whence the bodies had been taken, and on their return, carried away with them pieces of the wretched shanty, which has resounded with the moans and groans of so many murdered men."

—The Daily Phoenix
(Columbia, South Carolina), May 24, 1873

WHEN MORNING CAME, A SWARM of activity buzzed around the Bender farm once again, with at least fifty men and women wandering through the site. A group of people stood over the pit that had been the Bender cellar, and still more milled around the orchard, standing over the graves. One man had actually gotten into one and was rooting around for something. The bodies had been moved and now lay on the prairie, each draped with the same cloth that had covered them before.

I eyed the people suspiciously as I walked Surrey over to the site and tied him to a hitch with several other horses. Some of the people were back from yesterday, but others seemed new. A group was systematically ripping pieces of the Bender cabin apart, putting them into a neat pile about ten feet away. Another man had set up a table in the pigsty. (The sow itself was now missing.) He had an assortment of breads and pastries, and a woman was lugging over more even as I watched.

Shove their face in the mud. Watch as they flail and spasm, trying to breathe.

No. I'd save that for the Benders.

Yes. The Benders.

The Voice purred at the thought, calming down in a way I'd never managed to soothe it before. I'd need its help, if I ever got the chance to face them.

If yesterday had felt like a group of people gathering to solve a problem, this morning already had the taste of a circus about it.

Leroy was there, though he had a crowd around him peppering him with questions.

A few weeks ago, I would have taken one look at all these strangers and turned right around. A part of me still wanted nothing more than to be rid of all of it, but I managed to ignore that part for the time being. Just because I hadn't found anything other than the slips of paper last night didn't mean there wasn't anything else to be found, and I wanted to be sure to know as much as I could before I left.

I wasn't planning on returning to the Bender farm ever again if I could avoid it.

The papers themselves still sat in my saddlebags, and I resolved to always keep Surrey in sight today. With this many people around, there was no telling what someone might try.

The place only got busier. Many people rode up individually, but some came by the wagonload. News had spread about the bodies, and rumors were already swirling around what might happen next. The people with the odds and ends of the Bender cabin were selling them to onlookers. Why someone would want a piece of that place was beyond me, but already some were buying the more significant pieces of the property. Parts of the front porch. Identifiable pieces from the window frames. The large main beam had been sawed into chunks, and the seller was telling everyone how the holes in the beam were from gunshots from the Benders' victims.

Those who didn't want to pay a premium just walked over to the cabin and grabbed almost anything. Pieces of furniture no bigger than my pinky were being pocketed left and right. Not enough on their own to amount to much, but with the number of people showing up, it was clear there would be nothing left of the place within a few days, if this kept up.

I stayed to listen to all the buzz around the Benders. Already some were saying with authority that they'd headed to Indian Territory. Still others swore they were on their way back to Germany with a chest full of stolen treasure. One particularly inventive man was certain there was a hidden entrance to a large cavern somewhere not far away, where the Benders waited even now to come out and resume their villainous ways.

And what those ways were, exactly, also grew with the telling. Ma and Pa were uniformly described as demons in human form. Hulking brutes who could barely speak a word and cared only for the taste of human flesh. John was either a mastermind or a simpleton, but the real discussions all centered around Kate. She had sold her soul to the devil in return for a beautiful body. She bathed in moonlight and had regular gatherings with a coven of witches. She was hideous and only ensorcelled her victims to make them believe her lovely.

If all I was hearing were those wild rumors and stories, I wouldn't have lasted long before I gave it all up. But I also came across more important tidbits. Members of the victims' families were showing up, searching for answers about how their loved ones had died and what might have become of them.

From them, I learned many of the bodies we'd found had been regulars in the area, known to many of the residents. Some had been simply passing through, but the Benders hadn't seemed to care who they killed. A number swore their relatives had been almost indigent, though others had been traveling with a fair amount of paper money. These stories convinced many that the Benders had to have been hiding their loot somewhere, concluding that because they'd left in such a hurry, there was a good chance they hadn't had time to retrieve it.

Hole digging became a favorite pastime of the day. If you asked anyone about it, they'd swear they'd seen something that made them suspicious there was another body to be found, but no more came to light, and neither did any mound of stolen goods.

The more I thought about it, the more convinced I became the Benders had someone they used to move their haul. Another contact who could take it away and sell it in a place where no one would connect it with the Benders.

It made sense that they would head to see this contact, if for no other reason than to retrieve their share of the proceeds.

With that in mind, I asked around to see if anyone had seen repeat visitors at the farm. Perhaps in the middle of the night? But the close neighbors had refused to come back, no doubt warded off by the memory of what had happened to the German last night. In any case, no one was willing to say one way or the other about strangers connected to the Benders. No one with any actual experience, that is. More than a few made outlandish claims. Anyone was willing to say anything, if they were offered a small incentive, of course.

A part of me said I should be taking this time to do something more constructive. Cleaning my guns, for example. They hadn't been oiled regularly or checked for rust, and now that I'd steeled myself to the fact I might want them working as well as possible, it would be smart to make sure they were in working order. But I didn't want to sit around preparing to kill them. I wanted to get closer to having the chance.

Why was I trying to do things I was bad at? Anyone could poke around here trying to ask questions, but no one here had any answers. If they did, they'd already be off tracking the Benders down. No, it would be smarter for me to do what I did best: Think. Plan.

I rode off to the side of the site, close enough to see if anything different began to happen, but far enough away to have some privacy. Sitting there astride Surrey, I took out the map I'd brought and began to reason things through.

The Benders hadn't had enough horses to rely on a mounted escape, and the horses they'd had weren't good enough to last long, anyway. No, if I were them, I'd have headed for a train station. Somewhere near enough to get there quickly, but not so close that people would recognize me easily. I'd have taken the wagon, which was missing, and a wagon as rough as theirs would be something that might stand out.

There was a station in Thayer, to the north, that might be a good candidate. Sweeping down to the east in an arc from there were Galesburgh, Ladore, Parsons, and Labette. To the west and south, the options dried up. We were still too close to the edge of civilization for the railroads to have gone much farther.

Now that I had some experience searching for people, I knew

just how much time it would take to work my way through five different towns, asking around, avoiding suspicion, and finding out enough to be certain the Benders hadn't passed through. I could easily lose another week or more.

There had to be another option. It felt like one was tickling the back of my mind, but I couldn't pin it down.

I rode Surrey around the site some more, hoping it would come to me.

As I crisscrossed the farm, listening more than I talked, images from yesterday kept flashing through my head. The rotting calf. The growing collection of bodies. The man hanging from the rafters. The baby's ashy face.

Father.

They'd been with me during the night as well, of course. I'd just kept my mind busy with thinking. At this point, most of that thinking was wearing off, and the Voice was all too ready to remind me of every grisly detail.

A group of men rode up together, talking excitedly about the journey they'd just returned from. Someone had sworn they'd seen the Benders in a cabin ten miles to the south, and so of course a vigilance committee was formed to investigate. They acted as if they'd done something brave, and they hinted that "the Benders won't be a problem anymore," but when I asked for details, they hardly had any. No one even mentioned John's grating laugh, and I had a hard time believing anyone could have been so lucky as to avoid hearing it, even if John's life had been threatened. My guess was he laughed more when he was nervous, not less.

No one spoke of seeing the Benders writing strange numbers on pieces of paper, and there were no rumors of hidden messages being passed between them and any conspirators. The stack of notes in my saddlebags felt like they were getting brighter and brighter, as if someone should start to notice them and wonder why I hadn't shown them to anyone else.

Should I? Was it a mistake for me to hold back something that could help everyone find these murderers? There was no guarantee I'd be able to solve the code after all, and more eyes would increase the odds of getting it done quickly.

But I knew why I wasn't telling anyone else. The Voice whispered the reason in my ear, laughing. I didn't *want* just anyone to find the Benders.

I didn't want anyone else getting in the way of me making them pay.

The memories from yesterday might have been grisly, but at times I had to struggle not to dwell on them. There was a part of me that was excited by that gore. Entranced by it. I hated it, but I'd have been lying if I'd said I wasn't a little…envious. Angry that someone could just give in to that sort of emotion and not feel so conflicted all the time.

That's what was different about me now. I wasn't going to be the same conflicted Warren who'd made such a mess of this search.

I'd always been attracted to violence. Now was the time to use that to my advantage.

The whole time I was walking around the Bender farm, I looked at the people and wondered what it would feel like to actually kill someone the way the Benders had. What sort of jolt did the hammer send up your hand, when you struck a head? What kind of pull did a neck make on a blade?

The thoughts nauseated me and made me want to run and hide in a room, locked away from any weapons and anything that might help me hurt someone. But I crushed those feelings the same way I'd held back the Voice for years.

If it took turning into a Bender to get revenge for Father, I wouldn't think twice about it. It would be impossible for me to go home and look the rest of my family in the eye and tell them how badly I'd failed. What sort of a Bullock was I, anyway? Father wouldn't have shied away from killing to stop the Benders.

Yes, I should show the coded messages to someone else. Turn them over to Leroy Dick and let him handle it, then rush home and resign myself to living a timid life. Would Father want me to avenge him? A good person wouldn't do that, would he? Someone who really cared about not hurting anyone else.

But I didn't want to.

Instead, I was set on cracking the code myself. Finding the Benders. Finding Kate. And asking them eye to eye why they'd done it. And then...

So I kept the pages in my saddlebags and kept my eyes and ears open.

By midday, I was confident nothing else noteworthy was going to happen, but I still had that nagging thought at the back of my mind that I was missing something obvious. The place had been picked over by onlookers so much that anything that would have been found, had. Everyone might have been there claiming they wanted to help, but they really just wanted to stare.

There was talk of special trains being arranged to bring even more people to the site. The mound of Bender wreckage was noticeably smaller. The man in the pigsty had sold all his baked goods and left, vowing to bring even more tomorrow.

The pressure building inside me to leave grew with each minute, it seemed, but still I stayed.

Until I saw him. A man walking around the scene, notepad and pencil in hand, talking to people. Writing down notes. That was all I needed for it to dawn on me.

Reporters.

Newspapers.

I loved reading, but I'd completely ignored that vein in my search. Why take so much time fumbling my way through interviews when I could just read through the writings of people who'd done that job for me? Perhaps I could make connections other people wouldn't see or wouldn't take time to think about.

Without hesitation, I clicked Surrey to a walk and headed over to the man. He had a thin beard and a pair of small spectacles perched on the end of his nose. "You're a reporter?" I asked him when I was close enough not to have to yell and draw attention.

He smiled at me. "Ben Treat, *Osage Mission Transcript*. And you are?"

"If I wanted to read old copies of the papers in the area, where would I go?"

The smile slipped from his face. "I don't—"

"I don't imagine there's a library in the area."

"No. Osage Mission has—"

"Too far away," I said. "I need something closer, if there is one."

"Pretty abrupt, aren't you?" he asked, scratching his head and trying to smile.

"New to the area, and I could use some help."

He peered at me over the top of his spectacles for several seconds, then grunted. "Not many papers in the area just yet. In addition to mine, there's the *Thayer Head-Light*, *Fort Scott Monitor*, *South Kansas Tribune*, *Hutchinson*—"

"But is there anywhere I could look through many of them at once?"

"Fort Roach Inn subscribes to them all," he said. "Over in Ladore? I'm not sure what they do with the old copies, though."

I turned and galloped off without another word, leaving the man calling after me in confusion. I didn't care. Ladore was fifteen miles away. If I hurried, I could be there before nightfall.

Galloping the whole way wasn't an option, of course. Not if I wanted to protect Surrey, and at this point, there was no way I'd risk him. So eventually I slowed to a walk, allowing him to rest.

Not that I didn't have anything to keep me occupied. With Surrey walking at a steady pace, it wasn't too much to reach into my saddle-bags and take out the coded messages again. In the light of day, and with some actual sleep, there was more to notice than I'd seen before.

For one thing, some of the messages had punctuation added, not just numbers. For example:

23261802, 23651705, 11202513, 26070604, 16030201, 01292703

I counted the numbers between the commas. Eight every time. What did that mean? Did each set of eight refer to a different letter? Were they coordinates on a map? For a moment, I thought I might have gotten the key. Maps were divided into degrees, minutes, and seconds! But that would just be six numbers, not eight. Though I supposed they could have added meaningless numbers to the beginning or end of each set of digits, which might mask the message even more.

But what good would coordinates be? Some of the messages had strings of numbers several lines long. If they were locations, why would you need so many? And if they were locations, then they likely would have all been clustered around similar spots. With latitude and longitude, most of the beginnings of the numbers would have stayed the same.

So that idea went out the window.

There seemed to be a pattern inside some of the combinations, with zeroes separating some of the numbers. Did that have something to do with anything, or was it just coincidence? Maybe the zeroes were another form of punctuation, or maybe you were just supposed to ignore the zeroes completely.

Or was it all just some strange form of insanity? For all I knew, John or Pa liked to scribble numbers in their spare time. I didn't really believe that, though. There was something to the numbers that seemed far from random, even if I couldn't put my finger on it yet.

In "The Gold-Bug" by Poe, they'd used a substitution cipher for their code, and Legrand just counted up the different symbols to get an idea which ones stood for which letters. I'd loved that story and read it multiple times. According to Poe, the most common letter was *E*, followed by *A*, *I*, *O*, and *H*. Legrand had looked for doubles to give him hints about other letter possibilities. Except in "The Gold-Bug," the message had been one long string of characters, and now I thought this one was clusters of eight numbers. Unless all the words were eight letters long, that didn't make any sense either.

At last I dismounted, thinking perhaps by giving my undivided attention to the task, the solution would come more easily. I scoured the rest of the messages, hoping for another clue or some bit of information that I'd missed, but nothing popped out. As I stared at those digits, how in the world was I supposed to just guess what the Benders had used to understand them? For all I knew, it was a code worked out with their conspirators ahead of time, with no connection to anything I could use logic to understand. What Legrand had done took all of half a page.

Clearly I wasn't at Legrand's level.

It might have seemed easy to ride Surrey and look at codes at the same time at first, but now that I'd been making no headway, I noticed everything that was making things more difficult. The glare of the sun. The constant swaying in the saddle. Flies buzzing around us.

I stuffed the sheets back into the saddlebag, feeling like a failure all over again. Perhaps with some more time for my mind to mull them over, things would make sense later in the day.

Before I got on my horse, however, I reached into my bags and took out the revolver and ammunition belt Leroy had given me. Part of me wanted to shy away from it, but that part was no longer strong enough to stand up to the rest of me.

I wasn't going to be able to do what needed doing if I weren't willing to even put on a revolver again. When I had the chance, I'd spend some time cleaning it and practicing with it again too. No use having it on if I couldn't hit what I aimed at.

I strapped the belt on, the revolver feeling much heavier at my side than I remembered.

When I arrived in Ladore, news of last night's discoveries had already taken grip of the town. People huddled in small groups, talking in low voices, and there wasn't a child to be seen on the streets. Several men eyed me suspiciously as I rode past—some of the women too.

I kept my eyes open for the Bender wagon. I couldn't imagine many people leaving a vehicle in such a shape, with its haphazard wheels and rickety seat and sides that seemed scrounged from driftwood. Surely no one would have bought the thing. Chances were it was abandoned on some street near the train station.

Nothing leaped out to me. There were wagons all over, but none that belonged to the Benders. I already knew what talking to strangers openly would get me: Osage Mission all over again. And the last time I'd been in Ladore had been a disaster. So I improvised.

I pulled Surrey up to a store, got off, and strode inside, trying to mimic the same looks everyone else had been shooting toward me.

Three men stood to the right of the door. They'd been talking animatedly when I'd ridden up, but they'd stopped as soon as they'd seen me coming their way. I walked up and eyed them as obviously as I could.

"You all from around here?" I asked, having to fight the temptation to lower my voice.

"Who's asking?" the man on the right, short and clean-shaven, asked.

"I'm only supposed to talk to people who've lived here. Long enough to trust." I wasn't old enough or strong enough that they'd believe I'd come here on my own. Easier to make them think I was just doing what someone else had told me to.

"Talk about what?" the man with the square jaw, standing on the left, said.

"About the murders," I snapped. "What else would I be talking about? What else is everyone everywhere talking about?"

"You know something about them?" This from the freckled redhead with more than a hint of an Irish accent.

"The Benders headed off on a train about two weeks ago," I said. "I know that much. But we're not sure where they got on or where they headed, so I've been tasked with asking around. Near as we can figure, though, they had to have someone working with them. So I can't just ask anybody."

"What is it you want to know?" Square Jaw asked, much of the suspicion gone from his voice.

"Anyone see anything out of the ordinary here over the past while? They rode out from their farm in a rickety old wagon, and we don't think they'd have gone very far in it. Likely abandoned it near whatever train they bought a ticket for. You seen anything like that?"

"There's a lot of rickety in these parts," Irish said.

"Sure," I said. "But this one's more than most. Mismatched wheels. Wobbles when it moves. I doubt they could have paid someone to take it from them, let alone sold it."

The men glanced at each other, but it was clear they hadn't

seen anything like what I was describing. It had been worth a shot. I thanked them for their time and asked where the inn was. They pointed it out.

As I headed over to the inn, I couldn't help but feel a swell of pride at how well I'd managed the conversation. It was a far cry from where I'd been when I'd begun this journey. I'd always been so worried about being around people, but something had changed inside me in that tornado and the time healing up at Leroy's. I'd had a lot of time to think, and one of the biggest thoughts that had occurred to me was how useless all that worrying had been.

None of it had helped me in the storm, and that was the most dangerous thing I'd ever lived through. Compared to that, talking to a few strangers didn't seem nearly as daunting.

At the inn, I asked the clerk at the front desk if they had old copies of the newspaper.

"We do," he said slowly, confused by the question. "We subscribe to all the area presses. Always prided ourselves on keeping informed."

"Where might I read them?"

"The old ones?" His eyebrows raised. "Why, same place everyone would read them. In the outhouses back behind the inn. Nothing better than old newspaper to…finish your business with."

My stomach sank. Some vital clue might have been casually tossed aside, but I couldn't give up. I paid for a night at the inn, then headed to get what papers were left.

That evening, I spread the papers across my bed, sorting them out by date and cursing the gaps. The reporter had told the truth, however. There were six different presses represented. I set aside anything from the past week and anything from before I'd met the Benders. The news I needed would have come when they'd made a run for it.

Page by page, I pored over the small type and narrow columns. The articles bled together, with little to separate them other than small titles interjected here or there. Advertisements broke up the stories, often seemingly at random, so it was anything but easy reading. One line I'd be reading about record snowfall in northern New York, and the next would be a description of a land auction.

The night got later and later. I kept pausing to rub my strained eyes. The lamplight was better than a kitchen fire but still didn't make for easy reading. It didn't help that I had no idea what I was searching for, if there even was anything to find. With so many people in the area, wouldn't someone make a connection with anything important, long before I could?

I kept reading.

The headlines blended together. *Police Court. Ice for All. Meat Market.* There were articles about the disappearances, of course. Guesswork about who might be behind them, and details of the missing people, but nothing that shed light on where the Benders might be.

Emigration Turning! How to Acquire Riches.

An article detailing hotel arrivals in Fort Scott caught my eye, but nothing came of it. Just a list of names, none of which was Bender.

A word caught my eye: *Mysterious*. I leaned forward and read the article in the *Thayer Head-Light*.

Our citizens have been in a state of perplexity for several days on account of the discovery of a wagon, a mare and colt, and a horse just outside the city limits south of town.

It continued for a paragraph but didn't have any information about what the wagon looked like or who might have left it there. Still, it was the closest I'd come to something that might be a real clue. I turned my focus to the *Head-Light* exclusively. Luckily, it hadn't been one of the editions to have suffered much in the outhouses of the inn.

An article a week later read *Foul Play*. It was more about the wagon. As I quickly skimmed it, a detail sprang forward.

On the bottom of the wagon we saw a piece of flooring board nailed over a hole, on which was daubed in rude letters GROCRYS. *The wagon has been considerably worn, the hind wheels are both dished the wrong way by being too heavily loaded, and two of the spokes of the right hind wheel are broken.*

I thought my heart would burst from excitement. This was it! Between the description of the wagon and that crude sign for groceries, there was no doubt this belonged to the Benders. I'd done what I'd set out to do: used my brain to solve a problem faster than simply running around asking questions could do.

Counting the days off on my hand, I realized the Benders had little more than two weeks of a head start on me. If I made it to Thayer tomorrow (and I should; it was only another fifteen miles), I could find out where they'd gone and be on their trail the same day. They'd think no one was following them, so they wouldn't want to do anything to raise anyone's suspicions. They'd take their time. Stay calm.

They had no idea what was coming for them.

CHAPTER SEVENTEEN

"The Benders have been tracked into the southern part of the State, where all traces of them have been lost."

—New National Era
(*Washington, DC*), June 5, 1873

⸺

THAYER ENDED UP BEING FARTHER away than I'd counted on, and no matter how badly I wanted to catch up with the Benders, I didn't want to push Surrey beyond what he could endure. Horses died that way.

So I spent the night camping on the prairie again. My first order of business was spending some time with the rifle. After a half hour of practice, old habits started to edge back, and I was confident I could hit what I aimed at within fifty feet. If I came across the Benders and needed to take action, I'd be able to do it without worrying about missing. Father had taken good care of the weapon, and a wave of guilt swept over me when I thought of how sad he'd been that I hadn't appreciated it as much as I ought.

I drowned the feeling by turning my attention to the revolver. My hands shook when I first picked it up with the intent to shoot it, but that subsided when I shifted to examining the gun to see how well it would work. It needed quite a bit of attention and supplies to make it reliable, however. Supplies I didn't have at hand. The action was far from smooth, and some of the bullets had the start of rust around the edges. When I had time, I'd buy some new ammunition.

It fired, though I struggled to hit anything farther away than fifteen feet. I couldn't tell whether that was due to the gun, a lack of practice, or the nerves that made my hands get jumpy when I pulled the trigger. Probably a mixture of all three.

I spent the rest of the evening poring over those coded messages. I tried parsing out the numbers in different ways, thinking perhaps the commas I'd found on the one message had just been some kind of fluke. I held them up against the light, hoping I'd see some sort of marks that weren't immediately apparent.

Nothing I did got me anything other than nonsense letters. For a while I thought perhaps the messages were in German, which could explain why none of them made sense, but even that idea came to nothing. There just were some letter combinations that didn't work in any language.

When I lay down to sleep, my dreams were filled with swirling numbers.

Thayer was small. Little more than a cluster of buildings, though more were being built as I rode up. The train station was new, and anywhere a train went, people were bound to follow. They just made travel so much more convenient. You could get from San Francisco to New York City in four days. It had taken me that much just to ride back and forth in this corner of Nowhere, Kansas.

I headed straight for the train station. No need to ask around about the wagon, when I already knew what the—

I stopped, staring down an alley at a wagon tucked beneath a staircase. A wagon in such disrepair, it seemed like it was halfway to falling apart, with missing boards and mismatched wheels. I turned Surrey toward the alley.

In the back of the wagon sat a crude wooden sign: GROCRYS.

Kill them slowly. Gut them and stake them to the ground to die by the buzzards. Listen to their cries as they—

I realized I was gripping my reins in white-knuckled fists, and I took a few breaths to calm myself. There would be time for handling the Benders later. Finding them would take a cool head, I reminded the Voice. It subsided to a dull mutter.

The wagon held nothing other than the sign. I continued to the train station and hitched Surrey outside. Calling it a station was being generous. A man sat in a small shack next to the tracks, his hat over his eyes, audibly snoring from ten feet away. Other people were about the town now, but none of them showed any interest in the station.

I rapped against the window, causing the man to start and glare up at me.

"Whaddya want?" he snapped.

"Looking for someone. Four of them." I expected him to cut me off, knowing full well I was asking about the Benders, because wouldn't everyone else have been doing the same thing, no matter what the newspaper had said? Instead, he just stared at me.

"We get people now and then, you know," he said. "You lookin' for four of 'em in particular, or will any four do?"

"An older couple. German. Not the nicest people, and closed-mouthed. Then a younger woman, outgoing, and a man who titters like a hyena every other sentence. They might have—"

"You friends with 'em?"

"No, I—"

"Don't blame you. The young man's simple, and that's puttin' it kindly. If he'd 'a laughed one more time when they was buyin' tickets, I'da shot him, and I'm not exaggeratin'. Two and a half weeks ago, the four of them waltz over here like they own the place, right first thing in the mornin', and demand two tickets to Saint Louis and two to Denison."

"You remember that much? You're sure?"

"Son, you get four people in here like that in Thayer almost never. And I remember being 'specially glad they were goin' far away from here. Saint Louis is too close, as far as I'm concerned. Three hundred and fifty miles? I'd rather it were a thousand. At least it's likely the young uns'll get shot in Denison afore they come back. That's only three hundred miles off."

"Do you know who they are?"

"I didn't ask any more than I had to."

"The Benders!" I exclaimed, unable to help myself. How he could seem so laid-back about all this was beyond me.

"What does that have to do with anythin'?"

"The ones who killed all those people at their inn?"

He frowned. "Somebody's been killin' people?"

"Never mind," I said. Apparently something that to me felt universally important really wasn't. "When's the next train coming to Denison or Saint Louis?"

"They're in different directions, you know."

"It doesn't matter. I just need to know which."

"Then it's your lucky day. Train that'll pass through Denison'll be here in a half hour, though I'll tell you what I told them. I'd sooner buy a ticket through the underworld as a ticket through Indian Territory. Takin' your life in your hands if you do that."

"It goes through Indian Territory?" I asked, my heart sinking. Newton's directions—and the many stories I'd heard since—all came rushing back into my head. Father had always said he'd be more afraid of the settlers than he would of the tribes, and my time with the wagon train had lined up with that statement, but it still made me nervous. When everyone says one thing, and you think something different, it doesn't hurt to consider that you might be wrong.

"Through Indian Territory?" the man asked. "It don't go around it, that's for sure. It's gotta get to Texas somehow, you know."

My hand fumbled the money as I tried to slide it over the counter. "I can handle myself."

"The place is lawless. We're always hearin' stories about what goes on beyond that border. Outlaws and tomahawks. No sir, I'll stay here in Kansas, thank you kindly."

If I had a choice, why not go to Saint Louis instead of Denison? Why not pick the easier of the two?

"Do you remember which ones went to Saint Louis?" I asked at last.

The man was trying to pry the money out from underneath my fingers. "What? The grumpy ones. Didn't speak much English and looked like a pair of gargoyles. It was the younger ones headed down to Denison. Like I said, older people know better."

So it came down to that. Did I believe Kate and John were nothing more than pawns in the larger operation, or did I think they were the two leading the charge? My first instinct was to go with the older couple. They would have more experience and more influence on the others over time. But then I thought of that séance and of the way Kate had smiled at me. None of it lined up. Either she was a victim in something larger than herself, or she'd been laughing at me behind my back, or there was something more at play that I just didn't understand.

Surely there were worse reasons to risk your life than to find out more about a pretty face, though I didn't know what they were. I bought a ticket to Denison for Surrey and me and headed out to restock before the train came in. Looking at a map posted on the station wall, I saw Denison was in Texas, north of Dallas.

The man behind the ticket counter had gone back to sleep. I carefully tore the map free of the wall, then slipped another dollar across the counter. That should more than cover the cost of it, and I might need this much more than he did, soon enough.

Was I sure I could handle the trip? It was one thing to try to appear confident in front of a stranger, but maybe it would be wiser to turn back. I tried to think through what I knew about the place, hoping focusing on simple facts would make the pit in my stomach go away.

There'd been a time when Indian Territory stretched all the way up to Canada and all the way down to Texas, and as far west as Mexico and Oregon Territory. Bit by bit, that had been chipped away as one piece after another was taken by an American territory and then eventually became a state. Wisconsin. Iowa. Minnesota. Dakota. Kansas. Nebraska.

Now all those different tribes had been shoved together into what was left. Chickasaw, Apache, Wichita, Cheyenne, Seminole, Osage, Pawnee, Cherokee, Kansas, Choctaw, and more. If you listened to some, simply crossing the border into Indian Territory was taking your life in your hands. In addition to everything else, there were outlaw colonies: places where bandits grouped together, outside the range of any law.

It made sense the Benders would have headed in that direction, but it was a large area to cover. At least knowing they were going in the direction of Denison gave me a starting point. If I were them, I would have bought a ticket for a place farther along than I wanted to go, just to further muddy the waters.

If they'd gotten off somewhere in the middle of Indian Territory, what would I do then?

Better to handle one problem at a time. Besides, could it really be as bad as everyone said? If it were truly that dangerous, then the railroad companies wouldn't have enough passengers ready to buy tickets. And I *couldn't* go home. Not without being able to look Mother and my brothers in the eye and tell them I'd taken care of this. I wouldn't have been able to stand it.

Still, the Voice wanted to know a few bits of information. What did it feel like when your scalp was peeled away from your head? What sound did it make? How hard did you have to pull? It sent shivers down my spine, but the Voice kept coming back to it.

Strangely, I had to fight the urge to check through my saddlebags for weapons, despite the fact I had one strapped to my leg. Habits died hard, and I tried to focus on killing that one inside me. Just because I had a weapon didn't mean I was going to use it right away.

Not when I was saving it for the Benders.

I ignored the thoughts as best I could, blocking out the Voice's longings for stabbing or shooting or worse. I had other things to focus on, after all.

Sooner or later, others would follow the same clues I had. I might be ahead of the curve now, but I wouldn't stay that way unless I kept at it. Standing there waiting for the train to come, I realized just how difficult this task would be. From here, they could have gotten off anywhere. Switched trains. Headed into the wilderness. Joined up with accomplices in an outlaw colony.

I wasn't a Pinkerton, with whole teams of investigators to back me up and track down leads. I could be persistent, but there was a limit to even that. I didn't have deep pockets. If this went on too long, I'd need to start cutting back on what I was spending, staying outside instead of sleeping in an inn, eating the basics instead of hot meals. If I kept rationing well, I maybe had another two or three weeks before I'd have to start finding ways to earn more money to keep myself going.

The large locomotive pulled into Thayer soon after, hissing and steaming its way into the station and bringing with it the smell of burning coal, grease, and horses. I led Surrey back to the corral car, but when I tried to coax him in, he reared back in protest. The conductor came to see what the trouble was, and between the two of us, we got Surrey on board eventually.

It was hard to look at my horse, standing there on a short tether in a strange environment that was going to rattle and shake for the next day, and not feel more than a little guilty. I glanced up toward the front of the train, where the passengers would ride.

If faced with choosing to be with Surrey or strangers, which would I prefer?

"Can I stay back here with my horse?" I asked.

"Nothing will happen to the animal," the conductor said. "We transport them all the time."

"Just the same," I said. "Would it matter?"

He shrugged. "Someone wants to sit in manure instead of on an actual bench? Who am I to stand in the way?"

I hadn't taken the train in five years. We'd never had cause. In my head, they were the best way to travel, zipping through the countryside on iron rails. That image was far from reality, as it seemed like dozens of things could go wrong to slow us, and I became intimately familiar with them the longer I rode. We had to stop about a half hour into the journey to fill our water tender. Everyone always focused on filling an engine with coal to keep it moving, but the coal was only there to boil the water. When you were out of water, you weren't going anywhere.

This wasn't just a quick pause either. It took well over an hour to get all the water we needed, though I understood there'd been some difficulty at first with the tower that had to be fixed before the refueling could really begin. We'd need to stop halfway through Indian Territory to top the water off again and get more coal, but they tried to limit those stops as much as possible. A stopped train in the middle of a place full of outlaws was a prime target.

When we weren't stopping for water, we were stopping for passengers. When we weren't stopping for passengers, we were slowing down for the different types of tracks. I talked to the conductor about it during one of the many stops. The railroad companies liked to brag about the transcontinental and how it could get someone from Iowa to Nebraska in just four days—a far cry from the six months it would take by wagon or the twenty-five days it took a stagecoach. But that was on rails that'd had special care taken when they were laid down.

In spots of the country that weren't as important? The rail wasn't so sturdy. Instead of going sixty miles an hour or more, at times we had to slow down to ten.

I didn't regret my decision to stay back with Surrey, however. The bulk of the train had been bought out by a "hunting expedition"—a group of men signed up to shoot buffalo herds from the train. Apparently the train companies didn't like the animals getting in the way of their locomotives, and the government didn't like the animals supporting the tribes. Having citizens shoot the creatures en masse solved both problems at once.

Not that we came across any buffalo. That didn't deter the men at all. They just kept drinking, which seemed all they really cared about, anyway.

I found an empty stall early on in the journey and made myself at home on the ground. It wasn't much different from camping, when you got down to it. Just harder on your rear end.

After the first while, I took out the Benders' messages and started examining them for what felt like the hundredth time. By this point, I wasn't even sure why I kept tormenting myself. It wasn't as if I'd come across any other clues, and I was to the point now where I'd memorized several of the clusters. The sheets held no new information, and without that, they were as good as useless. Except without the sheets, I felt like I'd be as good as useless as well.

Father always used to say when you got stuck on one path, the trick wasn't to just keep trying. Often it was quicker to find another way.

So what else could I do that might help me make some progress toward understanding the code? The papers couldn't tell me anything else. Could my experiences with the Benders themselves give me any hints?

None of them came across as particularly intelligent, other than Kate. But as I stared at the pages, it occurred to me Kate almost definitely didn't write those numbers. They were too blocky for most women's cursive, and I had the sense Kate would pay as much attention to her writing as she would to her appearance. I might have been wrong, but what would it mean if these were written by one of the others? John, for example.

If he were the one working out the messages' meaning (and writing other messages back to whoever had been sending them), then he'd want something straightforward. Something he understood well.

The train lurched to the side as it hit a weak spot on the tracks, but I barely noticed it. My eyebrows rose as I thought of one thing I hadn't noticed yet: any sheets of paper devoted to working out the codes. No notes. No calculations. It's possible they hadn't kept any of those, but again, the sloppy way they lived made me doubt that. They'd been storing these in a hiding place on purpose, and there would have been times when they'd have to shove them away on short notice, most likely. I doubted any of them would have worried about cleaning the hiding spot out much.

So the code was simple, or at least, perhaps I could move forward on that assumption. A straightforward way for them to pass messages back and forth. If I were going to send a message to John, what would I use? All I knew of him was the fact he tittered like a drunken horse, and he always had his nose buried…

In a Bible.

CHAPTER EIGHTEEN

"There's intense excitement all over the country, and a firm determination to ferret out the parties engaged in the murders. It is understood that a large reward will be offered by the community and the State for the arrest of the assassins."

—The Evansville Journal
(*Evansville, Indiana*), *May 13, 1873*

―――――――

J OHN HADN'T STRUCK ME AS a zealot, but he'd been reading that Bible over and over as if it held some deeper meaning. What if they'd picked a book to act as their code? What could be more universal than a Bible?

Eight numbers. Scriptures? My family had only a passing relationship with religion, so it wasn't as if I could fall back on my Sunday school lessons to give me some insights. All I knew of the Bible was the fact people liked to quote book, chapter, and verse when they were telling you what they thought you were supposed to be doing that you weren't or were doing that you shouldn't. As if the fact something appeared in a book thousands of years ago somehow made it more relevant today.

My heart thumped in my chest, but for a moment, it hit up against my limitations: How was I supposed to work anything out if the Bible was the key, if I didn't have a copy of it to work from?

That lasted a few seconds before I remembered I'd brought the Benders' own family copy from their house. Though the memory made me doubt myself. If the Bible really were their key to communicating with their accomplice, then why would they leave it behind?

Then again, that might make sense, if they didn't expect they'd need the code anymore and the book had just been for show in the first place.

I fetched the Bible from my saddlebags, checking on Surrey as I did so. He had settled down and didn't even rear back when I came up to him. I rubbed his back and told him how proud I was of him, then sat back down and opened the book to the title page. If I were going to devise a code using the Bible as my key, how would I go about doing it?

I could do it by page number, but that would require me and the person I was exchanging messages with to have identical versions of the Bible. What would happen if that got lost? I didn't think that would be a reliable enough approach.

By book, chapter, and verse? Those would be the same for all of them. It wouldn't have to be the whole Bible; I could just pick one of the books in it and use that as the key. I flipped through the pages, staring at the names: *Leviticus*, *Daniel*, *Mark*, *Acts*. It could take forever to try them all, but if you didn't just use one of the books, then you'd have to…

Let the other person know which book you *were* using.

I turned to the table of contents and glanced over all the books. There were dozens, but they always came in the same order in each Bible, didn't they? If I numbered the books from one to whatever, then I could start each message by using that number to show which book I was referring to. But how would someone know the difference between one and eleven or two and twelve? You could do it by trial and error, I supposed, but John didn't seem the type who would go in for that.

If, on the other hand, you used a zero in front of the single digits, the reader would always know that each number would have two digits: 01, 02, 03, all the way up to 99.

So the first two numbers in each eight-number set would be the book. The second two would be the chapter. The third two the verse. And the fourth? The number of the letter in the verse? That would mean it would take dozens of combinations just to spell out a phrase. The number of the *word* in the verse made much more sense.

I flipped through the sheets to find one fairly short, settling on the first one I'd looked at:

2451310629020030728251207
0311230403112300557020729

050421

I used a pencil to break it up into eight-number blocks.

24513106

29020307

23251207

03112305

03112306

56020729

050421

The last number set was left with only six digits, which made me doubt my entire line of reasoning. It had all made so much sense, but was it just wishful thinking? It would be easy enough to find out. I parsed out the first set of numbers.

24513106

The twenty-fourth book in the Bible was Jeremiah. Fifty-first chapter, thirty-first verse: *One post shall run to meet another, and one messenger to meet another, to shew the king of Babylon that his city is taken at one end.*

I counted off the words. If I was right, this meant "meet."

On to the second set.

29020307

Joel was the twenty-ninth book. Second chapter, third verse: *A fire devoureth before them; and behind them a flame burneth: the land is as the garden of Eden before them, and behind them a desolate wilderness; yea, and nothing shall escape them.*

The seventh word was "behind." My palms had started to sweat. The pages stuck to my fingers, and I fumbled around to keep going.

23251207

Isaiah was the book before Jeremiah. I could just picture John being too lazy to find a book much further away than one he'd already been using. The twenty-fifth chapter and twelfth verse: *And the fortress of the high fort of thy walls shall he bring down, lay low, and bring to the ground, even to the dust.*

The word was "fort."

I blazed through the rest of the message. They'd used the same verse for the next two words. Leviticus 11:23. *But all other flying creeping things, which have four feet, shall be an abomination unto you.*

"Creeping things." I frowned at this, not quite understanding what it meant. *Meet behind fort creeping thing?* Maybe the next word would make more sense.

Luke 2:7. *And she brought forth her firstborn son, and wrapped him in swaddling clothes, and laid him in a manger; because there was no room for them in the inn.*

"Inn."

And then I was at just six numbers. Had they left something off?

Meet behind fort creeping things inn 050421

Could the six numbers be a date? May 4, 1821? Just how old was this message? Then I realized that, of course, they wouldn't be care about the year. The time they wanted to meet would be much more important. May 4 at twenty-one? Twenty-one what? Or was it two one?

That stumped me for a bit, but as I looked at the other messages, it occurred to me that if you numbered the hours of the day from the first to the last, you'd get twenty-four. One in the morning would be one; one in the afternoon would be thirteen. If this was what they used, then the twenty-first hour was nine at night.

Meet behind fort creeping things inn May 4 at nine in the evening.

If there were a fort, and it had an inn, could it be called "The Creeping Things"? That didn't remind me of anything I'd ever heard. What were creeping things? Snakes? Mice? Bugs?

I stared at the message, wishing it would tell me something more. I was so close! Could it be they used some other kind of code for talking about specific cities? Or was this just coincidence?

Fort Caterpillar? Fort Cricket? Fort—

Fort Roach. I'd just gotten the papers there the day before. Perhaps if I'd been getting more rest, it would have occurred to me sooner, but once it did, it seemed obvious.

Meet behind Fort Roach inn at 9 p.m. on May 4.

Either that was the biggest coincidence ever, or I'd actually broken the code. I took out the coded messages and kept going. It was painstaking work. The code wasn't designed for someone to be able to read it quickly. Then again, it also wasn't intended for very long messages. They were all under ten words. After a half hour of cursing the train as it lurched back and forth and made writing a pain, I had the completed list:

sold horses seat 127

meet river bend March 18, 10 p.m.

good market wagons need more

no more wheat spoiled fast

no lies money you think simple you do pay me 580

sheriffs near. Wait month before beginning

send message store when coming

moving red river trade again spring

accident hurt miss month

other watching need moved house wait

sold all bring soon 586

round rock good no watch begin now

need better house more people what you think

not hear months send fort worth not more rock

fort worth many eyes leave now let know where

storekeeper trust but still use number

more safe follow cattle north cheese home wait

not care how know you not lie me pay now

wait after winter

looking good pair horses

I come June

not come till march

meet den is on store June 8 8 p.m.

seat sold 739

how much taken give fifth

ready meet September 14

floods road delayed

freedom city August 22

not keep message burn

last message not able read better care John fool

I stared at the piece of paper, trying to have it make more sense through willpower alone. It felt like everything I needed to know what to do next should be there, but I just couldn't see it.

Much of it could just be ignored, most likely. The squabbling about payments and the arrangements for meeting times. And these hadn't been written by John but by whoever was working with the Benders. I should have seen that right off. Why would the Benders have kept coded messages that were supposed to be read by someone else? But the content itself? It didn't matter that John couldn't write code well or that floods had delayed the mystery partner. Instead, I had to focus on things that mentioned places. I made another list:

River bend, red river, round rock, Fort Worth, vineyard, den, and freedom city.

Many of those were fairly generic, and I worried they referred to landmarks and not town names. Then again, "freedom city" could mean Independence, Kansas. Fort Worth was obvious. The

Red River was the border between Texas and Indian Territory, but it ran for miles upon miles. I couldn't very well ride up and down it, hoping to run across something like a clue.

And the "den" they wrote about? Was that some sort of thieves' lair? A bear den? A cave?

What did "cattle north cheese home" mean?

I stared out the window, watching the prairie roll by like an ocean of grass. If not for the billowing smoke and roar of the engine, it would be easy to think no one had ever come through this part of the country before. It just reminded me how big the country was and how hard it might be to find four people somewhere out in all that space. For all the talk of a buffalo hunt, we hadn't come across any actual buffalo yet.

Focus on the task at hand, Warren.

Most of the messages were clear. Maybe by focusing on the parts that seemed strange, more would make sense. *Meet den is on store.* Did it mean "meet at the den on top of the store"? A storage room of some kind? That was nonsensical. And why would they include "is" for that message, when they never did otherwise?

If they were to meet in a store, not a den, then "den is on" could describe the kind of store, couldn't it?

I'm ashamed that it took fifteen minutes for me to connect the fact I'd bought a ticket for Denison, Texas, with "den is on." So maybe when they couldn't find the exact word they needed in the Bible, they got creative.

Reviewing the messages some more, it seemed like their accomplice had moved a number of times over the years. They'd been in a place called "round rock," or something like that. Then I thought they'd moved to Fort Worth, since they'd written "send Fort Worth not more rock."

Was that where they were now? No, because they'd said, "Fort Worth many eyes." So that only left "river bend," "red river," "freedom city," and "vineyard." Of those, "red river" was the only one that mentioned an actual move. Had they moved *from* an area on the Red River or *to* that area?

And what did "cattle north cheese home" mean?

I did the only thing that made sense: I got out the map I'd taken from the train station.

It covered Kansas, Indian Territory, and Texas, reminding me of just how daunting the task at hand would be if I didn't have a solid lead. I'd spent days and days just in a tiny corner of southeast Kansas, and now the Benders might be anywhere.

I scanned over the names of the cities, searching for some of the ones that had been mentioned in the coded messages. Red River was right on the border of Texas and Indian Territory, and a dotted line passed right through it, going north to south. It was labeled *Chisholm Cattle Trail*.

I wasn't sure how it was pronounced, but I was willing to bet it sounded an awful lot like "cheese home."

I couldn't help but feel a buzz inside me. Since I'd left home, I'd felt like I'd been making one mistake after another. Yes, I'd made progress on a grand scale, but I was still trailing along after the Benders like a kitten after a leaky cow. I'd bumbled around in Osage Mission without the first idea of how I was supposed to do what I'd set out to do. I'd zigzagged across Kansas, ending up staying the night with the very people I was hunting and not even realizing who they were. I still didn't care to think about the séance Kate had put on for me. It had to have been fake, though there were things about it I couldn't explain.

Either way, I'd gone from that boy who didn't know how to do anything to the one here, breaking codes and having a firm destination in mind for finding the Benders, while the rest of the state ran around aimlessly.

But it wasn't enough to just tail them. Somehow, I had to get ahead so I could start making plans of my own instead of always responding to what they were doing.

What did I have that could help me with that? They knew more than I did about who they worked with and what their goals were. If I could talk to one of their accomplices without them knowing, then perhaps I could hope to—

The memory of the letter I'd found on the Benders' doorstep— the one with the first coded message I'd found—hit me like a hoof to the head. A sealed message to the Benders that they had no idea existed.

Where had I put it?

I rummaged through my bags twice before thinking to check my pockets. There it was, somewhat worse for wear, but waiting for me to read it. I took it out and spread the paper in front of me. By now, separating out the numbers into eight-digit clumps was second nature. I leafed through the Bible word by word, looking up citations and hoping all this gave me something useful.

Red river full moved wash it a five mile west small house three water fall meet there.

With a bit of punctuation and some reasoning that "wash it a" had to be another town name, it was clearer: *Red River full. Moved Washita. Five mile west. Small house. Three waterfalls. Meet there.*

Checking the map again, I followed the Chisholm Trail north from Red River. Toward the middle of Indian Territory was a small dot a little to the west of the trail: *Washita.*

I clapped once in satisfaction. This was the first time in forever when I felt like I was doing something right—something almost worthy of the Bullock name. I knew where the Benders were going. The facts lined up quickly in my head.

The Benders would have taken their time to get to Red River. Why would they hurry? The rest of the world hadn't even known they were criminals a week ago. Then it would take more time for them to meet up again, assuming Ma and Pa wanted to circle back to join Kate and John. Since they were bound for the person who'd been selling all their stolen goods, it only made sense they'd want to pay particular attention to that. My bet was they'd be there as a quartet.

With some time and effort, I estimated how far the Benders would have had to travel to get to Washita the normal way. Going through Indian Territory would have taken them straight across the Comanche and Apache reservations. From what I'd heard, those were some of the most dangerous ones. Before they even got that far, they'd be in Cheyenne territory, and even I'd heard of the battles Custer's Seventh Cavalry had been having there the past few months.

The Benders wouldn't go that way.

If they took the long route, they'd first make it to Denison in two days. According to the map, there was no train from there to Red River, so they'd need to go by horse or stagecoach for almost seventy-five miles. That would be around another week.

At that point, they'd head north another hundred and fifty miles to get to Washita. Two more weeks of travel at least—probably more like three, and then they'd still have to fumble around figuring out where exactly they were supposed to meet their accomplice.

According to the ticket agent, the Benders were two and a half weeks ahead of me, but it would take them four or five weeks to do this trip.

Meaning if I could get there in two weeks, I'd make up the time.

I knew just what a real Bullock would do. He'd take one look at the Cheyenne, Apache, and Comanche and not think twice about risking it. Any risk would be worth it, if the Benders were the prize.

A single rider, traveling light, could make it across that territory in two weeks, if he knew what he was doing. And if he managed to avoid getting killed in the process.

It wasn't even a question for me. Somehow, I had to be able to live with myself after this journey was through. To be able to look my family in the eye and somehow feel I was worthy of our name. Anything I could do to make sure the Benders didn't get away, I would do.

Whatever it took.

CHAPTER NINETEEN

"There have been numerous reports of the arrest of the old man, but the persons suspected to be him have heretofore always established a different identity."

—Daily Morning Call
(San Francisco, California), April 7, 1877

WHEN I GOT OFF THE train in Eufaula, the temperature had dropped, and it was already well into the evening. The town was even less of a presence than Thayer had been. Little more than a train station for loading and unloading cargo, though there were signs of new buildings going up here and there. Something that might have been the start of a church stood not too far off, but the place wasn't designed for travelers.

Surrey was still skittish from the ride, so I decided to travel a few miles west before making camp. No one looked twice at me. No one seemed to take any interest at all. I pestered a few people in town for general directions through the state. Most of them gave me odd looks when I said where I was going, but they were happy enough to point west.

"Just keep going until you hit something or something hits you. First main river you come to'll be the Canadian. After that, ask someone closer to you, if you can find one that won't shoot you."

Still, the ride through the dusk didn't feel any different from a ride through the dusk in Kansas, and sleeping by myself under the stars couldn't be any more foolhardy than turning in for the night in the Bender cabin.

By the time Surrey had the nerves out of him, the sun had painted the sky a brilliant orange, deepening to a bloody red toward the horizon. I'd had to use my hat to shield my eyes from the sun for the first while, but now it was actually comfortable. I'd left the roads behind me. Better to be away from anyone and on my own.

That first night passed without incident, but on the second, things became more difficult. Father had taught me every trick he knew about making a journey across the country in safety, but I'd been twelve at the time, and most of it hadn't stuck. After a long day riding across the wide-open plains, I'd been all too ready for a warm fire, even if it did come from cow patties. I hadn't remembered an open flame like that could be seen for miles around.

As soon as I caught wind of hoofbeats approaching my campsite, all of Father's warnings rushed back into my memory, too late to do any good.

Grab your rifle and start shooting. Aim for the horses first, then go in close and finish the riders off, one by—

I ignored the Voice, though I did regret not having kept the Remington strapped on. At this point, making any threatening movements was likely to get me killed, and whoever was coming toward me had a much better view of me than I did of them. Being by a fire made you blind to anything else out in the darkness.

A cold supper in a live belly beat a warm supper in a dead one, any day of the week.

Whoever was out there didn't come close enough to the fire for me to make them out as anything other than shadows. Four or five of them, empty spaces in the night sky, where they blocked out the stars. The hooves hadn't been shod, which almost certainly meant I'd attracted attention from one of the local tribes. Seminoles, if what I'd heard in town was correct. I knew nothing about them and had no idea what to expect.

I sat there, staring into the darkness, waiting for them to say something or make a move. They watched me in silence, their horses shuffling now and then. I raised my hands slowly above my head, though that was more to stop the Voice from yelling at me to grab my rifle and start shooting.

After a long period of silence, the forms turned and continued their ride into the distance. I didn't move until all sound of their travel had gone away, though it wouldn't have been difficult for them to have a few of their group peel off and come back to my site in silence.

I kicked dirt over my fire until all the embers had died, and I spent the rest of the night—and the trip—without more than a small fire to cook when I needed it, being careful to use every trick Father had taught me to keep the smoke to a minimum.

After that first blunder, I did a better job of avoiding any more. As I exercised more caution, the journey settled into something like a familiar routine: Get up in the morning as the sun rose. Break camp, which meant nothing more than putting Surrey's saddle back on and picking up the odds and ends I got out each evening—a blanket, a small frying pan, flint.

In many ways, it reminded me of my family's journey back from California. My older brothers had been off working a cattle drive, giving me more time with Father than I'd ever had. He'd made it a point to teach me anything and everything he could on that trip. How to hunt. How to track beasts and people. How to survive in the wilderness. What to do in just about any situation that might come up. They were lessons I'd forgotten in the years since. Lessons that hadn't immediately come to mind as I'd started out on this journey to find Father weeks ago.

How much of what I'd done would have been easier if I'd looked at this as something more than a quick ride to a neighboring state? In hindsight, I should have been treating Kansas like the wilderness all along. I might have ended up handling everything better, though I had to admit that wouldn't have been hard.

But day by day, many of those lessons returned to me. How to spot a snake den. How to keep from being seen. How to find plants I could eat. Out in the wilderness, I felt like I was connecting with an earlier version of myself. The Warren who used to just want to have fun. Who didn't brood about violence all day long and didn't think twice about weapons.

Each time the Voice started to whisper, I quieted it with a reassurance that there would be time for violence when I'd caught the Benders. Violence and then some.

In the wilderness, you can't dither too much over things that don't matter. My rifle wasn't something that had to be avoided. It was a tool I used to hunt, and I put it to use multiple times. Yes, the first time I shot a deer, my hands shook, and my breath came in short gasps. Killing a living creature was a far cry from target practice with bottles. After I'd fired, I had to sit down and wait for the panic to pass, but it did. Then I stood and walked over to see if I'd hit what I'd been aiming at.

I'd shot the deer straight through the heart. My aim hadn't suffered at all, somehow, and perhaps all my worrying about not taking proper care of my weapons had been just another instance of me making something out of nothing. I could force myself to use the rifle, but just handling it for day-to-day care? I wasn't doing enough of it, no matter what the memory of Father's advice to me kept saying.

The deer had to be skinned and butchered, and that meant

knife work. Did the Voice revel in that much blood? Naturally, but at the same time, it was a routine I'd done many times before. Falling back into it, I realized how much violence had always been a part of my life. Had I broken down and killed people before? No. Would I do it now?

That remained to be seen.

After my success with the rifle, I turned my focus to the revolver again. When you were fighting at close range, a rifle wouldn't work nearly as well as a handgun. I needed to know I could rely on the Remington and on my ability to hit what I aimed at, and I'd only really tried to practice with it once.

I took a break for lunch the day after I'd shot the deer, and I walked off a ways from camp, to keep the sound of the gunshots from bothering Surrey too much. He wasn't used to them the way a horse that had been in the war would have been. Years ago, Father had taught me how to draw and aim by pointing instead of taking a bead with the sight on the gun. I'd gotten to the point that I could fan off three shots in a row and hit what I was aiming for almost every time, and Father had said I'd only get better as I grew older and got stronger arms.

The Voice had put an end to that.

But here in the wilderness, there was nothing for the Voice to try to get me to hurt.

I took my time, aiming for a cow patty about ten yards away. You couldn't just pull the trigger on a revolver, of course. You had to cock it first. Feeling that series of four clicks brought back a sea of memories. I lined up the shot and pulled the trigger.

A puff of dust kicked up two feet in front of the patty. The gun wasn't the only thing rusty in this exercise.

With that first shot out of the way, it became easier for me to do it again, and by the fourth shot, I actually hit what I was aiming for. The fifth time I pulled the trigger, however, the gun just made a popping sound instead of a resounding boom. I cursed and half cocked the gun, removing all the spent rounds before taking out the base pin and the cylinder, which let me hold the barrel up to the light and look through it.

Sure enough, it had been blocked. One of the first things Father had taught me was the dangers that could happen with a revolver. For one thing, you always holstered it with the pin on an empty chamber. Bump the gun just wrong, and the firing pin could hit the bullet and cause it to fire, scaring you to death if you were lucky, and shooting you in the leg or the foot if you weren't.

But things could be just as deadly if the gun didn't fire correctly. Sometimes a bad bullet wouldn't leave the gun, leaving the barrel blocked. Anyone who tried to fire it again without first clearing out the blockage was liable to have the gun blow up in their face. It was called a squib round.

I'd worried the condition of the revolver and the bullets would make this likely, and having it happen the fifth time I tried to shoot made me that much more skittish about relying on the weapon. I kept practicing with it, and I had three more squib rounds in the next fifteen shots. Whatever had happened to the bullets or the gun, it clearly had done some real damage.

Better to stick with the rifle unless my life was on the line, and even then, I'd have to hope I got lucky. One in five odds of having nothing happen when I pulled the trigger wasn't odds I was too comfortable with.

There were scares over those two weeks, of course. A river crossing I chose turned out to be much worse than I'd expected. Surrey plunged deep into a sinkhole I hadn't seen in the middle of a fast current. My instincts kicked in, and I pushed clear of the horse, swimming diagonally downstream in long steady strokes. I made it, breathless and a little shaken, but Surrey came to join me soon after, looking no worse for wear.

He wasn't the fastest horse, but he'd more than proven himself over the course of this trek.

My biggest focus was on remaining unseen as much as possible. I chose paths below any hilltops or ridgelines, weaving in and around the countryside to make sure I didn't pop up against the horizon to anyone who might be looking. It meant I didn't go as fast as I'd like, but better safe than dead.

I saw signs of other people. Smoke on the horizon now and then. Tracks in the dirt. Three more times at night, I was sure something—or some*one*—was watching me in the darkness. But whether I was lucky or just good at following Father's advice, I managed to make it without any confrontations.

By the end of the first week, I was much more comfortable with my rifle handy and my revolver at my side. I'd practiced more with it, a few times when I could see far enough around me to feel somewhat safe making that kind of noise. Yes, it hadn't been taken care of perfectly, but it seemed to function, as long as the bullets fired. My aim wasn't as good at a distance, but that's what the rifle was for. If I had to go up against the Benders—or anyone else—close-up, I was confident I'd be able to hold my own, as long as I didn't lose my head and the bullets actually fired.

So while I went more slowly than I might have wished, I made better time than I'd feared. With just myself to worry about, I could break camp early and ride late. It felt like something was following me, driving me onward. Wherever the Benders were, I knew every day brought them closer or farther away. I couldn't assume I had any extra time. If they made it to Washita before me and left, I had no idea how I'd pick their trail up again.

Still, I was optimistic, and I began to nurture some hope that this would all work out. That God—wherever He was—knew I'd already paid my price of sorrow, and He was helping me now to make things right.

A week and a half into the journey, I saw something glinting in the prairie to the east as I was taking Surrey's saddle off. I paused, squinting into the distance. The sun perched right over the horizon behind me, so I had plenty of light to still see by.

The glint didn't repeat itself, and I wondered if I'd imagined it. It was the way I'd come, and I hadn't seen anything back there that might have reflected light. No water. Nothing man-made. It had been just a couple of quick flashes, there and gone in a moment, and I'd only seen them from the corner of my eye.

Perhaps I'd imagined it.

The memory didn't sit well with me, however. I couldn't stop fidgeting as I tried to fall asleep, trying to convince myself the light had been a trick of the sunset. At last I stole away from camp in the middle of the night, walking across the prairie by the light of a crescent moon. I wouldn't go far. Just enough to get close to where I thought the light might have come from.

Halfway there, I stopped when I saw a small tongue of flame in the direction I was heading. A campfire, tucked down in a gully to hide it from sight. Someone behind me, though it didn't seem like they were in any hurry to catch me. Perhaps they weren't following me at all.

I couldn't rest on that hope, however. Back at my camp, I made my best attempt at sleep, but I was up and leaving well before sunrise. I changed my course, drifting more to the south in hopes that would put more distance between me and whoever was following.

The entire day, I kept glancing back, scanning the area for any signs of pursuit. It didn't make sense that anyone would be after me. I had no money, and the days of Surrey fetching a high price were well past him, no matter how much he mattered to me.

Then again, if someone *were* following me, there was only one way they could find out if I was worth robbing or not.

I made it to a break for lunch without any signs of followers, and I was just beginning to feel the knot ease in my shoulders when a flock of quail took to the sky, not more than a half mile behind me. They might have seen a predator, but it made my neck itch. I ate as I traveled, walking so that Surrey got the rest he needed.

A few plumes of smoke rose lazily into the air to the southwest. Signs of a Kiowa settlement, if I was right about my general area. I'd been trying to avoid other people, but perhaps if I chose my angles just right, I'd be able to use them as a shield of sorts, in case my instincts about being followed were founded.

Surrey and I came to a stream, and I used the chance to hide my tracks somewhat. Father had shown me the basics. You focused on showing your tracks heading into the water in a certain direction, and then you changed course while in the water. It didn't take long to do, but if you could find a place to exit that didn't show tracks as easily, it could take someone following you quite a while to find your trail again. By that time, I'd have hopefully gotten far enough that the Kiowa were between me and anyone following.

Part of me felt foolish for going to such lengths. I was in the middle of nowhere, and I couldn't afford to waste time. But Father had always stressed how living in the wilderness could bring out instincts you didn't know you had. Something felt off, and the feeling was strong enough to override my need to just make good time.

I continued west once I judged the smoke trails to be far enough away for me to be safe. If someone was after me, they'd have to now find my trail and avoid the settlement. Hopefully that was enough to make them give up.

Several hours later, a few cracking noises came from far behind me. If they weren't gunshots in the distance, I didn't know what they were. None of my concern, though. Not unless they came close enough to change that.

That night, I tried backtracking again. This time, I found no sign of anyone at all.

If there had been someone back there, they might have given up following me, since there were no real signs that catching me would be worth more than minimal effort. I got some sleep that night and headed off again in the morning.

Shortly before noon, I heard something that might have been thunder in the distance. A constant, steady noise that rumbled almost continually. The skies were clear, however, so I dismissed it as a trick of the wind. Then that same wind brought me snippets of noise: a bellow or a low grumble. A calf calling out to its mother. Enough that I got off Surrey and crawled to the top of a low rise to see what exactly lay in front of me.

Buffalo stretched across the prairie, a continuous flow of

animals in either direction. Not densely packed together, but so many that I thought I must be seeing things. Bellowing and shifting and calmly chewing the prairie grass.

Right in the way of where I needed to go.

Circling around them wasn't an option. I had no idea how far the herd extended in either direction, and I couldn't afford to lose a day or more. The Benders weren't waiting for this. I couldn't either. As long as I didn't spook the herd, I shouldn't be in too much danger.

I hoped.

I'd stay on Surrey, move carefully, and do my best not to startle any of them. If they were to stampede, and I were in the middle of that mass of animals, I'd have almost no chance of coming through it alive.

If I spent much more time thinking about it, I was almost sure I'd come up with any number of reasons to avoid riding through the herd. Instead, I crawled back down to Surrey and set off.

The noise of the herd grew louder as I found a gully that led in the direction I wanted to go. If I was lucky, it might keep me away from the herd's sight almost entirely. Better to just deal with a few of the animals than the whole mass.

Instead, the gully sloped up about two hundred feet farther, and I found myself in the middle of the herd.

Surrey froze. I froze. The buffalo stared at me but continued with their activities as if they didn't see me.

Generally, when you're dealing with animals, it's best not to do anything obviously wrong. Don't get between a mother and her young. Don't challenge a male. In my experience, any creature could become violent if it felt threatened. The trick was not appearing dangerous.

I kept my head tucked down and Surrey's gait steady. I made no eye contact with any of the animals and did my best to stay as far away from any one of them as possible. This wasn't my first time around animals, and I wasn't scared of them. However, I also had a very clear picture of what could happen when a creature that size decided it didn't much care for you. We'd come across a fair number of cowboys on our journeys west and back again. One time I watched as one of them had a careless moment. The steer spooked, hooked his leg with a horn, and dragged him off his horse, then proceeded to try to stomp him to death.

He'd gotten away alive, but it had been close.

Still, I'd now made it thirty yards into the herd, and nothing had happened to me yet. In fact, the creatures seemed as set on staying away from me as I wanted to stay away from them. They moved to the side as I approached, making it feel like I had a halo of free space around me wherever I went.

I began to grow more confident, even as I was amazed at just how many animals were in this herd. True, I was in a bit of a low spot on the prairie, so I couldn't see as far away as I could have if I'd been higher, but I soon felt like I was in the middle of a sea of buffalo, with no end in sight.

They didn't seem to mind my presence. They moved and ate and jostled against one another from time to time, but I might as well have not even been here, for all the attention they paid me.

Behind me, a few of the buffalo grumbled in protest. I glanced back to see three men had just ridden to the edge of the herd. All three had rifles, and the one in front had his pointed straight at me.

Perhaps a half mile behind them, a group of Kiowa hunters galloped toward us.

CHAPTER TWENTY

"That a family of four persons could drive to the nearest railroad station, abandon their team there, take the train and escape all the officers and detectives set upon their track, was incredible."

—Morning Call

(Allentown, Pennsylvania), November 10, 1889

———

T HE WORLD SEEMED TO STOP as all my thoughts narrowed to that one barrel aimed at my head. The rifle looked to be a newer Winchester, the same as mine. If he were on the ground, with the rifle steady, I'd be good as dead. Mounted? It was far enough from a sure thing that I wasn't just going to give up.

"Hello," I said, scrambling to think of a way out of this. If he fired the gun, the buffalo might well stampede. If they stampeded...

"You come on back now," the man said in a nasal voice.

"Why would I do that?"

He scoffed. "On account of you not wantin' to be dead, I figure."

The Kiowa had already cut into the gap between us by a fair margin. I had no idea if they were coming to attack us, wanted to warn us away from the buffalo, or didn't even consider us at all.

It wasn't something I wanted to find out, no matter what experiences I'd had with other tribes on the trail.

I focused on the man again. "Something tells me seeing you any closer will only increase the odds of dying."

He frowned in confusion. "What?"

"They with you?" I asked, jerking my chin up.

"Who?"

All three of them turned, then swore in unison. I took advantage of their distraction to nudge Surrey back into a walk, deeper into the buffalo herd.

"Hey!" the man with the rifle yelled at me. "I told you to stop."

"You fire that gun, and you'll spook the buffalo," I said. "If they stampede, we'll all be in trouble. So how about you just ride off, and I'll keep going."

One of them muttered something to the others, but they were too far off for me to catch it. I turned to see what was happening. The Kiowa—if that's who they were—had come within five hundred yards. The three outlaws had split up some, their horses nervously shying as they sensed their riders' unease.

The middle one swore again and headed into the herd after me.

"What's so special about me that you want to catch me so badly?" I asked over my shoulder.

"Before I got in this situation, nothin' more 'n your horse and whatever you had in them saddlebags. But now? I like my odds better in the herd than I do with them Comanches ridin' down on us."

"Comanches?"

"Might be we got in a little disagreement with some of 'em, yesterday."

"Disagreement?"

"Shot at 'em. Hit a couple to keep 'em from following us. Might've killed one or two."

Surrey began to move faster, and I didn't stop him. "Maybe that wasn't such a bright idea," I said.

He didn't say anything in response.

The second outlaw moved his horse into the herd as well, but the third swore at the other two and aimed his rifle at the Comanches.

"Ritter, you fool," the first yelled. "You pull that trigger, and we'll all—"

The gunshot rang out across the plain, sharp and fierce.

Surrey reared in surprise, and I snapped at the reins, spurring him forward. It led me deeper into the herd, but I didn't see any other options.

The noise startled the rest of the herd around us, but it hadn't caused a full-blown stampede. It was more like the buffalo had all gone from placid to alert, and Surrey galloping forward wasn't doing anything to calm them.

When several of the Comanche fired back, the buffalo went from alert to panicked, and all chaos broke out. They didn't move with any sort of purpose. Getting away from here was about all they cared about, even if that meant they became more densely pressed together.

The man behind me had spurred his horse on as well. I steered Surrey in and out of the herd as the rest of the buffalo got closer together. Much more of that, and I'd lose whatever sort of lead I had.

I looked over my shoulder. Surrey had maintained distance from the outlaw, but I didn't know how long he'd be able to do that. The one farther back had given up on the herd and headed to the south. The one who'd fired at the Comanches had gone north, but he paused and fired again as I watched.

The herd ran faster, and Surrey and I careened into a large bull, the glancing force of it enough to cause my horse to stumble and almost throw me from the saddle.

I grabbed my Remington and shot into the air, hoping the noise would be enough to startle them and clear a path for me. It was a desperate move, but I was seconds away from being trampled if I did nothing.

Behind me, a series of gunshots rang out one after the other.

As a giant mass, the buffalo pushed away from the shots, giving me a little space because of the noise I'd just made, but that only scared off the creatures that had been close enough to know I was

the one who had made it. There were plenty more behind them
that only knew they were running away from something worse.

I sawed Surrey's reins to the left, turning him to follow the flow
of the stampede. He could run faster than the buffalo, but there was
no way for him to maneuver his way clear of them. They started
to press in on my sides again. If they came too close, I'd almost
certainly be dragged down. I remembered the bloodied, torn face
of the cowboy who'd been trampled. That had been by a single bull.
This was thousands of buffalo, each of them at least half as big as
that one animal had been.

Another shot from my revolver moved the buffalo back again,
but when I tried to fire a third time, the gun did nothing but give a
small popping noise.

Squib round. I wouldn't be able to fire the gun again until I'd
cleared it.

I jammed the revolver back into my holster and freed the rifle
from my saddle scabbard.

The outlaw behind me fired into the air as well, then screamed as
his horse faltered. When I risked another glance back, there was no
sign of horse and rider at all. I was surrounded by rumbling, bellowing, panicked animals. It smelled like freshly plowed earth, and I felt
like I'd been caught inside a thundercloud, the noise alone shaking my
body. If anything, it reminded me of my encounter with the tornado.

What sort of a fool got himself into such a predicament twice
in the span of a few weeks?

I needed to get out of the main flow of the herd. Find somewhere I could begin to further separate myself. When I fired my rifle, I pushed Surrey to the right, hoping to edge our way to safety. It worked, though not as much as I would have liked. I fired again and again, my heart thumping like a drum as I could think of nothing else but escape. It wasn't working fast enough. We'd be caught, and Father would—

No. I wouldn't give up until I went down, and even then I'd keep fighting. I hadn't come all this way to just roll over and die.

I stood higher in my stirrups, desperate to find a place Surrey and I might be able to take cover. It was hard to make sense of the sea of moving beasts around me. I'd lost my bearings, along with all sight of the Comanches and the remaining outlaws.

An entire ocean of stampeding buffalo surrounded me, unbroken by any—

Fifty yards ahead sat a small rise in the ground, a cluster of rocks that the buffalo were moving around. If I went too far past it, there was no way I'd be able to get back there, but if I aimed just right, I might be able to stop on the far side of the boulders, where a tiny open space lay before the herd joined back together.

Three more shots. I'd lost count of how many I had left. Surrey kept moving. Animals pushed against us, and my horse missed a step. For a sickening moment, I felt him stumble and begin to fall. I raised my hands as if reaching out to someone who might save me, but Surrey managed to regain his balance and surge forward again.

Another shot. One more. The boulders were coming up far faster than I would have liked. I had too far to go. We'd be swept away from that piece of safety, never to be seen again.

When I went to fire my rifle, it clicked instead. Empty. I didn't have any way of controlling the stampede at all anymore. Instead, I ducked onto Surrey and spurred him on. To have come this far and gotten this close to what might have been safety would be far too—

The boulders were there, and Surrey made one last lunge for safety.

One final buffalo rammed into his hindquarters, spinning the two of us around and almost throwing Surrey to the ground. The hit shot us forward again, however, and when he managed to get his legs under him just before falling, we'd reached that small oasis of safety.

Surrey didn't need me to pull him to a stop. He pressed against the boulders, every bit as terrified as I was.

But alive, and in one piece.

Around us, the buffalo continued to race by, so many that it was easy to think they'd never end. A laugh broke out of me, whether from relief or nerves or just sheer joy that we'd come through this, I didn't know. Once it was free, I couldn't stop. The thought of how ill prepared someone like me was for all of this was too much. That I was still breathing was perhaps the funniest thing yet. The laughter turned to a mix of shouting and rage as I yelled at the herd, holding my rifle in the air and no doubt looking like a complete fool.

CHAPTER TWENTY-ONE

"It is reported here that the Benders, the notorious Kansas butchers, have been tracked to Northern Mexico. In consequence of there being no extradition between the United States and Mexico, they cannot be brought back except by kidnapping."

—Muscatine Weekly Journal
(Iowa), December 26, 1873

―――――

I WASN'T SURE HOW LONG IT took for the stampede to run its course. Time blended in a bewildering way as the train of buffalo continued past in an unbroken mass. Hearing anything over the din of the hooves was almost impossible.

Individually, each animal that raced past us did something different. Taken as a group, they turned into a constant stream, almost like water. Now and then one would come around the rise more sharply than the others, forcing me to shy closer and closer to the middle of the open space, but none of them took real notice of Surrey or me. They just wanted to get to wherever all the other buffalo were going. I wondered how that worked. How long would they run, and when would they decide it was safe again? Would one of them just give up, and the others would follow suit? It was easy to think they'd keep running forever, watching them now. That years later, they'd still be out on the prairie, always raging forward.

But they weren't limitless after all. At some point, the mass of creatures on either side of me grew thinner, and then the flood of animals was surging off to the east, leaving me quite alone.

The ground had been completely flattened across a wide swath of the prairie, the grasses pulverized, and the earth churned up in places. There was no sign of the outlaws or the Comanches, and I didn't waste time staying put to see if anyone showed up.

The next few days went without incident. After facing down those buffalo, I felt changed, somehow. More confident.

I had more time to think as I finished the ride to Washita. It rained the next day, and nothing brought the spirits down quite like sitting on a horse for mile after mile with water pelting you in the face. A good hat only kept out so much.

The Voice kept me company as I rode, and while I was willing to listen to it now that the Benders were getting near, I couldn't help wondering what, exactly, I'd do if I found them. Was I prepared to set my rifle up on some sort of overlook and wait for the chance to pick the family off, one by one?

Get close. See their eyes when you plunge in the knife. Watch the blood ooze out of—

The Voice could say what it liked, but I wanted something reliable. Better the Benders dead than me being close enough to revel in it properly. The Voice seemed willing to compromise. A picture came clearly into my head. Leaning there with a rocky outcropping digging into my elbows, John's head in my sights as I eased my finger onto the trigger. His head recoiling as—

A few times I caught myself questioning my sudden willingness to team up with the Voice. Was that how the Benders felt before they murdered one of their victims? If so, how would I be any different if I were to kill them in cold blood? I'd had more than enough time to think about my actions. Wasn't I the one who'd always talked about the importance of law?

Each time, I crushed the feeling as best I could. The Warren who'd ignored the Voice had let his father die. I was a new Warren. A better one. The old one always had to think things through a thousand different ways before he was ready to make a single move. The rest of the world didn't seem to do that, and they all got along just fine.

Besides, all the worrying ahead of time almost never made any real difference in the outcome. I had liked to think that if I just took the time to look at a problem from every angle, then I'd be able to make the right choice every time. Yet all too often, what ended up happening was something I hadn't anticipated at all, and so I had to make a last-minute decision anyway.

I wouldn't make that mistake with the Benders.

The closer I got to my destination, the more I had to hold back my desire to spur Surrey on faster than he could handle. As I traveled farther west, the prairie bled into hillier terrain, peppered with stunted trees and sagebrush. It was harder riding for my horse, so my progress was slower than ever. The heat kicked up as well, and I had no choice but to take longer breaks. Surrey had been with me through all this, and I felt guilty for what I was putting him through. He didn't deserve to be out in the wilderness. He should be at home, eating some oats and having nothing worse to fear than a long day of pulling the plow. He didn't complain, but that just made it worse for some reason.

Still, the miles kept going by, and I kept making progress. I knew where I was going, and I spotted Washita well before I was close enough for anyone in the town to take notice of me. I didn't know what I'd expected: A throng of people shouting and dueling in the streets? Brawls at all hours? The buildings flush with the riches of ill-gotten gains?

Whatever it was, it wasn't what I got. The "city" was mostly tents, with three or four timber-framed houses that hadn't been constructed particularly well. Really, it looked like any other town you might find in the wilderness. I didn't go close enough to see exactly, but I could spot a few forms sitting around, drinking or talking.

Perhaps things livened up at night, or they might have been

waiting for an unsuspecting young man from Missouri to wander in, but on the whole, Washita was a disappointment to the Voice.

Not all evil was evil all the time, apparently.

In any case, I escaped any run-ins with more outlaws, and I made it to the far side of the camp without incident. I might have questioned my luck, but I'd had more than my share of bad since I left home. It stood to reason I'd have some good sooner or later.

The directions the note had given were vague: "five miles west, small house, by three waterfalls." But I had time, and "waterfalls" was more than enough information to narrow the hunt down. There were only so many streams five miles away from Washita after all.

When I found them, it turned out "waterfalls" was a bit of a stretch. When I'd first read it, I'd pictured mountains and long cascading brooks. This was a series of small drops in a row, snaking through the closest thing to a forest I'd been to so far.

I had to lead Surrey through the trees, though thankfully there wasn't much in the way of undergrowth. I hobbled my horse by the waterfalls, tying his forelegs loosely together so he wouldn't wander too far. I took out my rifle and checked to make sure it was fully loaded, then did the same for my revolver.

My mind kept running through different scenarios, and I chewed on the inside of my lip as I tried to think things through. What would I do if I got there and they saw me? What if they shot at me? What if they didn't? What if it was just Kate and John? What if they had too many—

No. The time for thinking things through was done. I'd find where they were, and then I'd make decisions based on that.

I used the lessons Father had given me about moving quietly in the wilderness: Taking my time. Stepping on the balls of my feet. Being aware of what was around me. It had been a while, but I'd practiced them enough over the years that I wasn't too rusty. The whole point right now was to find their cabin without being seen.

To do that, I paid attention to the sounds that were already around me, and then I did my best to make sure the sounds that came from me blended in with the sounds that were already there. I didn't have to worry about my scent, or at least, I hoped not. If they had hounds, I could be in trouble.

I slowly made my way through the forest, avoiding making loud rustling noises, and keeping an eye out for a clearing or a sign of life. My heart was pounding like a fast-beating bass drum, and my face felt flushed.

I took a few deep breaths, centered myself, and kept going.

About five hundred yards upstream from where I'd started, the forest opened in a small man-made clearing. It was so new, there were still tree stumps littered across it, though judging by the rot on those stumps, it was more a case of the people who cleared the area being too lazy to do it right.

In the middle of it sat a one-room cabin, maybe two-thirds the size of the Benders' place in Kansas. This one was more sturdily built, with thick log walls and a sense of stability the earlier one lacked. No smoke poured from the stone chimney; no animals were in sight outside, though a small building that could be used as a stable had been built thirty feet away from the cabin. All doors were closed.

I pressed myself against a tree, then settled in to wait.

After a quarter of an hour, my pulse had slowed, and I'd had time to examine more aspects of the cabin: The way the path up to the front door was scattered with dead leaves. How weeds peeked up from between some of the boards of the front stoop. None of them had been stepped on or appeared stunted. Either whoever lived here really liked having weeds take over their house, or no one had been here in quite some time.

Beyond that, there were no other signs of life. No noises from inside the cabin. No shifting of a horse from the outbuilding. Instead, I just listened to the breeze through the branches above me. Birds calling to each other. The stream burbling happily behind me.

Even then, I gave it another slow count to a thousand. I hadn't come all this way to be done in by impatience now, and just because I didn't think there was anyone there didn't mean they weren't about to come back.

Or had they already left?

I tried to ignore that thought and focus on the here and now. There'd be time enough for wondering once I knew what was really happening here.

At last, I edged back around the tree and crept forward the last twenty yards to the cabin. My eyes were stuck to the building's windows, straining to catch any glimpse of movement from inside. If someone were there, I couldn't imagine they'd be expecting me enough to lay an ambush, but I didn't want to be caught unprepared. I held my rifle cocked and at the ready, my finger next to the trigger.

Nothing changed.

Once I arrived at the cabin, I crouched underneath one of the windows, took off my hat, and slowly raised myself until I could just peek over the sill.

It was another one-room affair. A table, a few crude chairs, two sleeping pallets, and a hutch. The fireplace would be the only source of heat in the place.

And all of it was empty.

This presented a new range of problems, though it also let me breathe easier for the moment, some of the tension draining from my shoulders. Was it possible I'd already fallen behind them? The dates didn't add up, unless I'd misinterpreted some of the messages. If that were the case, then I had no idea where I'd be able to pick up the trail again.

It would be better if they hadn't arrived yet, but if that were true, why was the cabin empty? *Someone* had been sending those coded messages to the Benders. Someone had instructed them to come here. Why not be waiting here for them when they arrived?

They might be back in Washita, keeping an eye out for the Benders. Or could it be some sort of trap for the Benders, with the accomplice planning to ambush them? If I were to go into the cabin, would I risk stepping into the middle of something I didn't understand?

That had happened weeks ago, and I was still doing my best to drag myself out of the mess.

The likelier explanation was that the accomplice was in Washita and only coming here now and then to check and make sure the Benders hadn't somehow gotten by unseen. They'd then use this place for a few days to make their final plans and split the bounty.

It had now been an hour that I'd been scurrying around, trying to keep hidden. I didn't fancy the idea of spending another few days or a week doing the same thing, and another plan presented itself to me. If I could find a place to set Surrey up, I could move into the cabin myself and lie in wait for when the Benders—or anyone else—arrived. Set an ambush of my own. If I were to confront them with my revolver drawn and pointed at them right from the beginning, they'd almost have to go along with what I said, wouldn't they?

And if I did that, then I'd be able to find out if Kate was a willing accomplice or if she'd just been dragged into this like a victim. I was almost sure she was in on all of it, but in my heart, there was too much room between "almost" and "sure," no matter what my brain or the Voice said. The memory of the way she'd looked at me, full of admiration and respect, was just too strong for me to ignore. No other girl had ever done more than say hello to me.

I set my rifle down and got to work. The sooner I was in place, the better.

The outbuilding had spaces for two horses. I set Surrey up in one of them, reasoning that if—*when*—the Benders came, they wouldn't be likely to head straight to the stable but come to the cabin first. And if they didn't do that, I could still come out from hiding before they caught sight of my horse. The whole point was to surprise them, and if Surrey were anywhere else, it would be hard to be certain they wouldn't see him.

Besides, they might assume my horse just belonged to the mysterious accomplice.

I kept an ear out for any sounds out of the ordinary as I rubbed Surrey down and got him some food and water. The stable was stocked with fresh hay, so it definitely hadn't been abandoned. Someone was coming here regularly, which spurred me to move faster.

Once I had Surrey situated, I took my saddlebags and brought them into the cabin. I'd be able to live on the food I had on me without having to light a fire for a few days. By then, I'd have had enough time to come up with an alternate plan if I needed to. For now, I settled in for the waiting to begin.

It didn't help that there was nothing to see in the cabin. No pieces of paper. No books. No belongings. Nothing in the straw sleeping pallets. No hidden cellar of terror either. If it hadn't been for the note I'd found at the Benders' describing this location, there would be nothing here to lead me to believe it was special.

I spent the next two days in that cabin, trying to find the best way to keep an eye on the outside. There was a crack in the door about two feet up from the bottom. High enough that I couldn't just look through it while I was lying down, but low enough that I had to crouch to be able to see through it. I ended up stacking both pallets on top of each other and placing them right by the door.

With all the spare time I had, I should have been able to come up with a plan that would have been perfect for the situation, but I couldn't think of anything other than what I was already doing. If the Benders came—or anyone else—I'd surprise them with my gun drawn, not giving them a chance to fire back. I wasn't going to kill them in cold blood, but if they tried to get away or do anything suspicious, I wanted to be in a situation where I could defend myself.

I cleaned my revolver and my rifle, examining them both for any signs of wear. The rifle was fine, but the Remington still had issues no matter how hard I tried to fix them. I took out each bullet and studied them to make sure they were sound, though I wasn't quite sure how I'd know. I weighed a bullet in my hand. Something so small could do so much damage, just depending on how it was used. I wanted to be that sort of person. You didn't need to be well-known or rich or a genius. You just had to do your job and do it well.

The worst thing about those two days was the way the Voice would start up a conversation with me and never stop. It still obsessed over violence, but it also liked to tell me how I was doing everything wrong. How I was a failure, and how it was my fault all this had happened. Too slow to recognize evil when I saw it. Too gullible when I saw a séance. Too poor of an outdoorsman.

And I didn't disagree with any of it. Any of my brothers would have done a better job than this. I was the least equipped Bullock to try and handle it, a fact I tried to tell the Voice each time it popped those thoughts into my head. But each time, it was too easy for it to respond that Father had been younger than I was now when he'd been running back and forth with shipping caravans in the west, fighting off bandits and getting the sort of experience I'd admired so much.

I felt like a child who liked to play pretend but then had been thrown into the middle of make-believe made real. Hadn't I always thought when I was younger how I'd want to be the one to ride after a villain and bring him to justice? I'd played sheriff, mimicking what I'd see Father do. I'd read stories by Poe and Verne and imagined I was on an adventure, the hero of a story.

Adventures weren't nearly as nice when they came on you in real life. They had storms you couldn't handle and dangers you didn't suspect, and there was no one there telling you what to do or how to fix it.

Two days into my stay, someone finally came up the road to the cabin.

CHAPTER TWENTY-TWO

"The question was asked the Colonel whether he believed the murders were committed for money or on account of Kate's diabolism or superstition. Colonel York thought that robbery was the object of the murders. Kate was avaricious, and would go to any lengths to get money."

—Deseret News

(Salt Lake City, Utah), June 4, 1873

═══════════

T HERE'S ONLY SO LONG YOU can lie on straw, staring through a crack in the door, before you start to lose your focus. Yes, I took breaks to check on Surrey, eat, and do the other chores I'd mentioned, but most of the time, I did my best to stay on task, revolver and rifle ready, my eye scanning the path leading to the cabin for any signs of movement.

At least, that's what I thought I was doing. I saw two snakes, three foxes, a deer, multiple squirrels, and too many birds to count, but when a man actually appeared, I only noticed he was getting close because he was humming to himself. My eyes shot open, and I realized I'd fallen asleep at some point in my vigil. I gathered my thoughts and hurried to peer through the crack.

An old man with a long bushy gray beard strolled up to the cabin, only a little more than ten yards away. He was dressed simply, with a homespun jacket and pants and a brown hat that might have been eaten by a cow at some point in the recent past. He was rail thin, of average height, though with a stoop to his shoulders, and had a slight limp, favoring his right leg.

He was also unarmed.

I scrambled to my feet, grabbed my revolver, and threw open the door, stumbling a little over the pallets as I hurried outside. The man stopped in the middle of the path, his arms halfway raised, his jaw slack with surprise.

"Stay where you are," I said.

"Hold on there, son. Take it easy."

I strode up to him, keeping my gun leveled on him at all times. It didn't take long to pat him down to see if he had any weapons, and I came up with a large knife and nothing else. He let me do it, standing still the entire time. I swung around behind him on the path, then motioned with my revolver for him to head into the cabin.

"Is this some kind of robbery?" he asked, his voice a little quavering. "You been in my house. You know there ain't nothin' in there worth havin'. But you can have whatever you want, if you find it. I'd like to know what it is, though."

We went inside, and I pointed him to a seat. Again, he went along with my commands without protest. "You sure you got the right man, son?"

Shoot him between the eyes. Watch him slump down to the floor in a pool of blood, his eyes vacant.

"I know everything," I said.

"Then you're one up on me. I don't rightly know a thing. At least nothin' I'd go writin' home about. Care to fill me in?"

He didn't seem like the sort of person who would team up with the Benders. More like a likeable old grandfather, sitting at the table with his hands in the air. "You've been working with the Benders," I said. "I found your notes. They didn't see the last one you sent. Maybe you've been waiting for them longer than you thought?"

"The who? We didn't properly meet, did we? The name's Missouri Bill, since I come from Missouri. Ain't been back there in—"

"What have you been doing with them?" I cut in.

He put his arms down a fraction, then slowly began to lean toward the table. "Mind if I rest 'em on the table some? Got the arthritis in my shoulders, and if I—" His elbows reached the table, and he let out a long sigh. "There. That's better. Can't hardly think when I got my arms up like that. Havin' a gun shoved in my face don't help much either, though."

"What's your connection to the Benders?" I repeated, wishing I didn't sound so much like a whiny child.

"I have not got one single idea what in the world you're talkin' about. Benders? What do they bend? Do you mean some kind of blacksmith?"

"The Germans. Don't play the fool. You told them to meet you here. You've been fencing the things they stole." I couldn't keep the doubt from creeping into my voice, however. The man had been coming to the cabin, sure, but he had an open face with smile lines at the corners of his eyes. And that stoop made him seem even more harmless. What proof did I have that this was where the Benders were coming? There wasn't one piece of evidence in the cabin or the shed.

"You seem like a nice boy. A little addled, maybe, but I like the look of you. Why don't you put down that gun and just ask me for help like a normal person? Heaven knows you're gonna need it. Don't you know Washita's not more 'n five miles east of here? If I'd'a been one of them outlaws, you'd be suckin' air through a new hole in your face before you could've said more than two words."

Shoot him now! Rush forward and slice him open. Carve him up like a deer.

I almost squeezed the trigger before I caught myself. I was still in control, not the Voice. The Benders weren't here yet, so it would have to wait. My gun dipped slightly. How did I know the man was the Benders' accomplice? But wouldn't someone say the same thing, no matter what sort of person they were?

"What do I need to do to get you to trust me?" he asked. His voice was kind, if a touch exasperated.

"What were you coming out here for?"

"I'm supposed to keep an eye on the place. I don't know why. They don't pay me enough to ask questions like that. But once a week, I'm to come out here and make sure it's all in good shape."

That made sense. "Who pays you?"

"This close to Washita? A man who wants to live longer than five minutes learns fast not to ask questions like that."

"And you've never heard of the Benders?"

"I'd be on my way back to town ten minutes ago if you weren't forcin' me to sit here. If you don't want my help, could you at least just let me go?"

"Where would you go back to? I thought Washita was full of outlaws."

"It is. And yes, I live there. I wasn't the world's most honest man when I was twenty years younger. Let's just say there are some who'd love to see me at the short end of a long rope. I can't say I'm proud of what I done, but I did it, and that's that. And Washita ain't so bad, as long as you know how not to make trouble."

I edged a few steps closer to the table. "They're a German family. An older couple who don't speak much English, and two children a bit older than me. Kate's pretty, and John laughs like a hyena. You'd know them."

He twisted his lips to the side and stared up at the ceiling.

"Sounds like I'd know 'em for sure. But I ain't seen no Germans here in well over a year and a half, and those ones were all headed west for Oregon, if you can believe it. Why they picked the most dangerous spot in the world to travel through is beyond me, but you never know, with Germans."

I had to make a choice. Again. Either stand here with my gun trained on the man for who knew how much longer, or give him a chance. He was far from spry. What did I think he was going to do? Suddenly leap up and club me over the head? It would probably make him faint to move that quickly.

"They killed my father," I said, holstering my gun, but keeping track of the old man out of the corner of my eye. Instead of lunging toward me, he rested his forehead on the table for a moment, his shoulders slumping in relief.

He froze for a moment, then cleared his throat. "They killed… Are you sure?"

"I saw his body myself. Dug it up in their fruit orchard. Yes. I'm sure."

He shook his head, seeming to gather himself, then continued. "That's—*murdered*? I'm sorry about your pa. This world can be an awful place, and don't I know it. And, well, since it looks like you've decided not to kill me, why don't you tell me what's goin' on, and then I can see if I can't do somethin' to help."

I leaned away to stay mostly out of range, dragging another chair closer to me to make sure I had plenty of space—and my right hand was free to go for my gun, if it needed to—and then proceeded to launch into my story for what felt like the tenth time. In many ways, it reminded me of my experience with Leroy. I didn't necessarily believe in providence, but would it be too much to expect that after what had happened to Father, I'd get lucky enough to fall in with two men who could really help me, almost by accident?

Bill grunted with interest and kept asking questions, clearly amazed at what I'd been through and disgusted by what the Benders had done. "There's times I wish I lived closer to where folks actually have half a clue what's goin' on," he said. "I ain't heard nothin' like that before in my life. A whole family? The girl too?"

"I'm not sure," I said. "I think she must be involved somehow, but I'd like to think it's not entirely of her own choice."

"Never can tell, with women. 'Specially strange women, and from what you been tellin' me, she's stranger than most."

Don't trust him. Don't trust anyone. Not until we get to the Benders.

I didn't know what to say to that, so I said nothing. The Voice was calming down now, and I was feeling looser around Bill. To put things to the test, I moved nearer to the table, my hand ready for any fast moves he might make. He didn't try anything at all.

The past few weeks of travel had made me not trust anyone, but how many times had that proven to be unjustified? All of them, if you didn't count the Benders. Of course, that was a big exception.

I launched into a discussion of the coded messages I'd found and what I thought they meant. Bill listened and asked to see them. Once I had them spread out on the table, he examined them one by one, holding them up to the window as if he might see something I had missed.

"These Benders need to have their heads looked at," he said at last, putting the last message back on the table and sitting back.

"Do you think this is the right place?" I asked.

"I been livin' here for years, and I don't know of no other place next to three waterfalls. This is the only place it *could* be."

"So whoever's paying you is working with them."

He pursed his lips together and ran a hand through his hair, his eyes wide and bewildered. "I 'spose so. I only wish I knew who it was, so I could help you some. Was your plan really just to sit here and get the jump on 'em?"

"Unless you have any better ideas," I said. "It seemed reliable to me. No need to make an ambush any more elaborate than it needed to be."

He thought in silence for a while, and when he spoke, he sat up and almost managed to square his shoulders. "Oh, it's not a bad idea, exactly. But it's hard to do with just yourself. Four against one, and that's thinkin' they don't bring their buddy with them? Sometimes it don't matter if you get the jump on someone. You can't watch five people at once. Still, I feel responsible for it somehow. All that money I been takin' has come from folks with their throats slit? That don't sit too good in my stomach. You open to someone helpin' you with this?"

I couldn't keep the skepticism from my voice. "Do you have much experience handling murderous families?"

"I may have a gimp back these days, son, but I wasn't always sixty-two. You gotta be able to hold your own when you're livin' in a place as wild as Indian Territory. Besides, I count two guns and one person. Unless you got a talent for shootin' with both hands at the same time, you'd be better served havin' me standin' beside you usin' whichever of those you're worse at."

It was one thing to trust a complete stranger because they had an honest face. But to give him my revolver or my rifle?

He held up his hands again. "No, that was too much of me to ask, what with us only just gettin' acquainted. What if you was to give me one of 'em, but keep the bullets for yourself. Them Benders don't need to know I'm goin' in empty."

"And if they somehow fight back? You'd be helpless."

"Like I said, I feel responsible somewhat. A man's gotta pay his debts. Could be your pa's dead in part because of me. I'd like to make that up to you."

It was a ridiculous suggestion, but it also convinced me he was in earnest.

Shoot him. Hide the body and wait for the Benders. You need to know you can go through with it. Everything gets better with practice.

I took out my revolver and pointed it at the man, my finger on the trigger.

He licked his lips. "You need to think about this. I'm tellin' you, you need help if you're goin' up against four murderers."

Do it! Pull the trigger. Watch the spray of splatter bloom on the wall behind him.

It would be so easy, and I'd been waiting for so long. Didn't the Voice have a point? If I wanted to be ready for the Benders, I needed to know I could kill a man. Needed to be able not to hesitate.

My finger began to tighten, but then I remembered Father.

Justice and the Bullocks were supposed to be one and the same, and this man might well be innocent.

I'd told the Voice I'd follow it once the Benders were here. People who really deserved its attention.

I took my finger off the trigger, placed the gun on the table, and pushed it toward the man. "But don't shoot unless you absolutely have to," I cautioned him.

He took the revolver and spun the cylinder. "I hate to argue, but you might be better off assumin' you're gonna have to pull a trigger or two in the near future. In my experience, people like them Benders don't take kindly to bein' threatened. That said, I'm gonna tell you somethin' now, and I don't want you to go all squirrely on me because of it."

Something had changed in his tone, and my stomach plummeted.

Idiot! You had your chance, and you wasted it. Don't trust anyone. Kill them all.

"What are you talking about?" I asked, trying to keep my voice steady.

"It's just, I may not have been entirely tellin' the truth just a bit earlier." He snapped the revolver back together and put it down on the table. "In my experience, it's always a good idea to tell someone with a gun whatever it is they want to hear. But mind you, I'm still on your side. It's just I'd hate to start this under…less-than-favorable circumstances."

How long would it take me to grab my rifle and bring it to bear? Much longer than it would take him to shoot me in the head. Now I was the one frozen in place. How could I have come this far, only to make a mistake at the end? Any Bullock would have been able to tell who to trust and who to steer clear of.

"Breathe easy, son. I ain't gonna shoot you." He fished around beneath the table, then brought out a second revolver, held in his other hand. "If I'd wanted you dead, I could've tried it before now." He placed them both down, stood, and backed away from the table with his arms raised.

I darted forward and grabbed both guns, staring from them to Bill in confusion. "I don't understand."

"Me 'n' the Benders, we've had an understanding these past three years. They were stealin' from folks without the sense to steer clear of 'em, and I was takin' what they stole and sellin' it. Sure, some of it come to me a little stained, if you see what I mean, but them Benders swore up and down no one died. That's important to me. I may be a no-good thief, but I don't hold with murder. There's some things a man ain't supposed to do, and don't I know what's at the top of that list. I mean, look at the messages I sent 'em. Yes, they're mine. I was the one to come up with the idea for the code. Figured nobody would catch on to it, and there you done it in less than three blinks. But any which way, none of them messages talk about dead bodies or bloodshed."

"So you went along with it all this time, and you want me to believe you didn't know?"

Shoot him in the head. Club him over his ear. Take the revolver and shove the barrel down his throat and—

"I'd say I was sorry, son, but I know how empty that'd sound. And I'd like to make it up to you now, if I can. That's why I'm showin' you my cards, so to speak. Your pa's dead, and I regret it. The Benders are comin' here today. I seen 'em in town not more than an hour ago. We was supposed to balance the books and be done with it all today. I gave 'em directions to this cabin and said I'd go on ahead and get things ready. So if you and I—"

I held up my hand, cutting him off. It had been faint, but I had just heard…

Voices coming toward the cabin. John's titter cut through the air, sending a shiver down my back. It had been annoying before. Knowing what he'd done now, it was anything but.

"They're here," I said.

The Voice went silent, listening.

Some decisions had to be made in the moment, and right then I knew I couldn't watch Bill and get the jump on the Benders at the same time. So I leaned forward and put his gun back on the table, then signaled to Bill to get ready. "You welcome them in," I whispered. "I'll hide behind the door and ambush them once they're all here. No one gets away."

He grabbed the gun and hurried over to the door, waiting for me to get situated before heading out.

This was it. If he really was with the Benders, he'd only have to tell them I was here, and it would be five to one. If that was the case, I'd start firing at them as soon as I could—another reason I'd had Bill go outside. I'd rather be in a place I could defend if things turned bad.

"See?" Bill called out. The walls of the cabin did little to muffle his voice. "Safe as a sleepin' baby, just like I told you."

John answered, though it was harder to hear him. Kate said something as well, and I tightened my jaw in excitement and anger. I'd done it! Hundreds of people searching after the Benders, and I'd tracked them down hundreds of miles deep into the wilderness.

"Well, come on in," Bill said. "Set yourself down for a while. I got all the money down under a floorboard. We'll have it out and get it split."

My hands were shaking, and my right leg was following suit.

Was I supposed to use my revolver or my rifle? In a room this size, with them so close, the revolver would be more reliable, so I leaned my rifle against the wall and pressed myself next to it, trying to keep my breathing level. I didn't want to do anything that might let the Benders know I was here. What if they checked in the shed and saw Surrey? Or what if my horse made noise and attracted them? Who should I aim at to keep all of them in line? Was Kate the leader or a victim as well?

John would be the one who presented the most danger. Pa Bender might have been a threat when he was younger, but I doubted he could move very quickly these days, and Ma Bender didn't intimidate me at all. John, on the other hand, might overwhelm me if something went wrong.

"I want to be out of here in an hour," Kate said as they approached. "We don't have time for lazing around, after that delay in Red River put us so far behind schedule."

"Don't get antsy," Bill said. "If it were me, I'd take the chance to sleep somewhere with a roof over my head, but you can go on wherever you want once this is done. But I don't want any of you sayin' I pulled anythin' fishy. We started friends and we end friends, right?"

"Right," John said, his high-pitched laugh making it sound much more sinister than he might have intended.

I held the gun up in front of me, making sure I'd be ready as soon as they were all in. And if they came in one at a time, more slowly? My plan suddenly seemed to have a hundred different ways it could go wrong. I'd had the whole journey to think of ways I'd deal with the Benders when I found them, and I'd gone over many different scenarios in that time. None of them seemed to have prepared me for what I was facing now.

The door creaked open, and Pa and Ma Bender walked into the room, followed by Kate. Just a few seconds more.

The sound of heavy footsteps came from outside, as someone ran a few steps forward. Before I could understand what was happening, someone slammed into the door from outside. It hit me in the hand and then the face. My revolver went flying, and my head hit the wall.

I had enough time to feel the sick twist of dread and confusion before whoever had hit the door gave it another blow, and I blacked out.

CHAPTER TWENTY-THREE

"WHEREAS, said persons are at large and fugitives from justice, now therefore, I, Thomas A. Osborn, Governor of the State of Kansas, in pursuance of law, do hereby offer a REWARD OF FIVE HUNDRED DOLLARS for the apprehension and delivery to the Sheriff of Labette County, Kansas, of each of the person above named."

—Topeka, Kansas, May 17, 1873

—————

A BUCKET OF WATER HIT ME in the face, and I spluttered and spat in surprise. I tried to sit up, only to discover my hands had been bound behind my back. Some kind of rag had been shoved into my mouth and tied there, tasting of dirt and grease. I blinked my eyes clear.

"Free piece of advice," Bill said, looking down at me. "You should learn to be a little less trustin' of people you don't know." The rag muffled my cries.

You're a waste of life. A dishonor to the Bullocks. Completely incompetent.

The Voice had already given up on me.

Bill walked back to the table, where the Benders were sitting around, staring at me. Pa had a dark expression, holding a hammer that he kept flipping around in his hands. Ma slumped in boredom or fatigue, wearing the same black dress I'd seen her in the first time, though she'd added a belt that had a large knife sheathed on it. John had his elbows on the table, leaning forward and smiling at me. Kate had her arms folded and her head down in a way that was hard to read. I lay in the far corner, my feet tied together as well.

Bill continued. "We just been havin' a bit of a discussion around what we should do with you. Pa and Ma were all for slicing your throat, but I told 'em I wouldn't be part of it."

"I don't know why," John said, then laughed. "We been killin' the rest of 'em."

"It's completely different when I have to look at it," Bill said. "I don't abide killin', and that don't enter into what I been doin' the past three years. I'm a thief, not a murderer. If I'd wanted him dead, I'd'a shot him before you came."

"So what do you think we should do with Warren, exactly?" John asked. "You goin' with Kate, and you wanna bring him with us?"

"This is ridiculous." Kate stood up and put her finger in John's face. "We don't know what he knows. You were the one who said we'd be completely safe here. What if he talked to someone? What if he told someone where he was headed?"

John waved his hand in dismissal. "He don't got the brains for that. He fell for your séance routine, didn't he?"

"That wasn't a routine, and you know it," she snapped back.

He swallowed, a flash of unease passing over his face before he regained his composure. "I ain't got time for debatin'. I went along with it, just like I always do, didn't I?"

John turned to his parents and switched over to German. They responded with what sounded like short answers. I couldn't tell if they were angry, or it was just that the language made them sound that way.

"No fair speakin' so the rest of us can't follow," Bill said.

"If I wanted you to understand, I'd talk so you could," John shot back. The discussion quickly deteriorated into a shouting match, with John and Bill leading the argument, but Pa and Ma inserting comments in half English now and then.

It felt like someone had carved out my insides. How could I have fallen for Bill? Father wouldn't have done something that boneheaded. He would have been able to handle the entire trip on his own. No Leroy. No tornadoes. He would have caught the Benders the moment he walked into their cabin back in Kansas.

Except he hadn't, had he? He'd gone into the Benders' cabin, and he hadn't come out alive again. And why had I even ended up in this place to begin with?

A hot ember of anger grew inside me. With as many brothers

as I had, why in the world had it fallen to me to do this? I was doomed from the beginning, and by all rights, I never should have gone. Why hadn't I just given in to the Voice long before? Killed the Benders in their sleep. If I'd never fought against those thoughts, I wouldn't be here either. Any other decision I'd made along the way would likely have led to a better outcome.

And yet here I was.

"There's no way I'm bringin' it all out in the open with you all here," Bill shouted. "I'd have to be as dense as a bag of bricks to fall for that. Four on one, and the four with all the practice in the world at killin' folks?"

"So you expect us to just let you leave and trust you gave us our fair portion?" John asked, then tittered as if he'd made a good joke.

"I got it all wrote down," Bill said, slapping a piece of paper on the table. "Every penny. I may be me a thief, but I ain't a cheat."

"We could kill you now, when we wanted to," Pa Bender chimed in with his thick German accent. "Easy easy."

"And I could have run off with all the money and left you nothin'," Bill came back. "Easy easy. I don't figure how you trust a man for three years and then all of a sudden think he's gonna turn on you at the last minute."

"Money does strange things," John said. "And Pa don't think what you wrote down is enough."

Bill's face had darkened to a deep purple that seemed even starker against his white beard. "He don't, don't he?"

Pa took a small booklet out of his jacket pocket and held it up. "I have also notes taken," he said. "Everything."

"That's as may be, but you can't just go around sellin' stuff that's stolen as easy as you can in a store."

On and on they went, with no sign that they were going to reach an agreement anytime soon. They broke things up now and then by turning the subject back to me, as if by switching things up, it might give them some resolution to something. Anything. After long enough, I closed my eyes, wishing it would all just end now. I didn't see a way out of this for me. My only consolation (if you could call it that) was that Kate didn't want me dead, apparently.

"You've got to help me," Kate said in a low voice.

I opened my eyes to see she'd left the table and come to sit on the floor next to me, though she was watching the argument, not me. The Voice flared back to life.

Lunge forward. Knock her to the ground and rip at her throat. Blood all—

If I could have said something back to her, I would have tried. As it was, the cloth muffled everything. If I thought about it too much, it made me want to gag.

"None of this is going the way it was supposed to," she continued, her voice rushed, with more than an edge of panic. "I'm worried. Ever since this began, it's only gotten worse, and now I feel like we're all doomed to die for what we did. And I know what you must think of me and what I deserve, and I can't say I blame you for it.

It's how I would feel if I were on your side of this. But you have to *understand*. And maybe if you can understand, then—then perhaps you'll be willing to help me at least live past the end of the day."

I continued to stare, not quite sure of what I was hearing and struggling with the thoughts the Voice was shouting at me.

You've got one more chance at revenge. You said you'd kill them when you could. You could at least kill one of them before the rest of them get you.

"We didn't come to America to do this." Her voice was shaking. She took a deep breath to try to calm herself, then put her back against the log wall. "All we wanted to do was come and make a place for ourselves, just like everyone else. But we couldn't seem to get ahead of anything, and things went from bad to worse. It didn't help that so many people looked down at us for some reason. So we couldn't spell. So I behaved a little differently. I tried *so hard* to fit in. It never worked."

The Voice quieted. For a moment, I saw far more of myself in her than I wanted to. Was she just trying to manipulate me, or did she mean it? And did it matter? She was talking to me. Was there some way I could convince her to let me go, even if I couldn't speak?

"The first one was the hardest. We didn't even know who he was. He came to stay the night, and he...tried to be with me while we slept. John came running over and hit him on the back of the head with a hammer. We weren't sure what else to do. We didn't kill him. Not at first. But the hammer blow had done something to his brain. He wasn't the same, and we worried what would happen if anyone were to find out."

My eyes flicked from her face to the argument to the door and back again. I raised my eyebrows to try to show the movement had meaning, and I jerked my head toward the door as well. Would she understand? If she was so worried about what was going to happen, we could just run away while they weren't looking.

I might as well have not done anything. She just continued. "Killing him seemed to be the charitable thing to do, at that point. Ma said so, at least. The first blow had been done in self-defense, and letting him live like that for the next ever? God wouldn't want it. So Ma sliced his throat, the same way she did when she was butchering hogs. You'd think it would be different: killing pigs and killing people. You'd think something would happen to stop you. Murder is evil, or so I'd always thought. God hated those who did it. But God didn't do anything to stop her. It was just another Tuesday, though I wish I could forget the way the blood drained down his throat and into his shirt collar."

Bill and John were standing a foot apart, yelling into each other's faces as Bill jabbed his finger into John's chest repeatedly, but by now, Kate's words had transfixed me. Or at least, they had transfixed the Voice. She was talking about what it had always wanted me to do.

"It only made sense to sell what the man had brought with him. That's what John said, and he convinced Pa and Ma of it as well.

We couldn't very well let other people see all the man's possessions. They might get the wrong impression. Folk aren't so trusting on the frontier after all. You could get a stretched neck long before you could offer a reasonable explanation. John had met Bill in Ladore a half year before, and the two of them had become friends. My brother said Bill had a…more relaxed view of morality. He broached the subject with him, carefully of course, and he came to an arrangement. Bill would sell what we had and keep forty percent of whatever came in. John brought all of it over to Bill in the middle of the night, and just like that, the man we'd killed had effectively disappeared."

She smoothed her dress out on the floor and then picked at a loose splinter on one of the floorboards. The argument from the other side of the room might as well not be happening.

"None of that changed the fact I couldn't sleep for a week. It felt like I couldn't close my eyes without hearing the way he'd gurgled at the end. After a month, Bill brought us our part of the proceeds. They came at a perfect time. We hadn't had enough to eat for a week, and it was looking more and more like we were going to have to give up on our dreams. But with that money, we'd be able to last at least another few months. And as much as it had disturbed me, I had to admit nothing had come of the killing, though some boys had found the man's body floating facedown in a river. It didn't seem like anyone cared. What was one more dead person in a place flooded with strangers?

"And it had been so *easy*. John kept coming back to that fact, and then he began to talk about how we might do it again, if we wanted to do it on purpose. If there were just a curtain strung up across the middle of the room, he could wait behind it, and we could usher a guest into the seat right next to the curtain. If it were loose enough, John could strike the blow without even having to see the man, so long as he could see the man's shadow against the curtain."

Was she telling me the truth? The way she said it, it sounded so reasonable, as if anyone could have made the same decision in her shoes.

"We'd only kill people who deserved it. I insisted on that, though I prayed to God afterward that I had done more to try and stop it. But I was weak. Somehow it seemed to make sense that it would be all right if they were bad. We'd meet them, see what they were like, and decide if they were someone who had a right to the life he was living. Only men too. They'd be all too willing to come see us, on account of me. John even encouraged me to dress more provocatively. It would be easier to tell what sort of man we were dealing with that way. Faster too."

What had they thought about me? And how had they justified killing George Longcor's baby? And my father? No. What she said didn't add up. I refused to believe anyone would think Father worth killing. Yes, he had a temper, and he could be preachy and obstinate at times, but if those were killing offenses, most of the country would be long dead.

"You know what I learned from all of it? The worst of all?" She looked me in the eye for the first time in a while, and I tried to encourage her to let me loose again, but her eyes were far away.

"Everything becomes normal after a while. The second time wasn't as difficult as the first, and by the fifth, even I wasn't offering much of an objection, though it shames me to say it. We killed at least fifteen or twenty men over the past three years. Enough that they began to bleed together in my mind. Each time was the same. Dead, they're just like any other carcass. Alive, they weren't that different either. We wanted to kill you, that night. John did, at least. I was against it. I said you hadn't done enough to deserve it, and you had a kind face.

"But we'd killed your pa, and you seemed like you wouldn't give up about it. And then that séance...I'd never had any of them come on that strongly. Ordering you to come to Indian Territory? Where had that come from? It scared me. Made me think perhaps something from the beyond would come for us. After you left, I decided enough was enough, and I was finally strong enough to convince my family to put an end to all of it. We packed up what we needed and left that very night. We'd had plans in place. Though we didn't think for a minute anyone would ever be able to guess where we were headed and get here ahead of us. Then again, we also hadn't counted on missing Bill's message or the mess that ended up being in Red River."

She blinked, her eyes focusing again, though she still took no real note of me, instead turning her attention back to the argument. It had quieted down a few levels, with Pa speaking in a string of German in a low tone, John translating for Bill.

"I don't know what they expected," Kate continued in a murmur. "This was always waiting for us, sooner or later. I've been around Bill enough to know he can get violent, and my brother isn't exactly someone with a long temper. If things take a turn for the worse, it would be helpful to have someone with me who'd be willing to stand up for me."

After all the hints I'd been trying to send her, it took me a moment to realize what she was getting at. I made eye contact with her and tried to say something again. She leaned forward and untied the rope around my face, then took the rag out of my mouth. "But stay quiet," she said. "They're only distracted for now."

Wait. Yes. Wait, and you can kill them all.

None of the others took any interest in us. It helped that we were off to the side, away from any of their sight lines. It also helped that they were just a few degrees away from punching each other.

"How much of this were you really involved with?" I asked in a low voice.

Her shoulders slumped even farther, as if my words had made her wilt. "Of course. Why would you believe anything I had to say?"

"I couldn't," I admitted. "But I'd feel better helping you if I could."

"You're helping yourself at this point," Kate said. "As soon as they've finished bickering, they're going to start wondering what to do about you again. Knowing my family, there's only so long I can keep them from killing you. And at this point, I'm beginning to be convinced there's only so long before they decide to kill me too. John's already been calling me weak. He says I'll end up giving the rest of them away."

At least she had the courtesy to sound like she'd regret my death.

"What would we even do?" I asked.

Grab a knife and let yourself loose. Give in to what you've always been meant to be. Stabbing. Slashing. Cutting. Sawing. Twisting the blade after it's in. Feeling their flesh—

"If we could overpower Bill, that would be the first step. He might talk about how he doesn't like to kill, but I've heard what people in Washita say about him. Seen how they look at him when he walks by. Maybe it's because I've already been around so many murders, but I can feel when someone's capable of it. Bill isn't just capable. He's done it plenty of times before."

"I don't have my guns," I said. "All it will take is for one of them to notice us and then pull the trigger."

"I took them outside," she whispered. "Told them I couldn't think with them in the same room and that we'd all be a bit safer if there were fewer ways for things to go wrong if tempers went south. But that doesn't mean I didn't have a plan of my own."

She glanced back at the rest of them again, then flicked her dress away from where she'd spread it out on the floor, revealing a pair of long knives gleaming softly in the afternoon light. "If we both were to come at them at once, we should be able to overpower them before they know what's happening. Once that's done, we tie them up, and I'll help you bring them back to Kansas. I may be damned for eternity, but that doesn't mean I can't at least try to atone for some of what I've done."

"And you think killing someone else is going to help with that?" My voice came out as a tight hiss.

Her eyes widened. "I didn't say 'kill.' There's been enough of that already. But if we tie them up, then we can bring them back to Kansas alive. Maybe I'll have a chance of escaping the hangman's noose, and even if I don't, I'll be able to walk up the steps to the gallows with my head higher than it would be otherwise. I have to think about what it'll be like when I meet my maker, after all."

Make her think whatever she needs to. Just get the knife.

Did she mean it? I couldn't tell, but what were my options at this point? If I stayed the way I was, I'd be killed. Of that I had no doubt. Maybe if the Voice and I worked together for once, I could make it out of here and see tomorrow.

Kate was still staring at me, waiting. And could the curve of her chin and her smooth skin have had some sort of influence on my decision? I'd be lying to deny it. I nodded once. "Fine," I said.

She glanced behind her, where Ma now seemed to be leading the argument. No one was watching us. "You go for John. I don't

want to have to fight my brother. I'll take care of Bill. Ma and Pa…
they're weak enough, we should be able to hold them off, if we can
get the other two under control fast enough."

She grabbed one of the knives and sawed at the rope holding
my hands in place, though she froze before they were completely
cut. "I can trust you?" she asked, her voice level.

"I'm not the one who's been killing people," I said.

"Fair enough." She finished the cut, and I moved my hands
from side to side, trying to get the circulation going again as Kate
sliced the bonds on my legs. "Ready?"

I snaked my hand out and grabbed the other knife. Its handle
was smooth, and I fought back a shudder as the Voice cackled with
glee. I nodded. "Ready."

We stood and rushed toward the table as one.

CHAPTER TWENTY-FOUR

"It is rumored that the notorious Bender family is hovering around this community. Our detectives are on the alert for them, and should the suspected parties prove to be the Benders, their capture is certain."

—The Madisonian
(*Virginia City, Montana*), *October 16, 1875*

═══════

M Y FOOT CAUGHT ON THE floor after three steps, so I ended up more sprawling into John than actually slamming into him, which had been my plan. He turned in time for me to catch a glimpse of his mouth open in surprise, and he swung his hand around reflexively to ward me off. I didn't have the grace to avoid it, and it threw me further off-balance. My momentum carried me forward as I fell, my shoulder connecting with John's chest. The two of us tumbled to the ground in a pile.

I kept my hand gripping the knife like a vise, afraid I'd lose it in the chaos. This wasn't going as it was supposed to. In my head, I would have knocked John to the ground in one swift blow, surprise more than overcoming any hesitance I had for actual violence. Now John was slamming his fist into my ribs, his knees jabbing toward me, the pain driving out any plans I'd been making. Part of me was as afraid of slicing myself with the knife as I was about John's attacks.

The rest of the cabin was filled with shouts and commotion, but I didn't have the chance to pay any attention to it. Somehow, I managed to get on top of John, straddling him as I raised the knife up, point down in a stabbing position. "You need to—"

Before I could get any more than that out, John freed his left arm from my weight and lunged up to grab me by the right wrist. I thought he would just be focused on keeping me from attacking, but he held on to my wrist and then swung his elbow around, twisting my whole arm to the point where I thought it would break. I screamed in agony and tried to move the angle to alleviate the pressure, but he kept twisting, and my grip loosened.

John kept applying pressure, swinging around until I was so far to my right that I fell over. In an instant, he was on me, punching into my head as we rolled around on the floor. I tried to shield myself from the blows, mostly unsuccessfully until I managed to connect with my knee between his legs. He doubled over in pain, giving me a moment to gather my bearings.

I glanced over to see Bill with his hands around Kate's throat, her face turning purple as Ma and Pa watched from behind. If I didn't do something quickly, Kate and I were both dead.

I shoved John away, my twisted arm protesting the sharp movement, and scrambled to my feet, rushing over to knock Bill free of Kate. For once, it went as planned. I somehow got on top of him, and whether it was the better leverage or the advantage of fighting someone more than twice my age, I was able to do more damage. I'd lost any ability for coherent thought. I had no strategy. No consideration of what might come next. No Voice. Instead, I found myself grabbing Bill by the hair and ramming his head into the floorboards over and over, wanting nothing more than for this to be over.

Something smashed into my left shoulder, and I looked up to find Pa looming over me, his clawed hammer coming back for another blow. I left Bill senseless and threw my arms around Pa's legs, bringing him to the ground. But though Pa looked ten years older than Bill, he moved like he was ten years younger, and he had plenty of experience with that hammer. It felt like he was hitting me with the flat end from all directions. A blow on my right hip, my left leg, my stomach. I had my hand in his face for a moment, clawing for his eyes, but before I could gain purchase, he drew his head back and bit at my fingers.

I grabbed his hand by the wrist, trying to learn from my encounter with John moments before, but whatever he had done was harder to do than it seemed. Pa manhandled me on the ground until he had my arm bent back at an impossible angle, the whole joint screaming as I tried to wriggle out of it. I might as well have been pushing against a brick wall, for all the good it did. Pa was pulling against my arm from behind, leaning back with his whole weight as I was facedown on the floor, straining to crane my neck around so I could see what was going on. It took every bit of strength I had to keep him from pulling it any farther back—and quite likely breaking bone—but I had no luck getting myself free. We were both out of the fight until the stalemate broke.

But then a pair of worn brown boots appeared in front of me, a black hemline cloaking almost everything but their soles. I followed the dress up to see Ma standing like a giantess armed with a knife of her own. Had the *whole family* brought weapons to this meeting?

She crouched in front of me and grabbed me by the hair, pulling my head backward, exposing my throat. As she snaked her knife forward, ready to draw it across my neck, I tried to turn away, but I might as well have been tied to an altar, for all the good it was doing. We made eye contact. The knife's edge was cold against my skin, and her lips peeled back as she began the cut.

Until a different knife sprouted from her own neck and then tried to rip its way forward, getting caught in the neck muscles or bone as it did.

A gush of blood spurted from her throat, and she screamed in pain and rage—or tried to. What came out was more of a shrill gurgle as her windpipe fought to keep itself clear. She dropped her knife and slapped her hand to her neck, her left hand beating away Kate, who'd come up from behind her to make the blow. The floor around me began to fill with blood, coating my chest and face as I continued to struggle, and it took a moment for me to realize some of the blood was my own. In the shock of seeing Ma get attacked, I hadn't felt her knife make any real cut into my neck, but she must have, as my neck now lanced with pain as I moved.

It took Pa a moment to realize what had happened. He bellowed and let go of me to rescue his wife. I ignored my wound and grabbed his belt as he scurried past me, pulling him to the ground, where we once again tumbled in a flurry of fists, elbows, and knees. The horror of what I'd just seen—and the fear of just how badly I was injured—gave me new strength.

Somewhere above me, John's scream cut through the air. "Ma!" Amid the struggle with Pa, I heard John pick something up from the floor, and then Kate called out. I found Pa's neck and clamped my right arm around it, pulling it tightly to cut off his air as he beat at me blindly with his hands. This time I had the right angle, though, and his blows fell short.

Locked up for the moment, I could take stock of the rest of the room. Bill's body was a lifeless heap on the floor next to the table. Ma was lying on the floor, blood now also streaming from a blow to her left temple. She thrashed back and forth, in pain or rage, her dress and face slick with blood, each breath a struggling hiss that carried through the whole room.

Kate and John stood facing off by the door, each of them with a knife at the ready.

"What have you done?" John asked, no trace of a laugh about him for the first time since I'd met him.

"Exactly what you all were planning to do to me, if I'd waited."

"We never—"

"I heard you, John. *Heard you.* If you plan to strangle someone in their sleep, you'd best be certain to talk about it where they can't hear you."

John lunged forward, blade first, aiming for Kate's gut. She swung to the side and sliced down with her own, cutting into John's shirt on his forearm and landing a superficial blow to the flesh beneath. He gasped and drew back, circling again.

"I don't know what you heard," he said. "More of that nonsense of your séances, no doubt. Ma and Pa and I would—"

"Some of us will be dead in a few minutes. I think we can stop with the family nonsense, don't you?"

John managed a giggle at that statement, though it sounded more like nerves than anything else. "We can stop with any nonsense you'd like, as long as this useless fighting stops. There's more than enough money for all of us. We were supposed to kill Bill, not each other."

"That's the problem with planning to betray someone," Kate said, making another feint with her knife. She seemed very comfortable with the weapon. "You start thinking: *If they'd be willing to kill them, would they be willing to kill me?* That's what made me start to listen for it in the first place."

"We don't even know where the money is," John said. "If Bill dies, we'll never get it."

"He's not dead yet," Kate said.

Pa continued to thrash in my arms, but his blows were getting weaker. The strength had gone out of Ma's struggles, and the amount of blood around her and across the floor was alarming. I glanced down to see Pa's head covered in blood that was streaming out of my own neck wound. Was I beginning to feel faint?

I tried to think through my options at this point. Any pretense Kate had made of capturing the rest of the family and bringing them to justice was gone. If John survived against Kate, he would kill me without a second thought. If Kate survived, was I any safer? But then again, if I fled, what good would that do? I'd come to confront the family.

Time to see it through. I would help Kate and then turn on her as soon as John was taken care of. I wouldn't kill her, but knocking her out seemed more than reasonable.

Pa went still in my arms at last, and I left him to get to my knees, fishing around on the floor for the knife Ma had tried to use on me. Its hilt was slippery, so I wiped it off as best I could on a piece of my shirt that was still somewhat unstained. Then I stepped forward to stand next to Kate.

She jerked in surprise for a moment, then saw me and nodded. Two on one. I just had to be sure to leave myself in a position that once John was finished off, I could take on Kate.

"I'll swing behind him," I told her, then began to circle the room, shoving the table and chairs out of the way to give us more space. The dizziness had left me. Perhaps the cut on my neck wasn't as bad as I'd feared.

John switched his knife from hand to hand, seemingly more than familiar with using it to fight. But he couldn't watch both of us at once, with one in front and one behind. He didn't wait for me to get in place, instead rushing at Kate and swiping at her face. She leaned back, dodging the blow but slipping on blood and falling to the ground.

Before John could leap on her, I lunged from his right, aiming for his rib cage. I'd hunted enough to know what happened to a creature once one of its lungs was punctured. John turned and hit my arm away with his free hand, grabbing for my wrist, though this time I was smart enough to stay out of his grip.

Kate lashed out from the floor, slicing at John's legs. He jumped over the attempt and brought his foot down on her left hand, hard. Her bones made a wet crunching sound. She screamed and dropped the knife that had been in her other hand. John kicked it away from her, and it skittered across the floor before ending up in the far corner.

As John was still focused on Kate, I stepped in, stabbing my knife toward his unprotected neck. He dodged to the side, but I still connected with his shoulder, the blade hitting bone before glancing to the side. John tittered, his eyes wide and intense. He moved his arm around, testing to see if I'd incapacitated it. Whatever I'd hit hadn't been enough. It didn't seem to have slowed him much.

For all the Voice had whispered to me for years about how dangerous I could be, causing real violence turned out to be much harder than I'd ever worried, and it had gone completely silent now. In my mind, I'd always been a sneeze away from killing someone, and I'd only kept myself from it through sheer willpower. I thought of all those times I'd searched through rooms, sometimes repeating the effort three or four times, just to make sure I kept other people safe.

I might have been many things, but it was clear I was no natural killer. What a time to discover that simple truth.

John ran toward me, closing the distance in a few steps. I held my knife out in front of myself, as if that would ward him away. He swiped it to the side and plunged his knife down, scoring a direct hit on my left upper arm. The knife went so far in, its point cut through my shirt on the opposite side. I gasped in pain and dropped my knife, all my focus suddenly on getting that *thing* out of my body. The sight of it—the hilt sticking in one side, the point out the other—made me lose track of everything else.

It took John two tries to jerk the knife out, blood welling from the wound, though not gushing. No arteries had been cut. I backed away until I was pressed against the far wall. For a moment, all desire to fight left me. At that point, I wanted nothing more than to find a safe spot and curl up and hide until this all went away.

That wasn't an option, and I hated myself for even thinking it.

Father wouldn't think like that. No self-respecting Bullock would. They'd see this through, no matter what it took.

John surveyed the damage around us: Pa motionless a few feet from Ma, who lay facedown in a pool of blood. Bill lifeless, ten feet away. Kate cradling a hand with fingers that bent in the wrong directions. I had no idea how long we'd been fighting. It couldn't have been more than a few minutes, but I was breathing heavily, my eyes had trouble focusing, my neck throbbed, and my left arm felt like it was on fire from the stab wound. John's arm was bleeding as well, but he didn't seem to mind it. I wondered if he was fully sane.

"How'd two on one work for you there?" he asked. His laugh sounded more like a hyena's again. "You should've known better than to put in with Kate, Warren."

I picked up one of the chairs and threw it at his head, running in behind it while he was distracted. That had been the plan, at least. In reality, John simply stepped to the side and let the chair hit the floor behind him. He punched me in the face with the hand that was holding the knife. My vision went dark, and the next thing I knew, I was staring up at the ceiling.

John was crouched next to me, smiling down at my face. "You're the cause of all this, you know," he said. "Things were fine until you came to our cabin. You made Ma and Pa all jittery, and Kate didn't know which way was up after that. They wanted to kill you while Kate and I were away. They should have, but then Kate came back, and she was all soft on you. We ended up leaving weeks before we should have, which meant we missed the message from Bill. Three years—*three years!*—living in that hell of a house in the middle of nowhere, smiling at all them people, tryin' to make them believe I cared what they thought. They hated us. You could see it in the way their expressions would change when we walked in a room. Oh, they'd perk up right proper when it was Kate. The men would, anyway. But me? Ain't nobody had time for yours truly. Not so much as a kind word neither."

I tried to reach up and hit him, but he put his knife to my neck, and I froze.

"I can finish what Ma started, easy enough. And I will, just as soon as—"

A bellowing scream cut through the cabin, causing both of us to turn and see Bill kneeling over Pa, a knife held in both hands, raised to strike down at the old German.

"None of that," John said, standing, still sounding confident. "There's been enough—"

Bill slammed the knife into Pa's stomach and then twisted the blade. I watched, stunned. Pa gasped, his eyes opening and his body convulsing in pain. His arms beat around on the floor, searching blindly for anything he might use to defend himself. He found the clawed hammer, gripped it, and swung it up at Bill in one motion.

The clawed half sank deep into Bill's left cheek, just below his eye. Pa managed to rip it out and land another blow before his wounds overcame him. Bill knelt there, the knife still buried deep in Pa's stomach. He stared out at nothing, the hammer hanging from his face, dripping with blood. Then he lost his balance and toppled face-first onto Pa.

"No!" Forgetting everything else, John stomped over to stand next to Pa's body. He began kicking the old man in the head, blow after blow. "You. Weren't. Supposed. To. Kill. Him. Yet!" He screamed wordlessly again, staring at the ceiling and then breathing heavily.

I backed up on my elbows, trying to put more space between us. John nudged Pa with the toe of his boot, then giggled. He turned his gaze to me, and his eyes were white around the edges, a half smile on his face. "Three years," he said again, quieter. "And all that time, I bit my tongue, knowin' someday I'd get what was mine. I knew we could trust Bill. The man was like a puppy, wantin' to be loved that bad. And it would have been fine if…"

"You killed my father." The words sounded stiff, coming out of my lips reluctantly. I spat out a tooth John had knocked free with that punch.

"And now it wasn't even worth the effort, was it?" John shrugged. "Though I suppose at least it was somethin' to do. I always said I—"

The door of the cabin slammed closed. A quick glance showed Kate had left. She was the only other person left breathing. John stared at the door for a beat, then slumped his shoulders. "She always did want to do things the hard way. I'll be damned if she gets away this time. Ain't no way I'm gonna feel better until she's as dead as the rest of 'em." He hurried out after her.

I was alone in a silent cabin with three corpses. From outside came the noise of horses galloping off and distant yelling. I collapsed on the floor, staring at the ceiling again and wondering what I was supposed to do. None of this had gone the way I'd thought it would. I'd only proved to myself again and again just how incompetent I could be. Yes, three of my father's killers were now dead, but it didn't do anything to heal the empty feeling I'd had upon seeing his rotting corpse. I wasn't sure if that feeling would ever go away.

I propped myself up, my body protesting the movement. I was hurting in places I hadn't even realized I'd been hit. I took one last look around the cabin, taking in the carnage John and Kate had left in their wake. This wasn't done, and it wouldn't be done until all the Benders had paid for their crimes or I was dead myself.

And I wasn't dead yet.

Limping into a slow run, I headed out the door in pursuit of them once again.

CHAPTER TWENTY-FIVE

"Neither Kate nor John Bender, nor their parents, Mr. And Mrs. Wm. Bender, has ever been captured and I am satisfied that none of the reports of their death, which have been circulated from time to time, were founded upon fact."

—Topeka State Journal

(*Topeka, Kansas*), *August 5, 1911*

OUTSIDE, THE TREES WERE BATHED in red from the setting sun, the sky on fire with orange and purple. Surrey was still in his stall in the shed. I didn't want to take the time to saddle him properly. After waiting this long to find the Benders, I wasn't going to risk letting them get away, even if half of them were now dead.

I put the bit and halter onto my horse and led him outside. Someone had taken my Remington, but the rifle had been left lying in the middle of the clearing. I stooped to get it, then took hold of Surrey's mane and lifted myself onto his back, my muscles groaning in protest. My left hand didn't want to grip as tightly as it should have.

A few weeks ago, I might have dithered, worrying how I'd find Kate and John. By this point, all the lessons Father had given me over the years had settled into my brain again, and all it took was a glance to see the broken twigs and crushed grass leading off to the west. I leaned forward and clicked Surrey into a trot.

Whatever was happening in front of me, it wasn't just important that I get there in time—I had to make sure I didn't walk into another ambush. Besides, a horse could only gallop for so long. Judging by the trail Kate and John were leaving behind them, I'd have no trouble knowing which way to go, and they had their horses going at full speed. You could tell by the length between the hoofprints.

Surrey sensed my nerves and kept wanting to go faster. I could relate, but I reined him in each time, keeping an ear out for any signs of fighting ahead.

We rode into the setting sun, the light growing bright enough to hurt my eyes. Staying on Surrey was harder than it should have been. I'd never ridden him bareback for very long at home. Without the saddle, I felt every hoofbeat through my whole body, and I juggled the reins and my rifle to keep my balance. I squinted and used my hat to shield my eyes from the worst of it, though that made it so I only had a general idea of what was in front of me. It had to be affecting Kate and John the same way and was likely the reason Kate had chosen to come this way in the first place.

I took turns paying attention to the track and to what lay ahead of me, dodging tree limbs and rocks and trying to keep Surrey at the same steady clip. What would I do when I found the two of them? I had my rifle, but they had my revolver. If I stayed at a distance, I ought to be safe. The rifle was much more accurate beyond twenty yards.

So I could threaten them, but I couldn't get close enough to force them to do anything, unless I was willing to shoot them.

Was I willing to shoot them? Having just witnessed the deaths of three people, my taste for it was about as low as it could get.

But if they got away instead?

The Voice grumbled, but it felt softer.

I'd deal with the question when it was in front of me. I hoped it would be enough to hold my rifle on them and persuade them to go along with what I wanted.

The trail continued, plain as day. After a while, the horses started to tire. The first horse—Kate's—had a shoe with a gouge on the right side. You could tell by the way the second horse's tracks sometimes covered the first. If I was reading it right, her horse was slowing more than John's.

About two and a half miles from the cabin, I pulled Surrey to a stop. The sun dominated the sky in front of me, making seeing anything ahead impossible, but the wind had carried a trace of a voice. I listened, focusing on ignoring the background noise.

There—to my right, faint yelling. Not screaming but arguing. I nudged Surrey into a slower pace until I was close enough to make out words. Then I swung off the horse, almost falling in the process.

I crouched and crept forward, placing my feet deliberately, testing each step to make sure it was free of dried branches or anything that might make a noise. I came over a slight rise in the land, and John and Kate popped into view in a clearing next to a small stream. Kate was lying on the ground, defenseless. John stood over her, my revolver in his hands, pointed straight at her head.

Without thought, I cocked my rifle, aimed, and stood. "That's enough," I called out, my voice somewhat slurred from the missing tooth.

John and Kate turned to me, relief on Kate's face, and surprise and then the same on John's. The gun didn't move an inch.

"It's just you," he yelled back. "You had me worried there for a second."

"Put that down," I said.

"You shoot me, I shoot her. Is that what you want?"

"Do you?"

He laughed. "At this point, I don't think it much matters anymore. Not since Pa went and killed the only one who could make the last three years worth my while. Bein' on the run when you're poor is a whole lot less fun than doin' it when you're rich, I figure."

I began to edge forward. Five years ago, I could have made the shot without too much worry. Now? With my nerves and my rusty aim? I'd want to be a whole lot closer before I had any confidence I'd hit what I intended.

"I don't think I like you comin' closer," John said, then tittered.

"And I don't think I care," I said, not stopping.

"I'll kill her."

"You'll be doing her a favor. A shot to the head's faster than a dance at the end of a noose."

He licked his lips, his eyes darting from me to Kate and back again. "So what do you want then?"

"I want the two of you bound, on a horse back to Kansas."

Kate managed to find her voice. "Just shoot him, Warren!"

"I'm doing what I want now, thanks very much," I answered.

"That's fine and good," John said. "But you just said it. Better to die fast than die slow. I don't think Kate or I fancy the idea of a judge and a courtroom any more than we wanna see a vigilance committee."

"Who said you'd die fast?" I asked. "A gut shot can take weeks to kill you."

He laughed again, high and grating. "Takin' a page from our book now, ain't you?"

I stopped twenty-five yards away. Any closer, and my advantage would be gone. I wasn't sure how good John's aim was, but I really didn't want to find out. "Put the gun down."

"You know," he said, tilting his head to the side. "You been talkin' more than a little, and it occurs to me I ain't never seen you do anythin' that makes me think you're given to violence. No temper, even when you were lookin' for your pa. If I were you? I'd have pulled that trigger as soon as I laid eyes on me."

"My father was a lawman," I said.

"Then he'd have told you the same thing." He pointed the gun lower and pulled the trigger, the shot lashing out across the clearing.

Kate screamed and put her hands to her leg, doubling over in pain.

I stared, motionless, as John moved the gun away from Kate and turned it on me. "She ain't goin' nowhere now. Think I can put my full attention on you, and my, ain't it interestin' you still ain't pulled the trigger?"

All my determination had vanished, and I was back where I'd been weeks ago, so focused on not hurting anyone that I'd stopped living my life. My finger was on the trigger, my rifle sighted on one of the people who had killed Father, and here I stood, unable to do anything. To actually *kill* someone, not in the heat of a fight, but to look down the end of that barrel and pull the trigger?

The Voice flared back to life, though it felt changed. *Do it, you coward. You come from an entire family of killers. Bullocks know how to take care of people like the Benders, but not you. You'll never be half as good as your father.*

And still my finger didn't budge on the trigger.

John's smile widened, though his eyes stayed dead as marble. He walked toward me. Ten yards away. Five.

He raised the revolver slowly, cocking it, pointing it straight at my head. "You cost me thousands of dollars, Warren. Sure, I could respect you a bit for wantin' to get back at them that killed your pa, but now I see you can't even do *that* right. So all of it's been a waste. All those people we killed. All the years I stayed in that cabin with the three of them, pretendin' I was simple. Waitin' for the time when it would all pay off. And instead, it's done in by a yellow-spined fool from Missouri who wanted to play cowboy."

Pull the trigger, Warren! Pull it!

The rifle was right there. I couldn't miss. My finger wouldn't inch.

"I've killed more than a few people in my life," John said. "Enough that I've gotten a sense for those I enjoy more than others. Shootin' you's gonna be somethin' I remember fondly for years."

Father would have killed him and Kate and not thought twice. The Voice wanted me to do it. But staring at the end of that gun, one thing became more than clear.

The Voice didn't control me. It didn't even come close. I wasn't a killer. I was a person who had bad ideas and paid them too much mind, but I'd never be a cold-blooded murderer. Not the kind I'd been terrified I'd become.

John pulled the trigger.

It clicked, and the revolver let out a small popping sound. I winced, expecting pain, then opened my eyes and looked down. No bullet hole. No wound.

John frowned at the gun in irritation. "Damn fool can't even have a gun that works right," he said. He brought it back up.

And I shot him through his left eye.

I hadn't even realized I'd done it at first. The sound of the shot still rang in my ears, and a hole had taken the place of the blue of John's eye, fast as a blink. Smoke drifted from the barrel of my rifle, and the tension that had been building in my shoulders was gone.

His arm dropped, and his body slumped to the ground.

Kate had scrambled away from us, though she hadn't made it farther than a few yards. I turned my rifle on her.

She held up her hand as if to shield herself from a blow. "Don't! This isn't you!"

I paused with my finger on the trigger, the question echoing in my ears. It wasn't me? Pulling that trigger had been one of the easiest decisions I'd made in a long time, and I'd made it with the confidence that the Voice didn't control me.

Kate lay there, frozen. I had to say something, but even I wasn't sure what it would be until the words poured out of me.

"For the past three years of my life, I've been convinced I'm one sneeze away from doing something horrible. That in my heart, I'm an awful person. Every time I'd look at myself in a reflection, I'd see that evil part of me, just waiting to come out and ruin my life."

She lowered her arm but stayed quiet.

I continued. "When I think of the things I did to try and keep that part of me in check—the hours and hours I wasted doing everything I could to avoid killing everyone around me—I'm shocked. Stunned that it got to be that bad. It started with thoughts. Wicked thoughts, out of nowhere. Bad enough that I was scared to tell anyone else about them, since they'd no doubt realize how awful I was at heart. So I made all these rules for those thoughts. Ways to keep myself from following them."

I'd kept my rifle trained on her the whole time, but it felt a little silly now. There'd been more than enough killings for one day, hadn't there? I lowered it, and Kate's shoulders loosened. If I could just get someone to understand me, somehow I would feel a bit more like I hadn't made the journey for nothing. And if anyone could understand me, it would be her, wouldn't it?

"It got to the point that I looked at those thoughts like they were something different from who I was. In my head, it was like a demon sat on my shoulder all the time, whispering ideas of what I might do. How I might hurt people.

"Looking back on it now, I see that was foolish. But it wasn't until just now that I figured it out. That Voice wasn't a different part of me. It wasn't something I could just bundle up and blame on something else. It's a piece of me, but not the whole of me. When I look at you and your family—at what you've done and how you've lived—or how this final fight has turned out..."

I shook my head. "I'm not who the Voice wants me to be. It's not in me. I would *never* do the sort of things you've done. Not to innocent people or even to people who might not be so innocent.

Back in the cabin, that was a struggle just to survive, and it was horrible. I'll never forget that scene. And I shot your brother just now because if I hadn't, he would have shot me. But just because I killed him doesn't mean I have to kill you." I dropped the rifle to the ground, everything becoming so much simpler. I wasn't going to kill another person. There was no need. The Voice could whisper whatever it wanted.

I wasn't the sort of person who needed to listen.

Kate got to her feet, brushing off her skirt and running her fingers through her hair to remove a few stray leaves. She might've been shot through the leg, but it appeared that as long as she kept her full weight off it, she could manage. Her eyes were red and puffy, and she had a long scrape running along her left arm. The hem of her skirt was ripped, causing a loose strip of fabric to trail along the ground. Her eyes stayed on the rifle for a moment longer than they should have, then flicked over to where my Remington lay next to John's outstretched hand. "I knew you'd help me," she said. "You're not like the rest of them."

"Haven't you been listening?" I asked. "I'm exactly like the rest of them. I've got those same thoughts. The same capabilities. But I choose not to listen to them."

"Same thing." She limped in front of me to go over to her horse.

"I'm not letting you go," I said. "You're coming back to Kansas to stand trial."

"I'll do nothing of the sort. You've already shown me you're not ready to kill me, so why should I worry about doing what you tell me to do?"

"I don't have to kill you to tie you up. I don't need to murder you to bring you back."

She laughed, though it sounded forced. "Do you realize how hard it's going to be for you to get home? I don't know how you made it this far, but you've got to do that all over again. How in the world are you going to do that and keep track of a prisoner at the same time?"

I shrugged. "I'll work it out. It's gotten me this far."

"I'll kill you in the middle of the night. I can't be trusted."

"I'm good with knots," I said.

She ran to her horse, and I darted after her. The horse, meanwhile, was thoroughly confused by this commotion and kept backing up, staying away from Kate no matter what she did. I reached out to grab her by the collar, but she ducked beneath my hand and headed back to her brother.

And my revolver.

I'd never make it to my rifle before she could pull the trigger. That much was clear at the first glance. She'd planned the move toward her horse to get me away from my weapon, and I'd fallen for it, just like I'd fallen for everything.

"You don't want to pull that trigger," I told her as she straightened with the gun in her hand.

She had a fierce smile and a new edge to her look. She cocked the gun, using both hands to get it done. "Why wouldn't I?"

"Because of that misfire," I said. "Sounded like a squib to me."

"A what?"

"Squib. My father taught me about them, back when he was showing me how to shoot. It's when the gun goes off, but the bullet doesn't leave the barrel. I've been worried about that gun and those bullets all along. Their last owner didn't take care of them properly. If you're foolish enough to take another shot without checking first to be sure the barrel's clear, the gun's as liable to blow up in your hands as it is to actually shoot."

"You're making that up."

"Ask your brother how it worked out for him."

She furrowed her brow. "It's a bluff."

"It's fate," I said. "Do you know how many times I might have died on my way to catch you? I made just about every mistake you can think of, but each time, something came through for me. Some miracle occurred, and I kept going. If you ask me, this is the universe catching up with your family. Put the gun down and come with me."

Her lips tightened, and she brought up her other hand to steady the revolver's aim. "I'd rather die," she said, then pulled the trigger.

The barrel blew up, sending shards of metal flying. A few hit the ground in front of my feet, but I escaped unscathed. Kate, on the other hand, had been blown backward, though she was strangely silent. I walked over to her. She lay on the ground, opening and closing her mouth like a fish, her eyes wide and blinking. A piece of shrapnel had lodged itself in her throat, blood welling around the wound. Her right hand was a bloody mess, with at least one finger missing.

I crouched next to her. She lolled her head to the side to stare at me, but her voice wouldn't work.

"That's in your neck," I said. "I can take you to town and hope someone can look at it. I'm worried something important got cut."

She brought her left hand to her throat, patting around at the area until she found the shrapnel. She struggled to grip it in her ruined hands, but managed to pull it out on her second try.

Blood sprayed from the wound—more than had gushed from Ma Bender, even—and I had to sit back to avoid getting hit. Kate managed a few gasps, but she didn't say anything else.

In less than a minute, she was dead, and the clearing was quiet once again.

CHAPTER TWENTY-SIX

"The end of the Benders is not known. The earth seemed to swallow them, as it had their victims."

—Kansas Historical Marker, State Highway Commission

THE RIDE BACK TO LAMAR wasn't as bad as Kate had tried to convince me it would be. I left soon after she'd died, leaving her and her brother where they'd fallen. For a moment, I considered burying them, but it only took one thought of Father for me to dismiss the idea. I unsaddled their horses, letting them free. I wanted no part of the Benders in my life ever again.

Back at the cabin, I didn't return to the scene of carnage, instead going to the shed and saddling Surrey properly before loosing the rest of the horses. When I left, I didn't look back. Perhaps some of the outlaws from Washita would come looking for them, or maybe they'd lie there for the rest of time.

It didn't matter to me.

I circled well clear of the outlaw colony and rode east until I hit the cattle trail, joining a few cowboys who were driving their herd north. They tended to my wounds, and I kept to myself, helping as I could, but not saying much to any of them. I didn't have many words in me just yet. The Voice made a few grumblings, but I didn't pay it much attention. I'd made my peace with it.

I spent time thinking about what I'd seen and done since leaving home. There were questions I'd never be able to ask now. How the Benders had gotten the best of Father. Who they were, really. What had happened during the séance.

Death brought an end to all answers.

A few weeks later, we reached Abilene. I'd earned a bit of money working for the outfit, and I used it to buy a train ticket back to Missouri.

The journey seemed to take an age. All I could think of was the expression on Mother's face when I'd have to tell her Father was dead. I'd left with a simple job, and I'd completely failed at it. Yes, the Benders were done, but none of that changed the reality of our future.

And it wasn't just Mother. My brothers would hear about it, and how would they all react? More than anything, I didn't want to see the disappointment in their eyes, the knowledge that if they'd been there instead of me, it all would have gone differently.

There was a part of me that argued against that line of thought. At least I'd been there, hadn't I? At least I'd done what I could, and if it had fallen short, what fault was that of mine? Where had they been? What would they have done differently? But no matter how loud that idea tried to get, it couldn't overcome the knowledge that I was the worst Bullock.

I didn't belong in the family, and everyone knew it.

The closer we came to Missouri, the more that hole in my stomach ate at me—a dread so fierce, it was painful. In some ways, it felt like that train ride would never end. In others, I wished it wouldn't.

But hours later, I escorted Surrey off in Neosho, fifty miles south of home.

Walking along a well-established road that led through plowed fields and neat houses was a massive contrast to the wilderness I'd spent the past month or more in. It was hard to believe a train ride could take you somewhere so different. Planting season was well underway, which made me think about how much I'd missed at home. Not only had I failed Father, but it had taken me away for weeks.

I got a few strange looks as I went by, not that I blamed anyone. With my brown hat, leather jacket, and chaps from Leroy, and the well-worn condition of everything on me, I was still outfitted for a cattle drive or a gunfight.

At night, I slept fifty yards off the road, in a small copse of trees. My meal was simple, but I was used to it by now. With enough ammunition to hunt with, I could have lasted as long as I needed.

I wasn't pushing Surrey at all, so I had a second night under the stars. I stared at the sky, berating myself for delaying the inevitable. Even in this, I was nothing more than a coward. Would everyone be better off if I just never came home again? Heading back to the wilds seemed like it would be so much easier than what lay before me. Only my sense of duty kept me there. Mother deserved to know what had happened to Father. I could at least do that much right.

It was dusk when my house came into sight, though the place was lit with enough lanterns to host a party. A line of horses waited outside, each of them saddled for a journey. I frowned. Had something else gone wrong? Hadn't our family suffered enough?

When I walked in the front door, I found the kitchen crowded with five men huddled around a map. Newton glanced up, and I froze, any words trapped in my throat.

He glanced at me and said, "Another one? We appreciate the support, but I ain't too sure what we'll do with all of you. You can wait outside, and we'll be on our way soon enough, though." His glance dipped to the map again without a second thought.

"Newton?" I said.

The chatter in the room stopped at once, as if my voice had cast a spell. All eyes turned toward me at once, and I recognized all of them. Wyatt. James. Virgil. Morgan. All five of my brothers were home.

Mother pushed through all of them. "Warren?" She gasped and ran forward, throwing her arms around me. And that broke the spell of silence. Everyone mobbed me, and I was surrounded by smiles and shouted questions as they all tried to speak over one another.

"Where have you been?"

"We were just going to come looking for you."

"What's happened?"

There was no way to keep track of everything they were saying or to answer anything. It felt wonderful to have my family all there, but at the same time, it was even worse. I'd have to tell them all at once about Father. I supposed it might be easier this way, at least—get all the disappointment out of them at once.

Newton put his hand to his mouth and let out a sharp whistle. Everyone else quieted. "That's better," he said. "We all want to know the same things, but there's no way he'll be able to answer half of 'em if we keep peppering him like a steak. So just shut up for five minutes and let the man speak. Warren, where the hell have you been? And since when have you started dressing like a cowboy?"

Silence. Adelia peeked out from behind my brothers. Some of their wives poked their heads around the corner as well. Everyone waited for me to tell them. The words didn't want to come out of my mouth, and I almost just turned and ran from the room.

"I went looking for Father, as you all know." I needed a glass of water. Or a rock to hide under. "He—it took longer than I thought. And I didn't—I couldn't—it wasn't as if—"

"We know all about your father," Mother said, but her voice was kind, without an ounce of accusation in it.

"You do?" I asked, my voice sounding as bewildered and lost as I felt.

Everyone nodded.

"What do you think everyone came back home for?" Wyatt asked. "The whole country's talking about those Benders and their victims. It's in practically every paper in the country. The Governor of Kansas put out a two-thousand-dollar reward. But we all figured you were as dead as the rest. No word from you for over a month? We were just about to set out to find you or at least find out what happened. And then we'd see to the Benders after that. No way they'll hide from the Bullocks. Not with all of us here. You can come with us now on the hunt. You earned that much, at least."

"But they're dead," I said, my voice sounding small.

"I wouldn't make that assumption," Newton said, sounding gruff as ever. "Sure, there's plenty who say they already strung 'em up, but no one's come forward for the reward, and you can bet no one would pass up the chance at two thousand dollars and the fame that would come with it."

"It's not an assumption," I said. "It's a fact. I left their bodies in Indian Territory more than two weeks ago."

This was met with a chorus of confusion and disbelief. But Newton ushered us all back to the kitchen, and everyone found chairs, and they listened for the next two hours as I told them everything that had happened. I left nothing out. My initial blundering in Osage Mission. Sleeping at the Benders'. The séance. The tornado. The buffalo. And the Benders' ultimate fate.

They listened to it all with an expression of shock on each of their faces. There were questions here and there that I had to answer. It was hard for me to keep everything straight in my head, so I jumped around a fair bit. Mother brought me a meal partway through, and I continued my story between bites. By the time I finished, it was dark as sin outside.

"And that's everything," I added at last. "I know I didn't do what I should have, and I know it's my fault Father's—"

Newton placed his hand on my arm and stopped me. When he spoke, his voice was solemn, without a trace of the rough persona he usually projected. "Warren. You don't have a thing to hang your head about. You really think we're angry at you? Do you realize how many thousands of people are searching for the Benders now? And you tracked them down all by yourself? If I didn't know you better, I'd think you were lying through your teeth, but I believe you.

"Father died. Murdered. It happens, and we're all plenty mad about it, but that's on the Benders, not you. You headed out and did what the rest of us couldn't. We're not mad at you, Warren. We're proud."

I stared at each of their faces, sure I must somehow be misunderstanding them. I'd hated myself ever since I'd seen Father's corpse. I'd blamed myself for everything, and they were trying to tell me it was *fine*?

"But he's dead," I said.

"But you're not," Mother said. She came over to wrap her arms around me again. I did the only thing left I could think of.

I hugged her back and broke out in tears.

HISTORICAL NOTE

When I set out to write this book, I didn't think there'd be that much difference between it and *The Perfect Place to Die*. This is only twenty years earlier, after all. How hard could it be? What I failed to account for was the stark difference between city life in the 1890s and rural Kansas in the early 1870s. Practically nothing was the same. The clothes, the landscape, the conflicts, the people, the livestock(!)—all of it needed a different approach.

As usual, I've done my best with this book to insert the narrative into the history while keeping as much of the history intact as I could. The Benders really did exist, and they really did go on a years-long killing spree of visitors to their inn. (What's up with people using hotels to kill people?) I tried to describe them as they actually were, right down to John's irritating laugh. Kate professed to be able to speak with spirits, as well.

The victims are also all true to life, with the exception of Warren's father. In that instance, I based him on Dr. William York, who went looking for his friend George Longcor when George failed to show up on his way back to Iowa.

Warren, then, took on part of the role of York's brother, a State Senator who began to investigate the disappearances when William vanished. Like Warren, his hunt led him to the Benders, and like Warren, he continued onward without really suspecting them. The scene that happens when Warren returned to the Bender farm played out almost exactly as described, from the flood of volunteer investigators to the failed lynching of the German neighbor.

There is no definitive proof as to what happened to the Benders. Some believe they died at the hands of vigilante justice, but with a $2,000 reward on their heads, this seems doubtful to me (especially since killing the Benders probably would have been met with roars of approval and fame). It seems likely that they fled south, as depicted in this book, eventually heading into Indian Territory, where their trail disappeared. In the years after the killings, "Bender sightings" happened frequently across the country, as the story of their villainy had taken the entire nation by storm. (I tried to capture the spread of that notoriety by including newspaper quotes from as many different states as possible. There were more I could have put in. The entire nation was fixated on the crime.)

In 1889, two women in Michigan were found who many believed to be Kate and Ma Bender, to the point that a trial was held in LaBette County. Ultimately the women were found not guilty, though Leroy Dick remained convinced they were the two Bender women.

All told, it's estimated that the Benders murdered twenty people, though it's possible that number was higher. They were killing over the space of at least two years, and Kansas at the time was an easy place for people to vanish and no one to think twice about it.

As for the Bullocks, I based the family on the Earps (of Wyatt Earp fame). Warren, the youngest Earp brother, lived in Lamar, seventy miles away from the Benders at the time of the killings, and the Earps almost definitely heard about what had happened. This was well before the O.K. Corral, and the reality of the Earp family was problematic enough that, in the end, I just chose to keep it a loose connection.

To read more about the actual history of the Bender family, I recommend the following books:

- Jonusas, Susan. *Hell's Half Acre: The Untold Story of the Benders, a Serial Killing Family on the American Frontier.* Viking, 2022.
- Wood, Fern Morrow. *The Benders: Keepers of the Devil's Inn.* BookCrafters, 1992.
- Beach, David. *The Bloody Benders: A Compendium of Articles from Kansas Newspapers in 1872–1873 Covering A.M. York and the Bender Tragedy.* KOPCO, 2022.

CHAPTER ONE

Think of the list that follows: men and women, young girls and innocent children, blotted out by one monster's hand, and you, my reader, of a tender and delicate nature, will do well to read no further.

I WAS SEVENTEEN—OLD ENOUGH for boys to come calling, even though none of them had, and nothing Mother said could fool me into thinking there was a reason other than the length of my nose and the size of my chin. "Handsome" is about as good a compliment any boy paid me, and that was only when his parents were listening. But I was a hard worker, and I knew my way around a farmyard and in a workshop. Father didn't have sons, and Ruby wasn't worth a thing when it came time for work to be done.

The boys hadn't come calling for me, but they more than made up for that by lining up for my younger sister. She never had a moment's rest at the dance hall, and she'd have been out nightly if Father had let her. As it was, she still went out twice as often as she should have.

Father would scream at Ruby each morning, and I imagine she thought she had it pretty rough the way he handled her. However, he was careful to keep his blows to places where no one would notice the bruises—and she was careful to keep those bruises from getting noticed. I wasn't as lucky, but I made sure Ruby never had a chance to see what he did to me.

It's amazing what a family will do to make other families think everything is normal and fine.

But one evening Ruby came into the room when I would have sworn she was already on her way into town. I was in the middle of changing for the night, and there was Ruby, barging in through the door, all breathless and hurried as she searched for a missing earring she just had to have for the dance.

"Zuretta," she said. "Have you seen my—"

I tried to turn fast enough, but the way she cut off told me I'd failed. Her eyes widened, and the blood drained out of her face faster than if her throat had been cut. The two of us stared at each other, neither of us speaking, for a full minute—maybe longer.

"That was Father?" she asked me at last.

"It wasn't Mother."

She nodded. Once, then twice. "There's a lot there," she said. "On your back. How long has he been doing this to you?"

"Long enough," is all I said. I could take the blows, and I wanted things to stay the same between Ruby and me.

Ruby had never been the sort of person who let things be,

THE PERFECT PLACE TO DIE

though. She'd march straight to the store and elbow her way into the front of the line if she thought it was necessary. She didn't wait then, either.

"Come on, Zuretta," she said.

"What?"

"We're going, you and I."

"Where?"

"East. North. West. I don't care. Anywhere but Manti, Utah."

"But Mother—"

"Mother knew what she was getting when she married that man. You and I didn't ask for it."

"But what would we do?"

She rushed over to her dresser and took out a bag and began throwing clothes into it, almost at random. "Anything we want," she said, and then looked up at me as an idea struck her. "Chicago." Her eyes were bright.

"Chicago?" I sat down on my bed.

"The Columbian Exposition. Remember? People have been talking about that for months. We'll go to Chicago. We might even see the Pinkertons!"

"We can't afford tickets," I said, hoping some reasoning would work with her.

But Ruby was already packing again. "I'll take some money out of the jar on Father's shelf when we leave. That'll pay for the tickets, and when we get to the city, we'll get jobs and never come back. Real jobs. Maybe as maids in a fancy hotel. Meet people from around the world. Come on, Zuretta! We'll be free!"

I could see the future with Ruby there, just for a moment. Expensive rooms and swaying train cars. *Free.*

But Mother cried out in the room next to ours, and it all came crashing down. "I can't," I told Ruby. "She needs my help. *Our* help."

Ruby licked her lips, thinking. Then she shook her head. "Not from me, Zuretta. I'm sorry, but no more. We all have our agency. God gave it to us to make our minds up. I'm getting out of here now. Tonight. You can come with me, or you can stay here and get beaten whenever Father pleases. I know the choice I'm making."

And I could see that she did, but I knew my choice as well. I thought it was the right one. The sensible one. I said goodbye to Ruby that night.

I never saw her at home again.

———

She wrote me, of course, and I even got to read some of her letters. The ones Father didn't catch wind of, at any rate. (Until we learned to have them sent to a friend and cut Father out of the process entirely.) The letters were filled with marvelous stories of Chicago and the exposition. She'd seen a real-life Pinkerton Detective, and she'd found work as a maid. Though, she refused to let me know where she was living. Everything went to a box at the post office downtown, and she picked it up there. She worried Father might come looking for her, but I thought the odds of him making the journey from Utah all the way to Chicago were slim.

In some ways, the letters made things harder. Father's temper only got worse, and Mother didn't get any stronger. He blamed me for Ruby running off.

I thought I'd been hiding it all well enough, but the bishop called me into meet with him one Sunday. He had a stack of letters on his desk, at least an inch high.

"Do you want to tell me about your father?" he asked.

I did not, so he sat back in his seat and sighed. "What am I going to do with you, Zuretta?" As if I was something to be handled and passed around. A problem that could be solved if he found the right leverage.

I perched in the seat across from him, my back safely away from anything it might brush up against.

The bishop pointed at that stack of letters. "Your sister," he began, then added, "It's not just me she's writing to."

"I can handle him," I said, which was true enough. "Ruby's off enjoying life in a big city. Mother and I will be fine."

The bishop hemmed and hawed about it, but he let me go at last, with a request I tell him if it got to be too much. I promised I would, because a promise was only words.

It all felt worth it when Ruby wrote me about her secret engagement. She'd fallen in love with the man of her dreams, and they were going to elope to Europe at the end of the summer. She wouldn't give me his name or say what he looked like, nor even describe what he did for his career. She was free, and she was happy, and that was all that mattered.

Until her letters stopped.

They'd been weekly occurrences for so long, arriving without fail each Tuesday. When one went missing, I assumed it must have been because of some trouble in the post. By Thursday, I decided the letter must have been lost. Three Tuesdays later, and I could think of little else.

Perhaps she'd eloped early. Perhaps Chicago was simply too busy for the postal service to function properly. But the lies you tell yourself during the day don't hold up to the thoughts that come at night. Ruby might have been hurt. What if she'd been struck by a cart or fallen off a ladder? She might be all alone in a hospital, unable to write.

Then the dreams came. Ruby trapped and alone. Ruby crying in terror.

I might not have been willing to talk to the bishop and accept his offer of help when it was just for me, but for Ruby I'd do almost anything.

That is how I came to be at the train station two days later, a ticket for Chicago clutched in my hand, and not a single soul to see me off.

ACKNOWLEDGMENTS

As always, a big thank-you to my family for their constant support and willingness to go on crazy cross-country road trips to see sites from serial killer history. (You know you might have a problem when you begin to plan vacations around where certain murders took place.) My wife, Denisa, might not like the book covers (too scary), but she's always there to encourage me and help brainstorm.

Thanks to my agent, Eddie Schneider, and all the JABberwockians; to my editors, Annie Berger and Gabbi Calabrese; to my copy editor, Manu Velasco; and to the rest of the crew over at Sourcebooks. I'm continually impressed with how they approach the business.

A shout out to my patrons over on Patreon, especially since they do it more out of a desire to support me than to get anything concrete back in return (can you tell I feel guilty?): Kevin Angell, Gwen Coltrin, Samantha Cote, Phil Hilton, Karol Maybury, Glenn Miller, Theresa Overall, and Frank Petty. Finally, a special thank you to Van Lindberg, for being the brave lone alpha reader. He read a worse version of this book, so you didn't have to. :-)

Visits to the Cherryvale Museum (where they still have the murder weapons, along with a veritable plethora of Bender information) and the Osage Mission Historical Museum were both eye -opening, and both very worthy of a visit if you're in the area.

I also wanted to thank my longtime friend Brandon Sanderson for his ongoing professional advice. "Why don't you try sticking to one genre instead of fifteen?" might seem like low-hanging fruit, but it came at the perfect time.

ABOUT THE AUTHOR

© Jaime Ranger

Bryce Moore is the author of *Don't Go to Sleep*, *The Perfect Place to Die*, *The Memory Thief*, and *Vodník*. When he's not authoring, he's a library director in western Maine and a past president of the Maine Library Association. A graduate of Brigham Young University and Florida State, he's a fan of film adaptations, movies, and board games. He uses his spare time to fix up his old 1841 farmhouse, shovel snow, and spend ridiculous amounts of money feeding his Magic the Gathering addiction.

sourcebooks
fire

Home of the hottest trends in YA!

Visit us online and
sign up for our newsletter at
FIREreads.com

....

Follow
@sourcebooksfire
online